"THE SNOWFLAKE"

by

Chuck Fletcher

This is a work of fiction. Names, characters, place, and incidents either are the product of the author's imagination or are used fictitiously. Any resemblance to actual persons, living or dead, events, or locales is entirely coincidental.

Copyright © 2020 by Chuck Fletcher

All rights reserved. No part of this book may be reproduced or used in any manner without written permission of the copyright owner except for the use of quotations in a book review,

First paperback edition November 2020

ISBN 9798560085759 (Paperback)

Published Independently

PREFACE

"THE SNOWFLAKE" is set in the slums of a North-Eastern mining community, in the nineteen-forties. It tells the story of a gentle-natured young boy, who is far happier walking the moors, collecting wild flowers with his retarded sister, than playing with other boys in the street.

Yet through his environment and the people in it, he is turned into one of the most brutal street-fighters in the North of England.

The story contains all the elements of his environment at that time. Things such as foul language, crude sex and raw brutality, but it also contains love, gentleness and alas, great sorrow.

CHAPTER ONE

He was dying and he knew it - but death didn't frighten Jimmy Glave. No, he was more concerned with not letting his family see what he went through, in those last torturous hours.

For he remembered watching his own father die of pneumoconiosis, or as miners called it, the pit disease. Now, shaking his head at the memory, he thought, 'No, it's best they keep well out of the way till it's all over - there'll be a big enough mess to turn their stomachs after I've gone.'

He knew there wasn't long to go now and, as he heaved even more lumps of his life up on to the pillow, crystal clear images of his father's death came flooding into his mind.

Once again, he saw him spewing blood everywhere and writhing in pain like some demented animal. He also recalled how embarrassed he had felt, having to watch the wretched man going through the last throes of his life, for it seemed so undignified for a man to have to endure such shame whilst his family looked on, and it was for this reason he had decided to come up to the attic, so he could die on his own without being gawked at.

Having been born in May 1902, it would only have been another four months and he would have reached forty five, which he considered, for a niner, was not bad really. Especially one who had had the sort of hard life he had. For he had never been one to do things by half - he had always worked hard, drunk hard and fought hard, just as he had always been taught to and, just like his father before him, the pit disease had been the only thing strong enough to put him on his back.

As he coughed again, more black blood dribbled from his mouth, but he felt nothing now - only a numbness seeping through his body. Then a faint smile of relief flickered across his lips as he whispered to himself, "Almost over now - a few more minutes, then I'll be free; there'll be no more pain or struggling for breath, and no more humiliation at not being a proper man any longer."

For, since the disease had taken hold these last few months, life had become hell as it slowly turned him into a substandard being and, as Jimmy felt that once a man lost the ability to work or defend himself, he may as well call it a day; because there were those who lost respect, or tried to take liberties they normally would never have dared, if you had been your normal self. As had been the case with his elder son, Siddy.

The lad had stood by gloating as his father had deteriorated and, the worst Jimmy got, the cockier the lad had become. If it had not been for the presence of his younger son, Matty, god knows what Siddy might have done to him, as the hate between the two of them had grown to fever pitch in the last couple of years, ever since Siddy had realised why his father had made him and his brother fight each other for so long in the backyard.

Turning his thoughts to Matty now he smiled, for this lad was different. At eighteen, he was the younger of the two by three years, but of late Siddy had certainly come to fear him, and now, as the final dregs of life spilled from him, he felt a sense of satisfaction as he recalled the very first time, he had pitched his two sons against each other, almost six years ago.

The young one had been twelve then, a quiet, timid sort of lad, who had been far happier walking the moors with his retarded sister collecting wild flowers, than playing with his brother or any of the other kids in the street.

This though had bothered Jimmy, because Siddy was beginning to show signs of becoming a bully, and he reckoned that, if anything was ever to happen to him and the lad was left in charge of the family, he would lead them a dog's life.

He remembered how he had thought for days about the problem and the only solution he could think of to combat Siddy's bullying, was to turn young Matty into a fighter. He had carried a fair reputation himself for scrapping, so teaching the kid how to use himself would not be much of a problem. No, it was getting him to fight that would be the bugbear, and the only way he could think of was to make him keep taking on Siddy, until he realised the only way to stop the hidings was to fight back.

The lad had taken some fearsome beatings in those early days, but, as time passed and he grew both in size and knowledge, slowly the tables began to turn, until one day Siddy had worked out just what his father had been up to and refused to fight anymore.

It was then Siddy's contempt for his father had begun to show itself, but it was also about then that the pit disease started to take hold of Jimmy.

Yet, even though he had achieved what he had set out to do, there was still one thing about Matty that bothered him, and that was his lack of a killer instinct.

He, Jimmy, had carried one and so had Siddy, but Matty just seemed as though he would do enough to get the better of his brother and then he would stop. It was as if he knew who the better man was and felt he did not have to carry on to prove it.

'Still,' he thought, 'It's probably just as well the lad doesn't have a nasty streak in him, for with his size, power and ability, he really would be capable of killing somebody.'

Now, as peace drifted over him, Jimmy Glave felt at last, he was ready to die.

<u>Two Years Later</u>

'Quarter to four again', thought Matty, as he stretched out his hand to switch off the alarm clock. 'Still, it's Friday - get this shift over with and I'll have two whole days to myself, two days away from that shit-hole.'

He climbed out of bed and drew back the curtains. Although it was pitch dark outside, he could just make out the snowflakes falling against the window and, as they melted and ran down the pane, he thought, 'How sad.' For melting snowflakes always reminded him of falling tears - so gentle, yet so full of sadness.

An involuntary shiver ran down his spine, but it was not the coldness of the room, it was of what the snowflakes reminded him - gentle but sad beings who had come into his life at one time or another.

So far there had been three - Frank Robson, a crippled friend he had once had, Billy the Buck his pet rabbit, and Dotty, his retarded sister. Frank and the rabbit were dead now, but he still had Dotty, and as he dressed, he began to think of her.

At twenty two, she was two years older than Matty, but she had the mental age of a child of about four or five. Her body was not like that of a young woman either, she was built more like a lad of around ten, but she had the most endearing smile and the prettiest face he had ever seen, and where the rest of the family had dark features, Dotty was a soft pink colour. This, coupled with her big brown eyes and little button nose, made her look just like a doll. She had long, brown, shiny hair and when she smiled, two little dimples would appear in her cheeks.

As he finished dressing, his smile broadened as he pictured her in her white frock with different coloured flowers on it and a pink ribbon in her hair; he also heard her laughing with that childlike cackle she had, and he chuckled at the thought of it.

Leaving the bedroom and closing the door quietly behind him, he thought how clean and tidy his mother kept Dotty and, considering she did not do much else these days, he supposed that was something to be grateful for. She always washed and dressed her and she also spent hours brushing her hair - it was as if Dotty was the only thing she had left in the world. For, since his father's death, she seemed to have lost all interest in living.

Tiptoeing downstairs, another shiver ran down his spine, but it had nothing to do with snowflakes this time. It was the thought of what would be waiting for him when he got down to the kitchen.

When he reached the bottom stair, he steadied himself, then, taking three long strides, he leapt up on to the table. He then lit the gas mantle and, as it illuminated the room, he looked down at the floor.

It was just as he had thought - there were dozens of the little sods scurrying everywhere - black, shiny cockroaches, some almost two inches long and as fat as a man's thumb.

He knelt watching them for a few moments, as they frantically tried to hide from the light. Some of them darted under the armchair and settee, others dashed for the dresser, but most of them reached for the sanctuary of the crack-riddled skirting boards.

Before too many could get away though, he jumped down from the table and went after them with one of his boots, but, as usual, they proved to be far too quick for him and he only ended up managing to kill about half a dozen of the little buggers.

'Still', he told himself, 'It's one way of getting the blood warmed up on a winter's morning.' Then a mental picture of the neighbours going through the same ritual came into his mind, and once again he shivered as he thought about the amount of vermin these old houses must have in them.

He could even remember spotting a rat once in the back yard, but he did not tell anyone though, because the lavatory was out there and he did not want to frighten them. 'Besides', he thought, smiling, 'They would probably end up using a pail instead of the lavvy.'

Sweeping the dead cockroaches on to the dustpan, he then threw them on to the fire and, while they crackled and burned, he put the kettle on top of them, then went into the scullery for a quick wash.

The water was freezing, but he gave his face a good rinse, then a good rub with the towel. "That's better", he said, as he hurried back into the kitchen to comb his hair in the dresser mirror.

After doing his hair and giving his face the once over for any blackheads, he stood back for a moment and looked at himself. 'OK', he thought, 'So I'm not Errol Flynn, but I'm not that bad. Surely there must be a young lass somewhere who could take a fancy to me.'

Yet it was not his looks which were to blame for his not having had many girlfriends - in fact, he was quite good looking, with his jet black hair, brown eyes and strong, dark features. No, it was as much his shyness to blame as anything for not getting on with the lasses. That, and the fact that he had no decent clothes to wear.

He often felt self-conscious about his size as well, for at six foot two, and weighing eighteen stone, he was rather big. Yet, what made it even worse though, was the fact that all the lasses he seemed to fancy were the small, petite ones.

There had been a couple of lasses in the past, but no one special. Just people he had taken to the pictures or had gone for a walk with. He had never even had a lover, and he knew for a bloke of twenty, that was bad. He had come close a couple of times, with Kathy Purvis, but every time he was about to get there, she would stop him because he did not have any nodders. Twice he had gone to the barbers to get some, but had changed his mind at the last minute because of his shyness. He once thought about asking one of his workmates to get him some, but as usual, he had chickened out.

'Never mind', he thought forlornly as he mashed the tea and sat down in the chair by the fire, 'It's bound to happen one day.'

As he eased himself back though, a cockroach shot across the back of his left hand and ran down the side of the chair. He took a swipe at it but missed by a mile, then suddenly felt another slight shiver run down his back at the thought of one of the little bastards touching his flesh.

It also sickened him to think of the diseases they carried, and all the different places they could get into, like the butter dish or the sugar bowl. For time after time he had told his mother to make sure she put the lids back on these things when she had used them, but more often than not she would forget. Suddenly, a sense of sadness came over him as he thought about the conditions the family had been forced into since his father's death two years ago.

For when his father went, his brother Siddy seemed to take it as a signal to do just as he pleased. Some days he would work, other days he would not – it all depended on the mood. In the end, the colliery had sacked him for bad timekeeping, which meant there was only Matty's wage coming into the house. With four mouths to feed and clothes to be bought, it was not long before their standard of living dropped.

The worst thing though, was having to live here in the Market Place. For all it was, was a slum. All the poor families were housed here - the Markhams, the Coxons, the Reeds and lots more who were on the poverty line - and why it was called the Market Place he would never know, for no one ever remembered a market being there. All it consisted of, was a winding, cobbled road running between about thirty houses, setback some forty yards or so. There was only one gas light by the side of the road and more often than not, the damned thing did not work.

Finishing his tea, he banked up the fire, then put on his coat and cap and, despite the fact it was Friday, he felt really depressed. As he let himself out of the front door, he could not help thinking that, just this once, it might have been better if he had stayed in bed.

With there being no wind, the snowflakes were drifting down very slowly and, as he walked, he put out his hand to try and catch some, but as usual, as soon as they touched his palm, they melted, which prompted a little voice at the back of his head to whisper, "So gentle, yet so sad."

On reaching the far end of the Market Place, he turned, then stood for a moment looking back across it. "My god!" he exclaimed, shaking his head in despair, "What a sad, desolate place this is - surely there must be something more to life than having to live in a cesspit like this."

As he turned and carried on walking to work, his mood became even blacker as he thought about what would become of Dotty if anything ever happened to him. For he knew his mother could not provide for her and he knew Siddy would not. So the likeliest thing to happen, would be for her to be put into Ryburn Asylum.

'Maybe it's Frank and the rabbit who are the lucky ones' he told himself, as he felt tears of sadness welling up inside of him, 'And it might be a good thing if Dotty and I were to join them. For god knows, I can't see things ever changing for us - this is what we were born into and this is where we'll die.'

He had had the same battle with himself so many times, for he hated his environment. Now suddenly, his mood turned to anger, as it invariably did whenever he got himself as depressed as this.

For basically, Matty hated what he was. He hated being the hard man his father had turned him into. It made him sick to think people feared him - after all he was probably one of the gentlest men living in Houghton-le-Spring. The trouble was though, being who he was, he could never show it, for it was not the done thing in his environment for hard men to show gentleness. He could not talk about nature, flowers, or birds without someone sniggering behind his back and thinking he was a sissy or a homo, and the thought of it all only served to anger him.

By the time he had reached the pit, he was in a right stew with himself, and was grateful to hear the locker room banter. At least the noise and larking about distracted him from his own thoughts, which at the moment, he felt was a blessing.

The banter quietened though, on the cage ride down to the pit face, just as it always did. He felt his stomach churn as usual, and the old thoughts of not coming back up again crossed his mind.

One or two of the men had a half-hearted attempt at humour, but Matty knew they would probably be thinking the same thoughts he was, for no one ever looked forward to going down the pit.

He reckoned it was the hardest way a man could have, of earning a living, for if you did not get crushed or maimed, the dust would most likely get you - as had been the case with his father.

For Matty had watched him slowly die with it, and although he had not been there at the end, he could still remember the wretched state of his body afterwards, and he would never forget the stench of the bed, with most of his father's insides spewn all over it.

He also remembered vowing then that, if ever he was given the chance to get out of the pit, he would jump at it. Even though deep down he knew there would not be much hope of that, as pit work was the only thing he had ever done.

As was normal on a Friday, no one worked too hard and, back in the locker room after the shift, the banter was as loud as ever, in fact, most of the blokes turned into bloody lunatics. They ran around the place grabbing at each other's balls, flicking wet towels off each other's arses and generally giving each other abuse about what they carried between their legs.

It was all done in fun though and no one took offence; it also served to put them in the right mood for a night on the beer. For as usual, they would make arrangements to meet each other later on in the Jolly Farmers and by ten o'clock they would be pissed out of their heads, with any thoughts of the pit many miles from their minds.

Coming down the locker room steps, he was startled when he heard a deep, booming voice call, "Matty, how're you doing son, are you all right?"

He turned towards the pit yard gates and his face broke out into a beaming smile as he saw Big John Fenwick walking across the yard towards him. "Hello, big fella," Matty said, slapping Big John's huge shoulder. Then, pointing to his belly, continued, "That bugger doesn't get any smaller - what do you keep in there, a pig?"

They both laughed out loud, and suddenly Matty's cloud of depression seemed to lift. He was pleased to see the big fella and he knew the feeling was mutual, for there was a respect between the two of them Matty had never shared with his father. Big John would often call in at the Glaves' house when Jimmy had been alive, for they had been mates since they were kids and, even though they had both been hard men, Matty knew his father had been a bit of a bully, but Big John never had been. It had been John who had given Matty the rabbit for his fourteenth birthday, a big ginger Flemish giant he had named Billy after one of their neighbours who also had a mass of ginger hair and, seeing that he was also a male, his full name became Billy the Buck. Sadly though, Matty only had him for about three months, as he was found in the coal-house with his head stoved in.

"I haven't seen you down the Jolly's for a couple of weeks, son. What's Up, are you skint?" Big John asked him, as he pulled his collar up against a sudden chilly breeze.

If it had been anyone else asking him that sort of question Matty might have taken offence, but as it was Big John, he knew he was only concerned with his welfare. "Mmmm, that's about the top and bottom of it, big fella" he replied, jokingly pulling out the linings of his overcoat pockets, and once again they both burst into laughter.

As he had not been to the house for a while, Big John asked, "How's your mother and the lass keeping? Are they both all right?"

"Aye, they're OK. Well, you know what my mother's like - she just seems to drift from day to day - but on the whole she gets by."

They carried on talking for a while about nothing in particular, but Matty noticed that Big John never once mentioned Siddy, and he reckoned it was because of him that he did not come to the house much these days. For he knew that Big John had no time at all for Siddy and in fact he had seen the anger in the big man's eyes several times of late when they had been in each other's company.

Matty knew that it would not have taken much for the big fella to stick one on Siddy but, on the other hand, he was not alone in wanting to do that, for he was one of the most obnoxious people one could ever wish to meet.

Not only was he bone idle, he was also a bully who would not think twice about smacking someone for the price of a pint. He had no pride in his appearance either and Matty was sure he did not wash from one day to the next. The sad thing was that he had been quite smart once - he carried the same strong, dark features as Matty, he had the same black hair and brown eyes and he used to be a well-made man too - but since he had stopped working, he had let himself go. His muscles had turned to flab, he carried a beer gut now and he had taken to slicking his hair down with grease, which meant it was flat on top but ragged around the edges, making him look like the slob he really was.

"Are you down the Jolly's tonight then?" Big John asked, bringing Matty back from his thoughts.

"Aye, I might try and get down for a couple, but that's about all I can afford though," he replied, for he knew his mother would have been up to the pit today to collect his wages and, seeing that there were no shoes or anything of that nature to buy this week and, providing Siddy had not cadged too much from his mother, there might be a few shillings left for him to go out.

So, after agreeing to meet at the pub at about six o'clock, they parted and, as Matty slipped and slid his way home through the slushy snow, he smiled to himself as he thought about Big John.

One thing was for sure, the man was aptly named - standing six and a half feet tall and weighing the best part of twenty eight stone - there really was nothing else he could be called. Most of it was flab these days though, for since he had finished at the pit five years before because of the dust, he had led a life of leisure. He did the odd job here and there, like helping Pat Ridley shift things with his horse and cart, or he would do a bit of fetching and carrying for Bob Hunter, the landlord of the Jolly's, who always seemed pleased to have him around.

Matty almost chuckled out loud as he pictured Big John scratching his head, for he always lifted his cap up with the same hand as he used for scratching - he did not take it off with one hand and scratch with the other. What with the scratching, his bald head and his bulldog like cheeks, Matty reckoned Big John could have made a fortune as a circus clown. Yet, as he crossed the Market Place, he could not help but think what a giant of a man the big fella was, and it was not only in size, for John Fenwick was one of those people other men either feared or respected.

Everything was as normal when Matty arrived home, with his mother stretched out on the settee asleep, or pretending to be, and Dotty sitting in her chair by the fire looking at her flower books.

He hung up his coat behind the front door, took his fish and chips out of the oven, ruffled Dotty's hair as he passed her, then sat down at the table to eat his meal.

Dotty put up her hand and waved at him with her fingers, smiled, then went back to her books. This was her usual greeting to him, but as always, he had to acknowledge her first - it was as if she was far away in a beautiful land of flowers - and touching her brought her back to reality again.

As he buttered a slice of bread, he could not help but wonder if a cockroach had been there before him and he wretched slightly at the thought of it. This made him look across at his mother again and, as he did, he mentally shook his head in disgust. For he could see by the things on the table that she had not bothered to cover anything.

She groaned but did not waken and, as he looked at her pathetic face, he thought what a sad person she was these days. He reckoned it would probably have been better if she had died with his father, for she was only a fraction of the woman she used to be. Once she had been a happy-go-lucky sort of woman who had kept the house spotless and who had always been there for her children. Yet after his father went, it was as if her reason for living had been taken from her. Now, apart from tending to Dotty, all she ever seemed to do was lie on the settee all day, or go upstairs and lie on the bed.

No housework was ever done, she would only cook occasionally and, as far as doing the washing was concerned, she did that once in a blue moon - which meant that if Matty did not do these things, they were never done.

He had often had a go at Siddy about doing more around the house - after all, the lazy sod had little else to do - but he reckoned he should not have to do it because it was woman's work. Several times he had even threatened to throw him out, but had thought better of it as he knew it would upset their mother.

So, for the sake of peace, he would do what he could to keep the house tidy during the week and then at weekends he would do the washing - well, everybody's but Siddy's, because if he preferred to walk around looking like a tramp and smelling like a shithouse, that was his problem.

It had often crossed Matty's mind what Siddy would have been like these days if their father had still been alive. For he remembered how the old man used to rule by fear and it had been fear that had stopped his brother from running wild. He could recall many a thump he had given Siddy whenever he had stepped out of line, and many a thump when he had not. For when their father had had drink inside of him, he used to turn into a bad tempered bully. Matty reckoned that is was for this reason he had grown up hating bullies.

Yet, if the truth be really known, he had never liked his father, as he could never understand what sort of man could have deliberately set his sons fighting against each other, just so he could go down to the pub and brag that he had two hard cases for sons, instead of one. For this was the only reason Matty could think of for why he had done it.

He had also been aware that his father had never had time for Dotty. Yes, he had worked to clothe and feed her, but he did not ever treat her like a daughter and never gave her any affection.

This had sickened Matty, for the lass could not help being the way she was - it was not her fault she had been born retarded. Besides, her gentleness more than made up for any deficiencies she may have had, and many had been the time she had cheered him up whenever he had been miserable, for her smile was like a ray of sunshine on a cloudy day. It took just ten minutes in her company for all his hardness to disappear and be replaced once more by the gentle side of his mature, a side very few people knew he had. In fact, Dotty was the only one left now who knew who the real Matty Glave was.

As he looked at the back of her head now, he smiled affectionately and, as there was plenty of time before he would be getting ready to go out, he decided he would sit with her for a while.

So picking her up, he sat down on her chair and put her on his lap. He picked up one of her books and began turning the pages and, as he did so, she would make little cooing noises, then whenever they came to a picture of a flower she particularly liked, she would point to it and say, "Look Matty, nice eh Matty nice" and as always, he would nod and agree with her; then as he continued turning the pages, she would go back to making her little cooing sounds.

After about half an hour and, feeling totally at peace with himself, Matty decided it was time for a wash and shave. So he got up and gently put Dotty back down on the chair. Walking into the scullery, he suddenly remembered he had no money on him, so he went back over to the mantelpiece and took five shillings out of his mother's purse. It was not a lot, but enough for a few pints and a couple of games of dominoes. As he shaved, he could not help wondering just how much of his hard earned wages Siddy had managed to cadge from his mother.

Once he was ready, he kissed Dotty on the head, gave her a little finger wave, then set off for the five minute stroll down to the Jolly Farmers.

The Jolly's was not much of a pub - it only consisted of one long bar, there was no snug or lounge, which in essence, made it a man's pub. The seating was wooden stools and benches and the floor was only slabs of bare stone - it did not even have a piece of coconut matting covering it. Yet it served its purpose, for apart from having a few pints and a bit of a crack, the only other things the men wanted to do was have a game of dominoes and when they had had enough, a bloody good singsong.

When he got in, Big John and several of his workmates were there. Big John ordered him a pint and Matty almost sunk it in one go, which prompted the big man to say, "Bloody hell, Matty, it's obvious there's been no beer down that throat for a few weeks!" This of course set the whole bar laughing and very soon matters like pit work and poverty were completely forgotten.

By about half past nine, Matty was beginning to think about calling it a night. Even though there was still another half an hour to closing time, he felt he had had enough.

As he stood up to leave and was fending off jibes about going early, he noticed the landlord, Bob Hunter, beckoning him over to the bar. The place was crowded, but he managed to squeeze to within about two feet of Bob, whereupon he called, "What's up, Bob?"

Bob did not answer though, but glanced up to the other end of the bar, then beckoned Matty closer.

Becoming a little annoyed as well as puzzled now, he raised his voice and said again, "What's up?"

Bob could see the change in the lad's features so he answered quickly, "It's your Siddy - he's just come in and he's as pissed as a newt, and he looks in a bad mood with himself."

Matty felt his hackles rise as he turned his body square to Bob and in doing so, spilled the drinks of the men around him. Whether it was the fact that Bob thought he was his brother's nursemaid, or simply that the man was scared of Siddy, only served to anger him as Matty barked back, "So, what the fuck do you want me to do about it – it's your pub - you sort the bastard out."

Then he turned and made his way towards the door, spilling quite a few more pints as he did so, but as he reached the spot where Siddy was standing, he stopped and stood glaring at him for a moment.

Siddy had his back to him, so was totally unaware of his brother who was standing behind him, thinking, 'My god, no wonder I'm ashamed of him. What a fat slob he's turned into - has the bastard no pride?' Then he noticed blood on the back of Siddy's right hand, which made him think, 'And by the looks of that, he's been smacking some poor bugger tonight.' Then, shaking his head in disgust, he left.

Outside, he stood for a while with his eyes closed, leaning against the pub wall, breathing in the cold, crisp air. It felt good and it also served to cool him down.

After calming himself, he looked at his watch and saw it was a quarter to ten. Feeling beaten now, he decided to stroll home. He wondered if his mother would have taken Dotty to bed yet, for he felt he could do with some of her soothing influence, but on the other hand, if she had, he could always take a candle up to his bedroom and read some poetry, which unknown to anyone, was his secret pastime.

On his way home he thought about the first time he had ever read a poem – it must have been when he was about sixteen and just after he had met Frank Robson, for it was Frank who had introduced him to poetry.

Now, as he recalled that first time Frank had mentioned poetry to him, he smiled with affection for, as he remembered it, he had felt quite indignant at being asked whether he read poetry, for he had always assumed that sort of thing was for cissies and, on telling Frank so, his indignation turned to surprise, as the seven stone cripple gave him a real tongue lashing.

"Who in hell's name do you think you are, Matty Glave?" he remembered him saying, "Do you think that for one minute, because a man likes to read beautiful verse, he is somehow a lesser man than you?"

Then he remembered how Frank had gone on to tell him how some of the greatest men in history had either been poets or lovers of poetry. By the time he had finished telling Matty just how wonderful it all was, he could not wait to borrow one of Frank's books to see for himself.

It took some understanding at first, but finally the beautiful philosophies of those rhyming verses penetrated through to him Then with the understanding came the pleasure, and since then he had spent many hours engrossed in poetry. In fact, he had even written a few verses himself, but he had not shown anybody. For he knew that if someone like brother Siddy were to find them, he would never hear the last of it.

On reaching home, it did not surprise him to find Dotty on her own for his mother would often go upstairs for a lie down on her bed, if the pains in her stomach or head were too bad. As he hung up his coat, he was pleased really that Dotty was still up, for after the incident with Siddy, he felt her calming influence would do him more good than reading.

Walking towards her, he smiled at the fact that she still had not acknowledged his entrance, 'But, on the other hand' he thought, 'Her little flower world is probably far more important to her than somebody merely walking in the door.'

Stroking her hair as he knelt down beside her, he was just about to ask how she was when he saw that she was crying. As she was sitting with both of her hands pressed into the pit of her stomach, he assumed she had a tummy upset. So he quietly asked her, "What's the matter, Dotty, are you not feeling well, my love?"

She did not reply, but kept on sobbing. 'I know what I'll do' he thought, 'I'll get her to stand up and pretend to kiss it better - that normally works.' As he stood her up though and she moved her hands from the front of her frock, he gasped with shock when he saw they had been covering a large bloodstain.

He knelt, stunned for a few moments, then asked himself "What in hell's name could it be?" He knew it could not be a period, for he remembered his mother saying once that Dotty was not like other lasses - something about her being under developed and her body not functioning like a woman's. "So what the hell can it be?" he asked himself again.

It was then she lifted up her frock and cried "Kiss it better Matty please, kiss it better 'cos it hurts!"

The sight of her torn, bloodied vagina absolutely horrified him, and again he gasped. For a full thirty seconds, all he could do was stare at the terrible sight in front of him. Then he put down her frock and held her to him.

It was as if his hug had been the signal for release, as her sobbing suddenly turned into hysterics. He pulled her closer to him and began stroking her hair gently in an effort to calm her.

Her crying though had woken their mother, who came hurrying down the stairs, calling, "What's up with the lass, Matty, has she hurt herself or something?"

As she crossed the kitchen towards them, he put up his hand in a calming gesture, then quietly told her, "No, mother, it's nothing like that." Then he turned Dotty towards her and showed her the bloodstain, saying as he did so, "I don't know what's happened to her, mother, but by the looks of her frock, I'd say it was something bad. Can you take her into the scullery and have a look at the damage between her legs, then if you want me to, I'll run up and fetch Doctor Smurthwaite."

He peeled Dotty's arms from around his waist, then gently pushed her towards his mother, who in turn, put her arm around the girl's shoulders and began leading her towards the scullery. Suddenly she stopped and, with a puzzled look on her face, turned to Matty and said, "It couldn't have happened very long ago, because I heard Siddy's voice about nine o'clock and I'm sure that if she'd been in a bad way then, he would've got me up to her."

At the mention of Siddy's name, Dotty broke free from her mother and ran screaming back to Matty. Flinging her arms around his waist again, she clung to him for dear life and began wailing at the top of her voice.

Once more he held her to him, gently stroking her hair and trying to calm her. He sensed something was very wrong, but he was puzzled about what to do, so he just stood holding her until eventually her screaming once again subsided into a gentle sob.

Slowly though, his mind began to clear and a terrible thought came into his head. "Surely not" he said to himself, as his mouth fell open in disbelief. "No, he couldn't have done that - not to little Dotty."

Closing his eyes, he suddenly remembered the blood on the back of Siddy's right hand, and he screwed his face up in disgust as he pictured him tearing into her. 'Poor lass' he thought, 'What hell she must have gone through. How could the vile bastard have done it - surely there are enough bags in Houghton he could've turned to for a shag, without having to abuse his own retarded sister.'

Hugging her even more closely to him now, he slowly began to rock her back and forth, then as quietly as he could, so as not to alarm her, he asked, "Dotty, was it Siddy who hurt you?" He paused for a moment to allow her to answer, but when she did not, he said, "Come on now, Dotty, tell Matty if it was Siddy – it's all right, he can't hurt you no more, Matty's with you now. If it was Siddy, just nod your head darling."

She still did not reply, as he stood holding her and staring at his mother's face, which by now was aghast with horror at what Matty was implying. Then, very faintly, he felt Dotty's head move up and down as she nodded her reply.

Their mother had noticed it too and, as she gasped with shock, he could hear her murmur, "Oh my god, no!"

Calmly he loosened Dotty's grip and gestured to his mother to take her saying, "Here mother, see if you can sort her out, I'm off back down the Jolly's - I shouldn't be too long."

She grabbed his forearm and pleaded "No Matty son, don't - fetch the police and let them handle it – don't you go doing anything silly."

For the first time that night, his simmering anger exploded as he growled back at her, "No coppers mother, in fact I don't even want the doctor involved. Can't you see how shameful it would be for the poor lass if this got out – can't you see folk talking about her and laughing at her behind her back? Doesn't it bother you what filthy things will be said about this family? No mother, you stop and think about it – I'm sure you'll agree with me if you do."

He turned then and walked to the door, but before he went, he stopped and looked back at the two of them. It was such a pathetic sight, he felt his anger rise once again as he told his mother, "See what you can do for her, but please, don't fetch the doctor unless it's really necessary" and before she could say anything, he was gone.

Oblivious to the cold, he rolled up his sleeves in preparation. As he stomped back to the Jolly's, he was feeling such anger as he had never felt before - in fact, he felt positively evil. For not only did he want to kill his brother, he wanted to inflict as much pain on him as he could before doing so.

By the time he reached the pub, he was totally consumed with rage. He stopped for a moment with the intention of calming himself down, but after about five seconds, thought 'Fuck it' and went storming into the bar.

Just as he thought, Siddy was still standing in the same spot as he had been earlier. So, grabbing him by the shoulders from behind, Matty hurled him backwards, slamming him against the pub wall, and with an almighty crack, his head bounced off it and shot forward as though he were a rag doll.

Being in such a rage, Matty did not realise that the blow had knocked Siddy out cold, so from then on, no matter how much pain he inflicted, his brother would not feel it.

Which was probably just as well, for as he wallowed in the sadistic beating he was giving Siddy, some of the most hardened men in the bar shrank back in fear at what they were witnessing, as he held him up against the wall and sunk his head straight into his brother's face, crunching both his nose and cheekbones, sending blood spraying around the bar.

He let him slide to the floor then and started into him with his feet - firstly stamping on his already mangled face, then his chest, and with relish, his genitals. Then he stopped for a moment, leering like some raging lunatic and ranting "Filthy, dirty bastard!" over and over again.

He had not finished though, and the whole place cringed with horror as he jumped up and landed with both feet on Siddy's right leg. As it snapped like a twig, a sickening crack resounded around the now silent bar.

Then, still chanting "Filthy, dirty bastard!" he dropped down on top of Siddy and straddled his chest, then put both hands around his throat with the intention of strangling any remaining life out of him.

There was a tremendous thwack on the back of his head, but he was so beside himself with rage, he probably did not feel it as he slumped forward unconscious across his brother's battered body.

Bob Hunter stood leaning on the cricket bat he had just used to lay Matty out, shaking his head in disgust at the bloody mess on his pub floor. He had seen plenty of violence in his days as a street fighter, but never had he come across such viciousness, such raw brutality, as he had just witnessed. He knew it was obvious too, that if he had not stepped in, they would probably have had to scrape Siddy off the floor.

Suddenly the bar began stirring into life again and it sickened Bob to see the way several of the men vied with each other for a look at the carnage.

It was past closing time by now, but as much in temper as anything else, he yelled at the top of his voice, "Come on now everybody, let's be having you - come on – it's gone fucking closing time and I want this place cleared."

Some either did not hear him, or simply chose to ignore him and continued looking at the two brothers and discussing the merits of the hiding, so Bob called to Big John and asked him to clear the pub while he went upstairs to the living quarters to telephone the police, because by the look of Siddy, he reckoned he might have a murder on his hands.

Big John was also sickened by what he was seeing and, thumping the bar, he bellowed in his deep thundering voice, "OUT YOU BASTARDS NOW - COME ON BEFORE I LOSE MY FUCKING RAG WITH THE LOT O' YOU."

Even those who could not see him knew whose the voice was and began making their way towards the door, within a few minutes Big John had the place cleared.

What followed was pretty hectic. The police had turned up first and carted Matty off to the station, dragging him out to the Black Maria feet first. Then the ambulance arrived and rushed Siddy off to the General Hospital through at Sunderland and, although he was not dead, the ambulance men seemed to think he may as well have been, as by the state he was in they did not hold out much hope.

Bob and Big John reluctantly made statements to the police, but only brief ones, as neither of them was too fond of the law.

Then, after they had gone, Bob's wife Bella, brought pailfuls of hot water down from the living quarters and the three of them set about cleaning up the mess.

As he mopped, Big John reflected back on what had just happened and he could not help but mentally shake his head in disgust, as once again he pictured Matty trying to beat his brother to death.

He stopped mopping for a moment and just stood, staring at the floor. He began thinking about Jimmy Glave and wondered if the man would have felt sick or proud of what Matty had done to Siddy. For after all he had trained the lad, he had been the one to turn the young 'un into a hard case. Matty had never wanted to fight when he had been a child, but his father had forced him.

Big John smiled to himself as he remembered how thrilled Matty had been with the rabbit he had given him. He treated it more like a dog and would put a piece of string around its neck for a lead and take it for walks - he would rush home from school and sit on the back step, sharing his tea with it, his mother was always moaning at him for not eating at the table with the rest of the family.

He stopped smiling at the memory though when he recalled how Matty had found the rabbit dead one morning in the coalhouse. Everybody reckoned that Siddy had killed it, but he had denied it and when he had said "It was only a fucking rabbit", Matty had flown at him. That had been the first time he had ever attacked his brother.

Thinking about it now, Big John realised that he was not at all surprised things had turned out like this. Over the years, Siddy had behaved abominably to Matty - and their sister as well. He had got worse too since their father had died; he could remember Matty having to smack him a few times whenever his nastiness had got out of hand.

As he carried on mopping again, he was still puzzled as to what could have turned Matty as vicious as he had been. He could only think that it must have been something really bad and it must have been something that had happened up at the house, or the lad would have smacked him before he had left the pub the first time. He racked his brain over what it could have been - he kept asking himself over and over what Siddy could have done that was so bad Matty would try and kill him.

After about ten minutes, the only conclusion he could come to was that it somehow involved their mother, Lily. Then it hit him just what Siddy had probably done and, as his confusion turned to anger, he threw down the mop and headed for the door.

"I'm off up Matty's house" he said to Bob as he passed him, "I think I know what Siddy might have done to upset Matty like he did. I reckon the sod's been badly using his mother, so I'm going up there to see if she's all right."

It only took a few minutes to reach the house, where he rapped on the door and walked straight in. The kitchen was empty, but he could hear noises coming from the scullery.

So he quietly called, "Lily, is that you in there? Are you all right, love?" The noises suddenly stopped, then he heard a faint whispering and a few moments later Lily came into the kitchen, closing the scullery door behind her.

He could see by her eyes she had been crying, so gently putting his arm around her shoulder, he asked "What's up, lass, has your Siddy been doing something he shouldn't have?"

She burst into tears, so he held her to him while she had a good cry. Then calmly he said to her, "Well, one thing's for sure Lily, whatever it is he's done, he'll not be doing it again, for your Matty's just given him the hammering of his life."

He held her for a few moments longer but, as affection was not really one of Big John's strong points, he released her and, slightly embarrassed, stood staring at the floor waiting for her to say something. As the kitchen now fell silent, he suddenly became aware of someone sobbing in the scullery.

So concerned had he been about Lily's wellbeing, he had totally forgotten about the daughter. He held Lily's face up and scanned it for any cuts or bruising and, when he saw that there was no mark on her, it dawned on him then to whom the damage had been done.

As he brushed past Lily to go into the scullery, she grabbed his arm, saying "Please John – don't go in there!" He hesitated for a moment, then eased her hand away and went in.

There was no gas mantle in the scullery and, as the place was only lit by a couple of candles, it took his eyes a few moments to adjust to the light - but finally, he saw her.

She was standing in the far corner by the sink, naked apart from a towel wrapped around her shoulders, and the poor lass was shivering like some scared little animal. As he stepped closer to her, he also noticed the rivulets of watery blood running down the insides of her legs.

He shook his head in disgust at the thought of what had happened to the girl, then turned and went back into the kitchen. It was as much as he could do to stop himself shaking with anger.

"Has the bastard done what I think he has?" he asked Lily, clenching and unclenching his fists in temper.

She did not reply, so, glaring at her now, he barked, "Well?"

"Aye, you're right, John" she said, holding her hand over her mouth, trying not to cry.

Seeing the state she was getting herself into again, he softened his tone as he enquired, "Have you sent for the doctor yet?"

Shaking her head, she replied, "No, she doesn't need one – she's going to be all right. Besides, our Matty doesn't want anybody to know what went on here tonight."

They both stood in silence for a while, neither really knowing what to say, Big John wondered how he would have felt if it had been two of his children involved in that sort of thing, and this made him realise that Matty was probably right. But the fact remained that Matty could be facing the rope for murder if Siddy died - and that was something he would not stand for.

Then Lily broke the silence by asking, "Where's our Matty now, John?"

"He's down the cop shop - Bob Hunter had to lay him out with a cricket bat, 'cos he went that loopy."

"Is he going to be all right?"

"I can't really say, lass" he said, fiddling with his cap. "It all depends on what happens to your Siddy – they've got him through at Sunderland General now, but he's in a bad way and the chances are he could die."

"Oh my god, no!" she cried, and collapsed into Big John's arms, sobbing her heart out.

He let her cry on again for a little while, then took hold of her by the shoulders and gently shook her, saying "Come on now, Lily, pull yourself together - the first concern is that young lass in the scullery - I want you to get in there and see to her. There's nothing we can do about Matty tonight, I'll pop down the station first thing in the morning and see what I can find out. But I'll tell you this, Lily" he said, raising his voice, "Shame or no shame, I won't stand by and watch Matty hung for a twat like Siddy."

"So take fair warning - if he snuffs it, I'll tell the cops exactly what made him do what he did." Then, turning her gently towards the scullery door, he told her to see to Dotty while he made her a cup of tea.

Meanwhile, back at the Jolly Farmers, Bob was treating himself to a cigar and a glass of brandy. Having finished the cleaning up, Bella had gone to bed, leaving Bob to reflect on what was probably the bloodiest hiding he had ever seen anyone dish out.

For in his time as a street fighter, Bob had been involved in some fearsome set-tos, but nothing like he had seen earlier. In his mind he reeled off the names of men he had fought or heard about, who he thought might have taken young Matty, but he could not think of anyone.

Not even Joula Lowrey would have been good enough, and he had been the person who had put an end to Bob's fighting days. "Aye" he reflected, feeling the right side of his rib cage which Joula had crushed, "Lowrey was a nasty bastard, but he wasn't in the same league as the young 'un."

Now, as he poured himself another glass of brandy, he suddenly realised just how mundane his life had become since he packed up the fight game. Smiling sarcastically to himself, he looked round his pub; 'Some fucking pub' he thought, 'I've seen better sodding doss houses.'

"Still" he sighed, "What choice did I have? I couldn't really afford anything better and it's beginning to look as though I'm stuck here too, unless I'm blessed with a miracle."

The sad thing was though, in his heyday, Bob had had plenty of money through his hands, for it was not unusual for him to fight for fifty pound purses when in his early to mid twenties. In fact, on several occasions, he had even fought for seventy-five. Then there had been the side bets his handler had laid for him. "Aye" he reckoned "I must've gone through a few thousand quid and what have I got to show for it? Nothing but this shit-hole!"

The more brandy that went down his throat, the more nostalgic he became. He wondered how his old handler, Barny Finch, was making out these days, then he remembered his cuts man, Cuddy Wheeler - the best man he had ever seen with a piece of cat-gut and a needle.

He also missed the cheering crowds, the back-slapping and the popularity. Then there was the feeling of adrenalin pumping through the veins and, of course, the smell of blood.

"But that's all in the past" he told himself. Then, as he looked across at the spot where the trouble had been, an idea sprang into his mind and he suddenly became very excited.

"Just supposing I could get young Matty interested in the fighting game" he enthused, "Jesus, we'd make a bloody fortune - after all, I've got the contacts and I know the ropes, and it wouldn't take me long to teach the lad a trick or two - not that he'd need much teaching though. Then in about a month, I reckon I could have him ready."

So excited had he become, he had completely forgotten the reality of the situation. Then, when he remembered just where Matty was, and why, he threw his glass against the wall, hissing "Bollocks" as he did so.

He just sat then for a while staring at the floor, stewing in his disappointment, then went behind the bar to fetch himself another glass. Sitting down again, he filled it with brandy and tipped it straight down his throat.

After several glassfuls he then became maudlin. "Here I am" he lamented, "Thirty-five years old and what have I got? A broken down pub in a slum, no money, and now a shattered dream. God, the only good thing that had happened to him since he'd packed up fighting seven years ago, had been meeting Bella. She was a good homemaker, a good cook too, but most of all she was horny and, seeing as how she couldn't have kids, they'd had a great sex life."

Yet, deep down, he knew he wasn't domesticated, for he yearned for the old days. He missed his old drinking mates, the gambling, and of course, the fight scene.

Feeling depressed now, he looked up at the clock. It was half past twelve, so he decided it was time for bed, but as he went to put out the bar lights, a sudden thought struck him. 'I wonder what sort of sentence Matty will get if Siddy lives - they might only give him two or three years. There'd still be plenty of time for him to take up fighting for a living, but the only problem then would be persuading him to do it.'

"Still" he concluded as he closed the bar door behind him, "If he does only get a couple of years, that gives me plenty of time to find a way."

CHAPTER TWO

Never having woken up in a police cell before, it had taken Matty a little while to fathom out where he was and how he came to be there. He could remember sitting on top of Siddy, then being whacked on the head, but after that, everything became a complete blank until he had come round about ten minutes ago.

He touched the lump on the back of his head again, and "Jesus", did it sting! The throbbing did not help either – it felt as if someone was rhythmically hitting him on the head with a hammer.

'Still' he thought, as once again he pictured Siddy's battered body, 'Two aspros will see me alright, but it will take a lot more than that to cure him!' For even though he could not remember everything he had done to Siddy, he felt he had done enough to have killed the bastard.

To try to ease the throbbing, he decided to lie back down on the wooden bench he had woken up on. He closed his eyes to a slit and found to his relief, it did not feel as bad. Then, after a few minutes, he drifted off to a fitful sleep.

In his sleep he kept hearing Dotty's pitiful cry of "Kiss it better, Matty, please – it hurts, kiss it better", and he could see her blood-stained frock, then the awful mess between her legs. He could see the blood on the back of Siddy's hand, then he saw himself driving his boot into Siddy's groin and leering at him as he did so.

The images and the sounds went on and on, until suddenly he heard a rattling of keys, but he could not quite work out where this noise fitted in. Then he heard a strange voice telling him to wake up at the same time as he felt someone shaking him. He kept telling himself that he was not asleep, then suddenly he opened his eyes to see a young man in a police uniform leaning over him.

"Come on, Glave", the young copper said, putting a tray on the floor beside where Matty was lying, "There's a mug of tea for you and a bit of breakfast."

Matty lay still until he heard the door close again and the keys rattle, then he opened his eyes and gingerly sat up. He bent down very slowly and picked up the chipped enamel mug, but ignored the egg sandwich next to it. Thinking that the tea would somehow soothe his still throbbing head, he took a big swig from it, then swallowed it back. It was completely tasteless, just like drinking hot water, and it did not ease the throbbing either.

Then a thought struck him. If this was breakfast, then that meant it was morning, so he must have been here all night. 'Jesus Christ', he thought, 'I wonder how Dotty is.'

He then sat chastising himself for a while, for he knew he had not given one thought as to what would happen after he had sorted Siddy out, and he began to fret terribly about it. He looked around the cell for any sign of a bell he could press to contact someone, but there was nothing – there was not even a window he could shout through.

Over the course of the next hour or so, he banged on the door several times, but to no avail. Either he was being ignored or nobody could hear him, which only led him to get more irritable as the time passed. He had also become aware of an awful smell somewhere in this place, which he finally discovered was the pail in the corner. It smelt of a mixture of disinfectant and urine, and the more his irritation heightened, the stronger the smell became.

Then at long last, he heard the clanking of keys again and the cell door swung open, but it was not a fresh faced young copper who came in this time, it was a huge bear-like man wearing a grey raincoat and a brown trilby hat, with the front of the rim pulled down over his eyes. Immediately, Matty's instincts told him that this man was dangerous.

For a good five minutes the man did not say anything, he just stood, leaning against the white, glazed brick wall by the door of the cell. His eyes did not leave Matty's – it was as if he was trying to read his soul. Then, when he eventually did speak, Matty felt the hackles rise on the back of his neck.

"So – you think you're a bit of a hard bastard, do you sonny?" he growled, holding Matty's stare, "Well, I've got some bad news for you", he continued, "I'm a hard bastard too." Then, for the first time since he had come into the cell, he moved. He took off his trilby and wiped his brow with the sleeve of his raincoat. This gave Matty a better view of his eyes, which he saw were steel grey and looked as cold as hell.

"Shilton's my name" he said, cockily twirling his hat in his left hand, "Detective Sergeant Clive Shilton – ever heard of me?"

'So this is the bastard' Matty thought, but not once showing any sign of recognition, he just continued staring up at the Sergeant's eyes.

For eyes played a large part in the world of hard men. If he were to break his stare and turn his eyes to the floor, the Sergeant would have automatically taken that as a sign of submission, but, as he continued to hold it, that served to let the Sergeant know he was not going to be intimidated.

The Sergeant had studied him closely and had come to the conclusion that this was no ordinary back street yobbo, this kid had power running through his whole body – he also looked quite intelligent, which, considering where he came from, was unusual in itself. The eyes had told him the most though, for it was in those he saw that the lad also carried inner strength and he knew that playing the hard man would only antagonise.

So, softening his voice a little, he decided to try a different ploy. "Your brother's in a bad way – does that bother you?"

Matty did not reply, he just shook his head slightly.

'Well, I'll be buggered' the Sergeant thought, 'Not only is he not concerned how badly hurt his brother is, he doesn't seem too bothered what the consequences of his actions are going to be either.'

Just to confirm it though, he decided to ask him, "Does it not concern you that you almost beat the lad to death then?"

Finally, he got a reaction, as Matty coldly uttered, "Next time I'll make sure."

Again the Sergeant was surprised, for although it was obvious the kid was hard, he certainly did not mark him down as a killer. So whatever it was his brother had done, he concluded it must have been something dire. So again he decided to be direct, casually asking, "What was it he did then, that made you want to kill him?"

Matty just shook his head again, but this time he let his eyes fall to the floor. It was not a sign of submission though and the Sergeant realised that – he could see the lad was somewhere else in his thoughts – something was troubling him, and badly.

"What's up Glave?" he asked sharply, intending to bring Matty back from his thoughts, "Is something bothering you?"

At first he did not reply, then quietly he asked, "Is there any chance of me seeing somebody?"

'At last' the Sergeant thought, smiling to himself, 'Things might move now.' Then he replied "Of course you can" and attempting a joke, added "As long as it's not your brother that is."

Matty almost laughed and, looking up again at the Sergeant, decided that maybe he was not the nasty bastard he was supposed to be after all, and asked, "Can I see Big John Fenwick?"

"Mmm, John Fenwick" the Sergeant mused. "I wonder what that fat twat has to do with things." Then, putting his hat back on and turning towards the door, he told him "Of course you can, I'll arrange it for this afternoon." With that, he rapped on the door, but as it opened and he went to leave, he stopped and turned for one last look at Matty. "I don't think he's a bad 'un really" he told himself, "I just think something drove him to do what he did, but one thing's for sure, he isn't going to tell me what it was, so I'll have to start looking elsewhere."

Alone again with his thoughts, Matty's mind once more wandered back to Dotty. He had not given much thought to how she and his mother would cope without him and it seemed pretty obvious they did not intend to release him. That is why he had thought of Big John, for if he could have a word with him, he felt sure he would keep an eye on them. They did not eat a great deal so they would not take much feeding, and if he were to call at the house two or three times a week, just to make sure they were all right, he would be grateful.

Suddenly he felt very tired, so he lay back down on the bench and closed his eyes. All manner of things flitted through his mind, not just Dotty and his mother, but that copper, Shilton. He had heard a few tales of how the man had always considered himself the hardest man in Houghton, and wherever a violent crime was being committed, it would not be too long before he was on the scene. He had also heard he liked to smack people around, just to show them who was boss. Yet Matty was sure the man had shown concern, or on the other hand, it could have just been a ploy to make him talk; but whatever, he reckoned it best to treat the man with caution.

The pain at the back of his head had eased now, but that was another thing bothering him – who was it that had hit him and what the hell had he used? The only person he could think of with enough nerve to smack him was Big John, who, probably thinking he was going to kill Siddy, had belted him with a stool. He smiled to himself as he pictured the big man swinging the damned thing at him and he knew from the size of the lump it had been one hell of a swing.

Other things drifted in and out of his mind, such as Siddy, what prison would be like if he got time, how would things be when he came out and then it was back to Dotty again. Finally though, he fell into a deep sleep.

Meanwhile, Sergeant Shilton was sitting in his office, with his feet up on his desk, lighting his third woodbine. He had another coughing bout and wondered again if forty fags a day were too many.

'Aw – bollocks to it,' he thought, 'If it's not smoking that kills me, it'll be something else.'

For the last twenty minutes or so he had been deep in thought about Matty. Not about what he had done, for that was pretty evident – one only had to look at the state of his brother to see that – but the reason why was the sticking point. He knew from past experience that a man did not dish out that king of hiding for some run-of-the-mill falling out. He knew it had to be something serious, but the question was – what?

It obviously had not been over money, for that was one thing the Market Place families did not have. So he wondered whether it could have been over a girl. Maybe his brother had tried his hand with his girlfriend or something, or could it be something stupid, like going round telling everybody Matty was a homo.

'I don't know' he thought, 'but whatever it was, I mean to find out, and I think I'll start with fat John Fenwick.'

As he pulled up outside the Fenwick house, Big John was just going in through the gate. He wound down the window, calling "Fenwick, I want a word with you."

Big John stopped in his tracks when he saw who it was. He also felt his heckles rise, for if there was one man he could not stand it was this hard-nosed bastard. In his younger days he had crossed swords with him many times and, thinking back to them, he could still feel the bruises.

He closed the half open gate again and walked over to the car. "What the fuck do you want?" he barked, determined not to be intimidated by the man.

They looked at each other for a few moments, each sizing up the other. The Sergeant thought 'My God, he's still the fat, arrogant slob he's always been.'

Big John held his stare though and was thinking similar thoughts about the Sergeant, and though he suspected why he had come to see him, he decided to play dumb.

"You were in the Jolly's last night when young Glave gave his brother the hammering, weren't you?" the Sergeant asked, lighting a woodbine, but never once breaking the stare.

Big John's only reply was "Mmm, so what?"

"So I want to know why he did it," the Sergeant snapped sharply, then with venom added, "And I want to know now."

The painful memories of their past meetings came flooding back to Big John again, and he was wise enough to know now that once Shilton got his teeth into you, he never let go. Besides, he was too old for the aggravation, and with that, he broke the stare and looked down at the ground. "OK" he said quietly, "What do you want to know?"

Realising he had him by the balls, the Sergeant asked irritably, "I want to know exactly why Matty tried to kill his brother," then sarcastically added, "Now even a thick twat like you can answer that."

Big John felt his hackles rise again and he glared back at the Sergeant. He might be too old and he might be tired of aggravation, but there was no way he was being talked to like a piece of shit and it showed in his reply. "Even if I knew why he did it," he lied, "You're the last person in this fucking world I'd tell – now piss off!" With that last defiant gesture restoring his pride, he turned and went into his back gate.

This left the Sergeant fuming as he muttered to himself "Bastard, fat useless bastard," and his first reaction was to get out of the car and go after the fat pig, but he decided against it. For he knew he had riled the bloke and, given the mood they were both in, they would probably end up having a set-to, and like Big John, the Sergeant was also beginning to feel his age lately. At forty-eight, he too reckoned he was getting a bit long in the tooth for fisty cuffs.

He took off his trilby and took a deep drag of his cigarette and, eventually he calmed down again. Then it suddenly struck him that he had not told fat Fenwick that Matty wanted to see him. 'Still' he thought, smiling, 'I can send a couple of young constables this afternoon to fetch him – that'll be an experience for them.'

The next place he called at was the Jolly Farmers, but again he was met by a wall of silence, so he decided to visit the Glaves' house.

As he knocked on the door, he tried to remember what the woman looked like. As he recalled, she was a tall, stout person with jet black hair, but when the door opened, he was taken aback when a wizened old woman of about sixty asked, "Yes, can I help you?"

"I'm looking for Mrs Glave, love, is she in?"

"Aye, I'm Mrs Glave, what do you want?" she asked defensively.

"My name is Detective Sergeant Shilton. I've come to have a word with you about the trouble your lads had down the Jolly Farmers last night, D'you mind if I come in?"

She hesitated for a moment, then replied, "Yes, but you'll have to wait here a minute." Then she closed the door.

He imagined the house was probably in a mess and she wanted to tidy up first before inviting him in, but while he stood on the doorstep, he could not help thinking how terrible she had come to look. Then he turned and looked around the Market Place and asked himself, 'Is it any wonder, living in a shit-hole like this.'

The door opened again and she beckoned him in, then indicated for him to sit on the settee, which he did. As he looked around the house, he saw that it was no different from all the other slum houses, sparsely furnished, coconut matting for carpet, and wallpaper peeling from the walls. He also noticed the fusty smell of poverty this sort of place carried and he half expected a cockroach or a mouse to run across the floor.

Lily Glave sat down in Dotty's chair by the fire and simply ignored the Sergeant. She knew why he was here, for Big John had popped in earlier to tell her he had been down to the Jolly Farmers to ask Bob Hunter to ring the hospital and the police station. She knew Siddy had not died and that Matty was being held, but how long they intended holding him they would not say.

"D'you know how your son in hospital's doing?" he asked, as he took off his trilby and put it on his left knee.

"Well, I've heard he isn't going to die, but apart from that, they told me nothing."

"What about Matty – have you heard what's happening to him?"

She shrugged her shoulders has she replied, "You lot have him locked up, as far as I know."

"Aye that's right, and we'll probably keep him locked up for a long time if I can't find out what made him do it."

Up till then, Lily had not once looked at the Sergeant, but after his last statement she turned her head and glared at him. Then, with pure hatred in her voice, she said "I bet you feel pleased with yourself, don't you?"

"No, I don't Mrs," he shot straight back at her, "And furthermore, I think there's something about this whole thing that stinks. I know Matty's a hard lad, but there's nothing about him that makes me think for one minute he's a killer, and from what I can gather, if he hadn't been stopped last night, that's exactly what he would have turned into."

Lily turned her head away from him and went back to looking into the fire. She felt so tired, not just of Matty and Siddy, not just of Dotty either, but of living – oh, how she wished Jimmy had been here now – he would have sorted it.

She was not aware of them, but tears were slowly running down her cheeks, and when the Sergeant saw them, he felt a little guilty. For even though he was a hard man, he also had a heart. He could see the toll life had taken on the woman so far and he knew she probably would not be able to take much more – in fact what had happened to her two sons would most likely be the end of her.

A tear dropped onto her hand and she took out her handkerchief and wiped her eyes. Then she straightened her back and asked, "Exactly how long will you put Matty away for?"

He tried to be as gentle as he could with his reply, but he knew it would still hurt her. "Well, that depends Mrs, he could go down for three to five years, but if there was a good reason for doing what he did, there's a good chance he would only get twelve months – and with time off for good behaviour, why, the lad could be home for Christmas with any luck."

He hoped the last part might have cheered her up, but it did not. Instead, she put her head in her hands and sighed deeply. Then she replied, "So – even if you knew the real reason, you'd still lock him up?"

"Aye Mrs, we'd have to – you see, Matty's still committed a serious crime and the law demands he be punished for it. People can't just go around trying to kill each other, can they now?"

As she sat staring into the fire again, he could see she was in deep thought; he felt she was beginning to waver. 'Come on lass' he said to himself, 'Come on – just tell me once why he did it.' He was willing her to say it, but when she replied, his hopes sank.

"What's the difference – twelve months, three years – it doesn't matter – we'll never cope without him anyway, so as long as you're locking him up, all I can tell you is that there has been bad feelings between them for a long time and it all probably came to a head last night."

He took his trilby off his knee and stood up. He knew she was lying and it annoyed him. He walked to the door, then turned round to look at her; she was still staring into the fire. "When I first came in" he said gruffly, "You asked me whether I was pleased Matty was locked up -well, all I can say to you now Mrs is, I hope you are."

On the drive back to the station he was raging. He banged the steering wheel with his right hand and shouted, "Idiots, stupid sodding idiots – why do they always have to see the police as enemies, don't they understand that we're also here to help?" Then calming down again, he shook his head in despair, thinking, 'I don't know why the hell I even bother.'

Back in his office, he paced the floor in frustration. He had arranged for John Fenwick to be brought down to the station, he had rung the hospital for a progress report on Siddy; now for the moment, he could not think of anything else he could do. So, picking up his hat from the desk, he thought, 'Bollocks to it all – I'm off for a pie and a pint.'

When Matty came into the interview room, the first thing he noticed was how badly Big John was sweating. Sitting down opposite him, he asked, "Are you alright, big fella – you look a bit flushed."

"Aye, I'm alright, Matty – I just hate these bloody places, that's all."

"How's my mother and Dotty – do you know?" he whispered anxiously.

"Your mother's upset, obviously, but the main thing is the lass is going to be alright," he answered, lowering his voice at the last part, then furtively looked at the policeman standing by the door, hoping he had not heard him.

Matty whispered again, "Do you know what our Siddy did then?"

For a reply, Big John simply nodded his head, still fearing the policeman might hear his booming voice.

"And has my mother asked you to keep quiet about it?"

"Aye," he nodded, then whispered again, "But I'm not too happy about it son, especially since that Shilton's sniffing around – be careful of him, Matty, he's a dangerous bastard.

This perplexed Matty a little, for the man seemed hard enough, but he did not strike him as dangerous. So he asked Big John what he meant, "How do you mean – dangerous?"

Big John leaned forward, trying to be more discreet, and replied, "Because he's a sly bastard – he'll come on all friendly, but all he's really trying to do is get you to open up so he can make a case against you. So I'm telling you – be wary of the bugger!"

He could see the anger in the big man's eyes, so to calm him, he added "OK Big John, I promise I'll be careful what I say to him."

"Now," Matty raised his voice slightly as he asked, "Will you do me a favour, can you keep an eye on my mother and Dotty for me – they won't take much feeding and I'll be grateful if you could pop in a couple of times a week, just to make sure they're OK – especially our Dotty."

By the sound of Big John's voice, Matty felt he had offended him as he replied gruffly, "Of course I'll look after them – you know I will, so you needn't worry on that score."

He did not think he needed to ask, but, just to put his mind at rest, he felt he must.

They sat in silence for a few moments, then Big John asked if there was anything else. When Matty said there was nothing, he stood up and wiped his brow with his cap, saying, "OK then young 'un, I'm off then. Is there something I can bring down for you?"

Matty shook his head, then thanked him for coming and, as Big John was led out of the interview room, he suddenly felt very lonely.

Having finished his pie, the Sergeant was now on to his second pint. He was mulling over his meeting with Matty's mother, and there was something about what she had said that had him puzzled. "We'll never cope without him," she had said – but who, he wondered, was the 'we'? Surely she could not mean the brother, for he had gained the impression she could not care less about him. So, who could it be? He had not seen anyone else in the house, but on the other hand, when he had first arrived, she had closed the door for a few minutes. The question was though, why? Was she tidying up as he had thought, or was she hiding someone – in the scullery maybe, or upstairs? For the 'we' bit certainly had him baffled.

He did not know the Glaves that well, so it was possible there could be someone else in the family, and the Sergeant decided the only way he could find out was to ask.

As he walked into the cell this time though, Matty stood up. The Sergeant was taken aback at the size of him, for he had looked a handful sitting down, but now he was standing he looked pretty useful. "How're doing, Glave?" he asked casually, "Everything all right?"

"Aye, I'm alright," replied Matty, remembering Big John's advice about being careful.

"I went up your house earlier to see you mother – she seems a bit upset."

"That's understandable" he answered, standing square to the Sergeant, who could see by his stance, was not going to be intimidated.

So, leaning against the wall, he took off his trilby and began plucking at the band, saying matter of factly as he did so, "How many are in your family, Glave – surely there's more than just you two lads, isn't there?"

Matty heard the alarm bells of caution ring in his brain. He sensed the man was fishing and it was obvious that if he had been to the house and had not seen Dotty, his mother must be keeping her out of the way. So he quietly replied, "No, there's only the two of us. Why do you ask?"

Once again the Sergeant knew he was being lied to, for there was one thing he had learned in his twenty-eight years as a policeman – that was how to spot a liar.

Not wanting to risk upsetting Matty, the Sergeant decided to let it drop. Afterall, it was something he could easily find out by asking around. He stood playing with his hat for a while, then said "OK then Glave, we'll leave it for now." And with that, he left.

It was not until the following day that Sergeant Shilton found out about Dotty. He had been told that the girl was retarded and certain pictures began to formulate in his mind. Either Siddy had badly used the girl, or even worse, he had interfered sexually with her. 'But even worse than both of them, is the fact that the lass might be dead,' the Sergeant thought, curling his top lip in anger.

The first thing he had to do was see the daughter. If she was in the house and was all right then that would be fine – but if she was not, the whole lot of them had better watch out. For, as he told himself as he climbed into the car, 'I'll sort the lot of the bastards out – aye, and that includes him down the cells.'

He did not drive up to the house this time, instead he parked at the bottom of the street and when he got to the door, he did not wait to be asked in either. He simply rapped on it and walked straight in.

To his relief there was a girl sitting in the chair by the fire. 'At least she's not dead' he told himself. Then Lily Glave came in from the scullery wiping her hands with a tea towel. "What do you want this time?" she asked sharply, "And what's the idea of just walking in? Have you got no bloody manners?"

"I did knock twice, love, but I got no reply, so I thought you might be in the back yard" he lied.

"OK then, what do you want?" she asked again. Then walking over to Dotty said, "Come on pet, you go into the scullery while I talk to this man."

The Sergeant could not help but notice the lass was retarded, he also saw how she held her lower stomach as she walked and grimaced with each step she took, indicating she must be in a hell of a lot of pain. His instincts told him then, he had found the cause of the trouble.

Lily closed the scullery door behind Dotty, then turned, saying "Well, I'm waiting."

"Your Matty just asked me to pop up and see how the lass was, that's all, he said she'd been ill lately and was a bit concerned about her," he casually lied. Then added "Is the lass alright, she doesn't look too well to me."

He knew by her response she had not believed a word he had said, as she replied "Aye, she's OK," then walking to the front door and opening it, barked defiantly "Now get out."

They stood looking at one another for a few moments, both knowing the other was a liar, but as he had achieved what he had set out to, he decided not to antagonise the woman any further. So with one final glance at the scullery door, he gave her a curt smile and left.

Some minutes later, as he sat smoking in his car, he felt rather pleased with himself, for now he had something to work on. All he had to do was to get someone to make a statement saying what Siddy had done to the lass, and he would nail the bastard good and proper.

It was possible he could have kicked or punched her in the stomach, but he felt it was more than that, he was almost sure he had raped her and the more he thought about what Matty had done to the twat, the more sympathy he felt for the kid. For he knew fair well that if he had been in Matty's shoes, he would have done the same thing himself.

In the course of the next few days, he visited Matty several times, yet never once did he mention Dotty.

This struck Matty as rather odd, for Big John had been down to see him and had told Matty that the Sergeant was well aware of the lass. Which got him to thinking that, either the Sergeant had not found out what had happened, or he was playing some cagey game.

The truth of the matter was though, the Sergeant had given up trying to get anything out of Matty, for again he felt that if he had been in the lad's shoes, he would not have wanted people to know about it either.

Yet he still had his job to do. So the following week, when Siddy was considered to be out of danger, he paid a visit to Sunderland General.

As he sat by the bed picking at the band of his trilby, the Sergeant felt nothing but revulsion for the bloke lying on it. Even though his body was badly beaten and broken, he had to fight back the urge to lay into him.

For although Siddy was in a bad way, he had refused to answer the Sergeant's questions, saying he couldn't remember anything about the night, and even when he had threatened to break his other leg, Siddy still did not crack.

So as he left the hospital, Sergeant Shilton felt both subdued and frustrated, for he knew that by law Matty was guilty, but in terms of being a man, he was not.

That afternoon Matty was formally charged with Grievous Bodily Harm. It could have been worse, he could have been charged with Attempted Murder, but Sergeant Shilton had used his influence to get it reduced. Yet he still was not happy, for he knew the lad could still be facing three years or so.

The following morning, he decided to have one last go at John Fenwick. This time though it would not be in a hostile manner, he would try and appeal to the bloke's sense of decency, that was if he had one.

When he reached the Fenwick house, Big John was not there. His wife told the Sergeant that he was on his allotment at the top of Seaham Road, and seeing as he had never been to these allotments before, it took him a good twenty minutes and there were three stops for directions, to finally locate the big fella.

As nothing was growing on the allotment at this time of year, he walked straight across it to the big tin shed in the far corner and, as he opened the door, he couldn't help but chuckle to himself, for the first sight to greet him was Big John sitting on an old bus seat and warming his hands by an old stove.

The chuckle soon disappeared though, as the big fella's instant response was to bark at him "And what the fuck do you want? This is private property so piss off."

Sergeant Shilton could have reacted just as angrily, but he chose not to. Instead, he stood a large log up on its end, sat down on it and he too proceeded to warm his hands by the fire.

Big John sat in silence, inwardly raging at the cheek of the bloke, for this was his sanctuary, the one place no one was allowed but him. This was where he came in his sad moments or where he could think out his problems without being disturbed and it offended him to think the useless pig could just wander in as he liked.

Yet when the Sergeant did reply, Big John was taken aback by the softness of his tone, as he told him "Now, now, Fenwick, this is not the time for us two to be arguing. I think if the truth was known, I'm feeling as badly about young Matty as you are, and all I'm trying to do is stop an injustice. For if Siddy did to the lass what I think he did, then the wrong one's locked up."

Big John did not answer for a few moments, he sat staring into the fire thinking, 'Somebody must have opened their bloody gob then, cos it's obvious Shilton knows, but who could have told him. Surely Matty wouldn't, nor Siddy. So, either Lily had cracked or he's guessing.'

Then without turning to look at the Sergeant he asked, "How much do you know then?"

Sergeant Shilton sighed with relief at the mildness of Big John's reply, for he didn't want to be drawn into another confrontation with the big man. He was tired and as he looked at Big John out of the corner of his eye, he could see weariness on his face too.

"I'll be honest with you Fenwick; I've got nothing concrete on Siddy but I've seen enough to know he did something bad to the lass. Now if it's what I think it is, rape, then I reckon Matty should have been allowed to finish the job."

"But unfortunately, that's not how the law works so, I have to try and nail Siddy some other way. To do that though, I need help, I need someone like you, or his mother to make a statement. You know as well as I do the bastard shouldn't be allowed to get away with it and neither should Matty be sent down for three years when it should only be months."

Big John put another piece of wood on the fire and thought about it for a while. Even though it was wrong for Matty to do three years, he still felt the lad would prefer that to Dotty's shame. So almost in a whisper he said "No, I think things are best left as they are, that's how Matty wants it, so that's how it will be."
Puzzled and with frustration in his voice, the Sergeant asked, "What do you mean, that's what Matty wants?"

So Big John proceeded to explain to him the deep feelings Matty had for his sister and even though she wouldn't be aware of what folks were saying about her, both he and his mother would be.

He knew folks would point at her and whisper vile things behind her back. Like what the lass had had to put up with and how long had it been going on. Like what a bad mother Lily must have been to allow it to happen and was it only one brother that was abusing her.

"No," the big man concluded, "As I've said, it's best left alone, Matty's quite prepared to do his time to protect the lass."

Then as Big John lapsed into silence again and sat staring deep into the fire, Sergeant Shilton glanced at him. For a moment he wasn't sure if it was the wood smoke stinging the big man's eyes, or if he was crying. One thing was for certain though, he had come to realise that there was more to John Fenwick than merely a pair of fists.

A few minutes passed with neither speaking as they both reflected on their thoughts of Matty. Now the Sergeant could see the full picture he knew there would be very little chance of him ever making a case against Siddy. So if he was to help the lad, another favour would have to be called for.

"It's all his father's fault you know," Big John whispered again and bringing the Sergeant back from his thoughts. "The lad never wanted to be a fighter, but Jimmy forced him into it," he continued, "I suppose he must have had his reasons for doing so, but I've never been able to figure out what the buggers were."

"Maybe he didn't want the young 'un to be bullied by his brother," the Sergeant responded, "Or maybe he just wanted to keep up the Glave name for being hard men, cos he certainly was."

"I don't know," said Big John, sounding more weary than ever now, "But whatever it was, he's ball's it up now."

They sat talking then about the old days, which surprised the Sergeant some, for he never imagined he would find himself conversing with the likes of John Fenwick, in anything other than a hostile manner.

Big John had also told him about the rabbit and the cripple friend Matty once had and, as the Sergeant strolled back to his car about an hour later, he couldn't help but think just how much the big man liked the lad. Then he suddenly stopped and smiled to himself, as he realised how much he liked him too.

The following morning though, Matty was to receive even more bad news and, once again it was Big John who was to be the bearer of it.

As he entered the interview room, Matty could see that the big man was sweating even more heavily than he had been before, so he knew something was wrong as he asked sharply, "What's up now Big John, has the fucking house burnt down or something?"

Wiping his brow with his cap, the big man replied, "No, but it may as well have done, I'll tell you about that later though. I've got something far more important to tell you."

He hesitated then, as if fumbling for the right words, then he blurted out. "It's your mother Matty, she collapsed last night and had to be taken through to Sunderland General."

Then seeing the look of anguish on Matty's face, he put up his hand in a calming gesture, as he continued to tell him, "But there's no need to get yourself in a stew though, she's not ill or anything, but Doctor Smurthwaite reckons she's knackered and a good rest would do her the world of good."

Matty put his head in his hands and slowly shook it, as he replied sadly, "I don't know Big John, it seems to be one thing after another." Then a fearful dread came over him as he asked, with panic in his voice, "What's happened to our Dotty then?"

"Steady, steady," Big John said, making his calming gesture again, "You needn't worry about the lass, she's up at our place." Then he chuckled as he added, "My missus is fussing over her like an old hen, she's loving it."

Matty relaxed then and smiled as he thought about Mary Fenwick fussing over Dotty. 'Aye' he told himself, 'She'll be well cared for there alright.'

His gentle thoughts of Dotty soon evaporated though, when Big John said, "There's more bad news as well Matty," then sighing deeply added, "You've been finished at the pit, but not only that, your mother has a month to get out of the house."

"For fucks sake" he uttered, as Matty felt his temper coming on, "What sort of people are they. You risk life and limb for the bastards and all they can do in return, is to kick you when you're down."

He put his head in his hands once more and screamed to himself "My god, I've made a right balls-up of this."

Big John could see he was hurting, so trying to comfort him said, "Don't be too hard on yourself son, this mess isn't really your fault. It's all down to that bastard of a brother of yours, he's the one who's caused all this and, I'll tell you something else, if the twat ever shows his face around our way again, I'll flatten him."

An involuntary smile crossed Matty's lips as he looked up at Big John. Then suddenly he chuckled as he replied softly, "D'you big fella, I reckon you would do that."

Neither had anything to be happy about, but as they sat looking at each other, Big John smiled at him and nodded. Then stood up and slapped Matty on the shoulder, saying "Don't worry son, you'll get through this and when it's all over, the pair of us will go out and get pissed. Don't go worrying about the lass either, as I've said, we'll look after her."

Then as he headed for the door, he turned and called, "So keep your bloody chin, alright."

Matty sat for a few moments staring back at the door. Then he smiled at Big John's attempts to cheer him up. He knew the big man wasn't very good with words, but he knew his heart was in the right place.

No matter how much he tried though, he could not stop worrying about Dotty and that night he barely slept a wink thinking about her.

Even when he managed to drift into sleep, he would hear her pitiful cries somewhere in the darkness. Sometimes she would call him, but when he answered, she would go silent again.

So it was to be, he fretted in his waking hours and was tormented in his sleep.

It didn't take the Sergeant long to notice the change in him either, as he became irritable and depressed. So one night he decided to pay the lad a special visit.

As the Sergeant walked into the cell just after eight o'clock, Matty, thinking there was more trouble, immediately sat up on his bunk.

"What in hells name is wrong now?" he sighed woefully.

Instead of answering though, the Sergeant merely smiled and pulled open his overcoat to reveal four pint bottles of brown ale, sticking out of the inside pockets.

Matty grinned when he saw them and, when the Sergeant bit off one of the caps and handed a bottle to him, a sense of light relief came over him. For if nothing else, having a drink and a bit of a chat might help to take his mind off Dotty for a while.

In his attempts to cheer Matty up the Sergeant broached different subjects, such as pit work. But in the light of what Big John had told him about being sacked, the Sergeant did not get much out of Matty on that one.

Then he tried football, telling Matty he was a life long Sunderland supporter and he never missed a home game if he could help it. To which the lad replied curtly, "Aye, I'd be one too, if I could afford the bugger."

So the Sergeant tried history, the war and even politics, but all to no avail. Then casually he asked Matty did he ever do any reading, like magazines or books.

"Not really," he said. "Well not the kind of books you'd expect me to read anyway."

This intrigued the Sergeant and he began speculating in his mind as to what sort of books the lad read. He did not think it would be something porno, for the lad did not seem the type. Neither could it be the subjects they had already passed over, or he would probably have said something "So what the hell could it be?" he asked himself, more puzzled than ever.

As a silence then developed between the two of them, the Sergeant bit the caps off the remaining two bottles. Handing Matty his, he remarked, "I'm keen on a bit of poetry myself like."

For an instant Matty thought that the Sergeant had found out about his liking of poetry and was being sarcastic, but when he looked at the bloke's face and saw he was serious, he just shook his head slowly in disbelief.

Seeing the shake of the head, the Sergeant asked sharply, "And what's so bloody funny about that then?"

"Nothing at all" Matty replied smiling, "It's just that I like reading it too."

"Well bugger me," the Sergeant exclaimed, "Who would ever believe it, the only thing us two have in common, is a liking for poetry."

Then for the first time in a long while Matty burst out laughing, the Sergeant also saw the funny side of it and he broke into laughter too.

It wasn't long then before they began eulogising about their favourite poems and poets. The Sergeant went on and on about Keats and Kiplin, whilst Matty quoted passages from poems by Wordsworth and Burns.

The Sergeant was amazed at the depth of feeling Matty put into his quotes and it prompted him to ask, "Have you ever tried to write any poems yourself Matty?"

"Mmmm" he answered, smiling forlornly. "It was about snowflakes, about how gentle they are and when you try to catch one it melts, then turns into a tear of sadness. As if it had somehow fallen into the wrong environment and the only way it could escape, was to dissolve and then vanish."

Sergeant Shilton was totally transfixed as Matty carried on, unashamedly revealing his innermost thoughts.

"You see," he continued, "There are people just like snowflakes, people too gentle for this earth, especially somewhere like Houghton-le-Spring. For in a place like this the only way to survive is to be hard. If you show any gentleness, you are either considered soft, or a homo. Yet if you are a furry animal, or you have a mental or physical handicap, people expect you to be gentle. Oh they'll still abuse you, but at least your gentle ways would be accepted."

The Sergeant detected a tone of bitterness in the last part of what Matty had said, and he suddenly felt a cold shiver run down his spine. For in the light of what John Fenwick had told him of Matty's love for his rabbit, his crippled friend and retarded sister, he could not help but feel that the real snowflake he talked of was really himself.

Then later that night as the Sergeant drove home, Matty's words echoed in his head and once again he felt that cold shiver run through him. It was as if he somehow knew, that one day he would be called upon to confirm the death of a very gentle being, or in the lad's own words, a snowflake.

The following morning, Sergeant Shilton called in to see him again and took a couple of books for him to read. It pleased him to see that Matty was in better spirits, which was just as well, for the date of his trial had come through.

"You'll be up at the Assizes in about eight days" he told him solemnly, then added, "But don't worry yourself too much, for it won't be as bad as you think."

"Why's that then?" Matty asked jokingly, "Are you going to let me off or something?"

"No you silly sod" the Sergeant replied laughing, "But I don't think you will get the three years you were expecting."

After the Sergeant had left him, Matty tried to settle down to a bit of reading. But his concentration kept being interrupted by what the Sergeant had said about not getting three years, which finally led him to assume that someone had told him the true story.

Yet when he got to the Assizes, no mention whatsoever was made of Dotty and when he was sentenced to only twelve months, he shot a glance across at the Sergeant, who in return just smiled at him then winked.

Matty smiled back at him and thought 'Yes you sly old bugger, you've certainly worked a flanker here alright.'

Then as he was being driven up to Durham Prison in the back of a black maria, he reflected back on the courtroom and who had been there. But apart from Sergeant Shilton and Big John, the only other face he had recognised was, surprisingly, Bob Hunter.

CHAPTER THREE

The cell in Durham Jail turned out to be nothing like the one at Houghton Police Station. For a start, he had to share this one with two other blokes, which meant, not only did they share space, but also their moods, noises and smells.

There was no friendly copper either. In fact the warders were right bullies, who would constantly challenge Matty to prove just how hard he was, by taunting him with shouts of "Come on then, you big useless twat, try sticking one on me and see where it gets you." Or they would deliberately bump into him on the landing and ask who the hell he thought he was pushing.

Those first couple of weeks took some getting through as the warders set out to show Matty, that no matter how hard you were, they held the upper hand.

He also had a visit from the wing top-dog. A hard looking lad from Newcastle called Ron Sheppard, or as he preferred to be called, Shep.

It was whilst he was working in the boiler house on his fourth day there, Shep had ambled over to him and had quietly asked, "How about you and me taking a walk around the back?"

Matty had hesitated for a moment for he could sense trouble, but his manly pride got the better of him. So nodding his reply, then looking around to ensure there were no warders watching, they casually strolled round to the back of the boiler house, where they proceeded to eye each other up for a few moments in complete silence.

Shep was a hard man and Matty knew it, for you didn't get to be top-dog if you weren't, but Matty didn't fear him, nor was he the slightest bit intimidated by him, as he asked, "Well, now we're here what comes next?"

Then without warning Shep flew at him, but Matty side stepped his charge with ease. Whereupon Shep turned and came at him again. This time though he managed to get a grip on Matty's coat collar, pulling him sideways and making him lose his balance.

But as Matty went down, he grabbed at one of Shep's legs and lifted it upwards, also throwing Shep off balance.

Then they both wrestled with each other on the ground, both throwing short punches, but neither doing any damage and, it wasn't until Matty got Shep in a headlock, did they stop for a breather.

"Now what are you going to do, you cocky bastard?" Matty asked panting.

Shep didn't reply, mainly because he couldn't, as Matty had such a strong grip on him. So not really wanting to take it further as he knew he had the better of the lad, Matty said, "I think this has gone far enough now Shep. Besides, I don't want your title, you can be top-dog for as long as you want as far as I'm concerned. You keep out of my way and I'll keep out of yours, ok?"

He eased his grip a little to let Shep reply and when he nodded slightly, he let him up.

Shep stood glaring at him for a few moments, undecided whether to have another go or not, but in the end he thought better against it. For he could sense this bloke was something different.

From then on, even though Shep was still considered top-dog, Matty was treated with great respect by the rest of the wing, by everyone but the warders that was.

It was during his third week in prison that he was to finally have a confrontation with one of those too.

He had just finished rinsing out his slop bucket and was washing his hands, when an Officer by the name of Greenwood came up behind him and urinated in it. Then as he was putting away his penis, he sneeringly told Matty "Wash it out again."

Matty's temper snapped and he spun round and kicked the slop bucket, sending it flying across the room and crashing against the far wall, just missing the doorway through which Governor Warren was walking on one of his tours of inspection.

A hushed silence fell over the whole room as the Governor slowly walked towards Matty and Officer Greenwood. Then without a flicker of emotion, he stood directly in front of Matty and asked, "What's wrong Glave, got a problem have we?"

Having been so hyped up with temper, Matty was somewhat taken aback by the calmness of the Governor's attitude and, it was as much as he could do to utter, "N,No sir."

The Governor stood looking at Matty, then at Officer Greenwood. It was obvious he was aware of the tension between the two of them. So he stood for a while longer, until he was satisfied the heat had been taken out of the situation. Then he calmly turned to walk out, but telling Matty as he did so, "Get a mop and clean up the mess."

With the sting taken out of his tail now, Matty reluctantly got the mop and began swobbing, but all the while, waiting for the

Officer to make some sarcastic remark. For if he did, he would end up with a mouthful of his own piss.

What Matty didn't notice though, was the telling look the Governor had given Officer Greenwood, which was in fact, as good as a bollocking. So if any further trouble was to flare. up between them, they would both be in the mire and, being aware of this, the only comment the Officer made to Matty when he had finished was, "Right Glave, now let's be having you back to your cell."

"God you were lucky there Matty" Joe Coalflax the elder of his two cell mates told him when they got back to their cell.

"So fucking what" he replied sharply, still feeling the after effects of losing his temper.

"Look son" Joe pleaded, "Will you bloody listen to me, because if you don't, one of these days you are going to get yourself a damn good hiding."

"I'm not frightened of those bastards" he barked again.

"I know you're not son, but that's not the point" Joe told him calmly, trying to placate him. "There are a hell of a lot more of them though and, for every one of them you put down, two more will take his place, but not only that, you'll be thrown into solitary too and probably lose your remission."

"Besides, all they are really doing is putting you in your place, let you know who is boss like, that's all. If you just keep biting your tongue, you'll see, they'll get fed up eventually and leave you alone."

Feeling a bit miffed at being bollocked by a bloke half his size, Matty didn't reply. Instead, he lay down on his bunk, closed his eyes and thought about what Joe had said.

Then, after his temper abated, he came to the conclusion that Joe was probably right. The warders did have a job to do after all and, they had to be seen to be in charge. So it was only logical they had to impose themselves on the inmates. Besides, the one thing he certainly did not want to happen, was to lose his remission.

It took another couple of weeks though before the bullying actually stopped and he had had to do a lot of tongue biting to get through them.

An Officer named Pearce had been the one to let Matty know that hostilities were at an end, by offering him a sweet of all things.

"Go on" he had said, as he held out the packet to Matty, "The buggers are not poison you know."

In return Matty had smiled and taken one, then as they both gave each other a knowing nod, Matty couldn't wait to get back to the cell to tell Joe he was right all along. So being more relaxed now, the days seemed to pass, much quicker and his change of mood was also appreciated by both Joe and Dicka. In fact, as the days passed, the three of them became quite close.

Joe was the one he could relate to better though; this was probably because he was older and therefore more mature.

He seemed to be a well educated bloke too, which surprised Matty. For he had always thought that if a person had brains they got on in life. Yet it was obvious something must have gone wrong where Joe was concerned, for he was now doing his third stretch for burglary.

But as Matty sat studying him, he couldn't help but think just how much he looked like a burglar though. For he was short and wiry, with a distinct look of a ferret about him.

Dicka on the other hand was just the opposite. For although he was a likeable lad, he was as thick as a brick.

He was about Matty's age but nowhere near his size. Yet there was a hardness about him and he was forever going on about stoving someone's head in with a hammer. Inwardly, this made Matty smile, for even though the lad was hard, he didn't think that Dicka was the sort to use a hammer.

'Still' he reminded himself, 'The lad must have upset somebody, seeing as how he is doing two years for robbery with violence.'

He was a funny lad too and Matty was glad he was in with them. For whenever they got a bit depressed Dicka would cheer them up with one of his silly stories, like the one about his grandmother's cat.

Dicka reckoned he went to visit her one day, and not being able to see the cat anywhere around, had asked her where it was.

"Oh I've had to have him put down" she had told him sadly.

"Aarrr" he had replied sympathetically, "What for?"

"Well to stop it from getting killed that's why."

He never did finish the story, for Matty and Joe were so doubled up with laughter, he never got the chance.

Oh they had the occasional tiff of course, but no grudges were ever held. For they all knew just how much they relied on each other, to help them get through their time.

The nights were proving to be Matty's biggest problem now. As it was then he had time to think about Dotty and his mother. He was still troubled by Dotty in his sleep too.

Many a night he would hear her somewhere in the distance, quietly sobbing. She never called his name now, but he knew it was her and, he couldn't help but feel she was watching his every move.

It was after one of these nights that Officer Pearce came briskly into the cell and told him to dress quickly, as he had a visitor in the Governor's office.

As Matty entered, he was a little disturbed to see Sergeant Shilton sitting next to the Governor on the far side of his desk.

"Hello son" the Sergeant said, standing up and stretching out his hand for Matty to shake.

Matty took it, but as he did so he asked cautiously, "What brings you here then Sergeant?"

The Sergeant sat down again and the Governor indicated to Matty to sit on the chair, on his side of the desk.

"It's bad news I'm afraid son" the Sergeant told him solemnly. Then hesitantly added, "Your mother died about one o'clock this morning in Sunderland General."

Matty could only sit in stunned silence, with his face telling it all, for the news had completely shattered him.

They left him to his own thoughts for a few minutes, then Sergeant Shilton asked "Would you like to come through to the funeral Matty?"

For fear of bursting into tears, he didn't answer verbally. Instead he indicated with a slight nod of the head.

"OK then son" replied the Sergeant, "But I must ask you not to do anything silly when you get to Houghton."

Matty sighed, then asked him forlornly, "What do you mean, try to escape or something?"

"No I don't mean that" said the Sergeant, as a slight smile crossed his lips. "I mean your brother will probably be there and I don't want you thumping him."

At the mention of Siddy, Matty's remorse was suddenly replaced by anger and, as a sarcastic leer distorted his face, he replied "Will he now, are you sure he's fit enough?"

"Aye, he is" the Sergeant told him, ignoring the sarcasm, "He's out of hospital now and living through at Penshaw."

"Penshaw!" Matty exclaimed. Then asked, "Do you think four miles is far enough away?"

The Sergeant knew what he meant, but again he ignored the sarcasm.

Instead, he stood up and put on his trilby, but all the while studying Matty's face.
"Aye" he told himself, "He's only been in here for six weeks but already there's a change come over him. There's a brashness about him that was never there before. But on the other hand, is it any wonder, being banged up with the rest of life's shit in a place like this."

For he had often thought, that whilst prison was ideal for criminals, he doubted if it ever did the likes of Matty any good.

He walked around the desk and came to stand by Matty. Putting his hand firmly on his shoulder he said "I'll let the Governor know when the funeral is going to be son and he can make the arrangements for you to get to Houghton, but in the meantime keep your chin up." Then more as a plea than a statement, he added "And for god's sake Matty, try and get rid of that bitterness will you?"

A few minutes later, as he walked through the car park, the Sergeant stopped and turned to look back at the prison. A feeling of depression suddenly came over him as the word 'Justice' ran through his mind, for he knew, that in Matty's case, justice wasn't really being served.

The funeral was the following Thursday, at eleven o'clock, but so on edge was he, Matty had been dressed since eight.

Officer Pearce had purloined a navy blue overcoat for him to wear over his prison uniform, also a black tie. This though, proved to be a problem, for Matty had never worn a tie in his life.

Joe, spotting his dilemma, took the tie from him and, as not to embarrass him, said jokingly, "Here Matty, let me show you how to tie the famous Joe Coalflax windsor knot."

It took four or five tries, but finally Matty got there. In fact he was so impressed with himself when he looked in the mirror, he turned and, posing in front of Dicka, asked "Hey Dickson, which great Hollywood actor do I remind you of?"

Dicka looked up from his comic, distorted his face in puzzlement for a moment, then said gleefully, "I've got it, King Kong."

"You cheeky bastard" Matty called him jokingly, feigning to swing his right boot at Dicka, "King Kong indeed. I reckon I look a bit like Clark Gable myself, what do you think Joe?"

Joe simply raised his eyebrows, shook his head and replied "I wish it was time for you to go through to Houghton and I wish you would take that clown with you, maybe then I'd get a bit of peace."

Matty and Dicka looked at each other and though they tried not to, they both burst out laughing at Joe's stuffy attitude.

The laughter did not last long though as Officer Pearce suddenly appeared in the doorway and told Matty it was time to make a move.

He was surprised to see that the two guards acting as his escort, also wore overcoats and black ties. This he felt added a bit of respectability to things and, as they walked towards the main gate, Matty reckoned that it would take a good pair of eyes to spot who was the prisoner,

They drove him through to Houghton in an unmarked white van and parked about thirty yards from the church.

"We'll wait till the funeral cortege gets in first Glave" said Officer Gordon, who appeared to be the senior of the two. Then in a more authoritative voice added, "And remember, no contact with anyone, ok?"

Officer Gordon's warning seemed a little pointless as he was so far away from the rest of the mourners, he had difficulty making out who exactly was there.

Not that there was many, apart from Big John and Mary Fenwick, the only other faces he could be certain of, were Bob Hunter and his wife Bella.

Oh there were others he couldn't quite put a name to, like uncles and aunts he hadn't seen for years and one or two other people he didn't recognise from the back, but it saddened him not to see Dotty there.

When he thought about it though, he realised it was only common sense really. For if she had spotted him, she would probably have wanted to come to him and in the circumstances, he knew that would have been impossible.

Matty was in no way religious and, as he sat looking around the church during one of the prayers, he couldn't help but think what a waste of a beautiful building it was.

For most of the time it just stood empty and, the amount of flowers around the place must have cost a fortune, for there was every type of bloom he could think of, which automatically turned his thoughts to Dotty.

He remembered bringing her to his father's funeral, and he smiled to himself as he recalled the look of amazement on her face, for she was simply in heaven.

All through the service she had kept tugging at his coat and as she pointed to different flowers, she would say in her childlike voice, "Look Matty, look. Nice eh Matty, nice eh."

He remembered how it had taken him all his time to keep himself from laughing and, now as he fondly thought of his sister an involuntary smile crossed his lips as he wondered how she was keeping.

Officer Gordon swiftly brought him back from his thoughts though, by nudging him in the ribs and saying briskly, "Right Glave that's it, let's go."

It was all over so quickly he began to feel guilty. For the one person he hadn't even thought about was his mother.

So as he stepped into the aisle, he stopped for a moment and looked down towards the coffin at the front of the church.

"Ta-ra mother" he whispered, "You can rest easy now." Then for the first time since he had entered the church, he felt tears welling up inside. So he quickly took out his handkerchief and pretended to blow his nose and hoped neither of the guards had noticed his moment of weakness.

If they had, there was no comment, for the journey back to Durham was a silent one. Which gave Matty a chance to reflect on the funeral and to try and work out who had been there.

Then it suddenly dawned on him that he hadn't seen Siddy, so he closed his eyes and reflectively scanned the mourners. But the only person who looked anything like him, was a wizened old man who sat on his own, away from the rest.

'No it couldn't be' he thought, 'But on the other hand, the slicked-down hair did look familiar. So if it was him, the least I've done is age the bastard twenty years' and then he silently chuckled to himself.

But by the time he got back to his cell, a mood of depression had come over him as the full force of what had happened finally hit him. Even though in her latter years she hadn't been much of a mother to them, she was still their mother and, though it took some admitting, he knew he would miss the old girl.

Joe sensed how subdued he was and, when Dicka tried to cheer him up with a half-hearted attempt at humour he glared at the lad and silently mouthed, "Shut your fucking hole."

Dicka, of course, instantly took the huff and stomped out onto the landing, whilst Joe went back to reading his book, but all the while, keeping a weather eye on Matty, for he looked as though he was about to explode at any time.

But he managed to get through the rest of the day without any major incidents, the night though, was a different matter.

After lights-out, he lay in the dark determined not to let himself doze off to sleep. But by about one o'clock he finally caved in and, as he had expected, she was there, somewhere in the darkness silently sobbing.

But it wasn't only Dotty's voice he heard this time, for there was someone else crying too and it didn't take him long to recognise his mother's voice.

He never saw either of them, nor did they speak to him, but their sobbing simply droned on, hour after hour, until finally he was awakened by the sound of a bell ringing and the rattle of keys.

It was time to get up for slopping out, but at least it had broken his sleep and, even though he was only emptying his piss-bucket, he was still grateful for something to do.

The following few days were hell for Matty, but the Tuesday after the funeral was to prove to be even worse. For he was about to find out the real reason, why Dotty was not at the funeral.

He was in the woodwork room when Officer Pearce came over to him and said "You've got a visitor Glave, come on, I'll escort you through to the visiting room."

It wasn't an official visiting day, so Matty immediately knew something was wrong and, as he entered the visiting room half expecting to see Sergeant Shilton, he got a shock to see Bob Hunter, sitting at one of the tables smoking a small cigar.

"Hello Matty son" Bob greeted him, stubbing out his cigar as he did so.

Matty nodded slightly, but didn't reply straight off, for he was puzzled as to why Bob was here. Then after a few moments he asked "What's up now Bob. What brings you here?"

Normally confident with words, especially amongst his own kind, Bob suddenly found himself struggling to give Matty an answer. He had rehearsed what he was going to say several times in the car coming here, but now he was actually facing the lad, his words seemed to dry up.

Eventually though, he got control of himself again and, seeing the impatient look on Matty's face, he quickly said "It's your sister I've come about Matty."

"Dotty!" Matty exclaimed, standing up and knocking his chair backwards, "What in Christ's name has happened to her?"

Officer Pearce, who had been standing at the door, came over to him and snapped, "Now, now Glave, calm it down or you'll be straight back to your cell."

Matty stood glaring at him for a moment, then common sense got hold of him, as he nodded his submission, picked up his chair and sat back down again.

"Steady Matty" Bob whispered, "It's no good getting yourself all knotted up son, for there's not much you can do about anything, stuck in a place like this."

Matty sat wringing his hands, silently stewing, then hissed "Well, what the fuck's wrong with our Dotty then?"

So Bob, as evenly as he could, began to explain. "According to Big John, about two weeks ago, the lass refused to take any food or drink and she wouldn't even go to the lavatory. Which meant Mary had to keep cleaning her.

All she seemed to want to do was stare into the fire, she didn't even want to look at her flower books and, as the days passed, Mary started to get concerned, so she sent for Doctor Smurthwaite.

Well he examined her, but couldn't find anything physically wrong with her, so he recommended she be taken through to Ryburn Asylum."

Matty almost lost control again as he barked "Ryburn, that place is for fucking loonies, not people like our Dotty, surely they can't lock her up in there?"

Bob tried to placate him by explaining "No you're wrong Matty, it's not just for loonies, it's for anybody with mental problems, you haven't got to be daft to be put in there."

This last bit struck a chord with Matty, for he had often thought himself that if ever anything was to happen to him, Dotty would end up in there. So calming down again he asked sadly "Will she ever come out again?"

Even though Bob was a hard man and his only intention was to use Matty, he couldn't help feeling sorry for him, as he could see how badly he was hurting. But he thought it best to tell him the truth and get it over with.

"Well Doctor Smurthwaite reckons not" he told him sympathetically, "You see, she has withdrawn into herself and just refuses to communicate. The Doctor says she's had something traumatic happen to her to cause it, something that's scared her so much, she just wants to shut the world out."

Without looking at Bob, Matty asked "Did he say what it could have been that scared her?"

"No, he didn't know, but Big John seemed to have an idea though, yet when the doctor asked him what it was, all he could say was "Never mind."

"Of course Doctor Smurthwaite had a go at Big John for not telling him, but the big man still wouldn't let on."

"Did he tell you by any chance?" Matty asked him suspiciously then.

"No he didn't" Bob lied, "And I didn't ask either. As far as I'm concerned that's family, nothing to do with outsiders."

Of course Bob had prised it out of Big John, but there was no way he was going to let the lad know, for God knows what he would be capable of in his present mood.

Matty sighed and nodded his head slightly, to indicate he believed Bob. Then he put his head in his hands and closed his eyes tightly as Dotty's face came into his mind.

'Is it any wonder she's turned like she has' he thought, 'What with that business with Siddy, then having himself and their mother taken from her, and having to go and live with strangers.'

He mentally shook his head in despair and as he felt the tears welling up inside of him, he began apologising, over and over again to Dotty, until Bob finally brought him back from his thoughts by shaking him by the arm and saying, "Come on now son, pull yourself together, the lass will be well looked after in Ryburn. And as Doctor Smurthwaite says, it's the best place for her."

Matty sat for a few moments longer, then removed his hands and opened his eyes. "Aye" he said hoarsely, "You're probably right Bob, but I can't help feeling lousy about the whole thing though."

As Bob sat quietly twiddling his thumbs then, Matty studied him for a few moments. Even though he had known the bloke for a few years now, he had never really taken much notice of him. Up until now he had only been the bloke who served him his beer on a Friday night, but as Matty scanned his face, he felt he was seeing him for the first time.

He had never noticed the scar tissue around Bob's eyes before, nor the scar on the right side of his chin and, by the shape of his nose, that looked as though it had been smacked a few times too.

Then Bob looked directly into Matty's eyes and they held each other's stare for a few seconds. "I'll tell you one thing Bob" he said, as a faint smile crossed his lips, "You've turned out to be a friend I never thought I had."

Slightly embarrassed at Matty's compliment, Bob replied "Awe, get away with you lad, it's the least I can do in the light of what happened in the pub that night."

"What do you mean, involving the cops?" Matty asked.

Hesitantly Bob replied "Well, that and having to lay you out with the cricket bat."

"What!" Matty said, astounded, "You mean it wasn't Big John who smacked me, it was you."

"Aye, it was that" came Bob's nervous reply, "But I only thought I was saving you from committing a murder though. Matty, I hope you're not upset, are you?"

Matty chuckled and shook his head, "No I'm not upset Bob" he told him, "It's just that I've always thought it was Big John, cos he was the only one I reckoned would have enough guts to hit me." Then he chuckled out loud again as he uttered, "A bloody cricket bat."

"Aye, we can laugh about it now son, but at the time, you had me shit-scared, I can tell you. I've never seen anybody go so bloody loopy and I've seen a bit of violence in my time."

"Is that how you came by your scars?" Matty asked, looking him straight in the eye.

"Mmmm" Bob replied smiling, "And I did a stretch in here too."

"How long ago was that then?" Matty asked curiously.

"Oh a few years back now, but it doesn't look as though the place has changed much" he said, eyeing the walls and sparse furniture. Then he asked "Are the warders still bad bastards Matty, do they give you a hard time of it?"

"They used to" he replied with a note of cockiness in his voice, "But not now, we've got this little arrangement where they keep off my toes and I keep off theirs."

Bob chuckled, for that was exactly what he wanted to hear. Then with enthusiasm he asked, "Who's the number one on your wing, you?"

"No" Matty told him, again with that air of cockiness, "But he doesn't bother me either." Then he grinned broadly as he added "You see I've got the same arrangement with him, as I have with the warders."

This comment pleased Bob no end, for what was the point in investing in a fighter if he was only going to be second best.

So, satisfied things were coming along as he had hoped, Bob decided he had done his bit and it was time to leave. Then as he rose and put on his hat, he looked down at Matty and, as sympathetically as he could, said "I'm off now son, if there's anything you want, just drop a line to the pub and I'll sort it out for you and, try not to worry too much about the lass. As I've told you, she's in the best place, she'll be well looked after in there."

Matty didn't answer, he just looked up at Bob and nodded his head slightly. For now that Bob was leaving, a sense of loneliness came over him and his mind went straight back to Dotty.

Then as Bob went out of the door, Matty felt the tears once again well up inside of him and it was as much as he could do, to stop himself from openly crying.

For the remainder of the day, he was once again, hell to live with. So Joe and Dicka steered well clear of him and were both relieved when it came to lights out.

Matty wasn't though, for this was the time he had been dreading most and, as the night wore on, whenever he felt himself drifting into sleep, he would shake his head to keep himself awake.

But in the early hours of the morning, he could resist sleep no more and, as he had suspected, she was waiting for him. Yet she wasn't sobbing this time though, it was worse. She was screaming at the top of her voice, "KISS IT BETTER MATTY, IT HURTS MATTY, KISS IT BETTER."

She went on and on, repeating the same thing, until finally, in frustration he yelled back at her "FOR CHRISTSAKE DOTTY

LEAVE ME ALONE, IT'S NOT MY FAULT YOU ARE DAFT AND THEY'VE LOCKED YOU UP. NOW GO ON, GET AWAY AND LET ME GET SOME BLOODY PEACE."

He listened then for some reply, but there was nothing but silence. He strained his ears for any little sound but there was nothing. Then, after several minutes, just when he thought she had left him, he suddenly heard a distant sobbing, echoing somewhere in the darkness.

Instantly he was filled with remorse and began gently calling to her. "I'm sorry Dotty, I didn't mean to be nasty. You know Matty loves you, but I'm so weary my darling, there's so much happened lately. Besides, I can't do anything while I'm stuck in here, can I now?"

"But I'll tell you what my little darling, when I come out in November, I'll come straight through to Ryburn to get you and we'll go and live somewhere by the sea. Somewhere like Seaham Harbour, where we can get a little house with a garden and fill it full of flowers for you. Would you like that Dotty eh, would you like that?"

He listened again for a reply, but there was none. So he told her "I promise little angel, I'll come and get you, now you go to sleep and let me sleep too and, as I've promised, I'll see you in November. Ta-ra Dotty and remember, Matty loves you."

His pact with Dotty seemed to have worked for she never did bother him again and, the following morning Joe and Dicka couldn't believe the change in the lad, it was as if he had woken up a different person.

Yet that was exactly what Matty felt he was, for now he had something to aim for. Yes he would get her out of Ryburn and they would go and live by the sea, just how he would achieve this of course would be a different matter, but he was determined to try.

Firstly, he had to get himself fit, for whilst he had been in prison he had put on weight, which was unusual really, as most blokes tended to lose weight. But seeing as how he had been having three meals a day and not doing any work, which in both cases, was unusual for him, he felt he had at least put half a stone on.

So that night, during recreation, he went to see the Officer in charge of P.T., who turned out to be a Welshman by the name of Hughes.

He was a tall, thick set bloke, who had done a bit of boxing in his younger days and, though he looked about forty, as Matty watched him spar, there was no denying he was still useful.

He set Matty a training programme and, after a few weeks Matty began to feel the benefit of it, in fact he became so keen, Officer Hughes arranged for him to use the gym any night he wanted to.

One particular thing he looked forward to, was the sparring sessions they had at the end of training. But seeing as there was no one to match Matty, Officer Hughes would take him on himself.

Hughes was by far the fitter and, seeing as how Matty couldn't use his head, knees or feet, he didn't fair too well against the old boy.

As time passed though and with Matty getting fitter, the tables slowly began to turn. Until one night, after yet another vigorous sparring session, as they sat wiping themselves down with towels, Officer Hughes told him "I'll tell you what Glave, I reckon, when you get out of here, you could take up boxing as a career, d'you fancy it?"

Matty smiled inwardly as he thought 'what me a fucking boxer, no thanks.' Then to Officer Hughes, replied, "No, I don't think so, when I do get out of here, I'll have better things to do, than knock the shit out of some poor bugger for money."

As Matty carried on drying himself, Officer Hughes glanced sideways at him and couldn't help thinking what a nice kid he was. Then turning to look at him said, "I'll tell you what Glave, I reckon you'll do alright for yourself on the outside, you seem to have your head screwed on right."

He turned to walk away then, but stopped and added, "That is if you learn to keep hold of that temper of yours."

They smiled respectfully at each other, then went their separate ways.

Matty felt at peace with himself, but as he walked back into his cell, things soon changed.

"Matty, thank Christ you're alright," exclaimed Joe. Looking puzzled, he replied, "What the hell's wrong with you Joe?"

"I've just been talking to a lad along the landing and he reckons there's a new bloke just been brought in, called Bomber Foster."

"So," Matty said, sounding a bit annoyed.

Starting to shake now, Joe replied, "He's already done Shep, our number one, now he reckons you're next, because somebody told him you were the real hard man in here."

Matty sat down on his bunk and looking up at Joe asked, "What does he want to have me for, I can't afford to have any trouble, I'm getting out in about five months' time."

"Because I hear the useless bastard likes to smack big blokes, seemingly, the bigger, they are, the better he likes them and you Matty, are one of the biggest in here son."

Matty felt the hackles rise on the back of his neck as he jumped down off his bunk and began pacing the cell floor. "Surely to God he wouldn't start anything with me, would he? Not with me only having a short time, surely not."

"Look Matty son" Joe said, as calmly as he could. "You know as well as I do what these bastards are like, your circumstances won't matter a toss. If this bloke fancies having a go at you, he will. The only thing you can do, is steer well clear of him." Then he looked down at Matty and, raising his voice to emphasise the point, added, "Have you got that?"

Matty didn't answer straight off, for he was too deep in his thoughts of this new bloke. Aye, he knew fair well what bullies were like, after all, he'd been brought up with one. But even though he knew he wasn't scared of this bloke Foster; he also knew he would have to avoid him at all costs. Because if he was to get into a scrap with him now, he would be sure to lose his remission and, that was one thing he couldn't let happen.

So, a little subdued, he finally answered by telling Joe "Aye, I suppose you're right, even though it goes against the grain, the best thing I can do, is try and avoid him."

A strained silence developed then, as Matty got up and stood leaning against the cell wall with his hands in his pockets and Joe sat staring at the floor. It was Dicka who finally broke it though, with one of his pearls of wisdom, as he said "And if it does come to a scrap Matty, stove his head in with a fucking hammer."

Both Matty and Joe looked at each other and burst out laughing. "You simple gob-shite" Joe called to Dicka, "Where in hell's name is he going to get a hammer in here?"

Dicka, of course, took offence, replying sharply "Alright, fucking know all, I'm only concerned about the bloody bloke, that's all."

Matty walked over to him and, putting his hand on Dicka's shoulder, told him "It's OK Dicka, I know you are worried, but you needn't be. I'll be alright, you'll see."

He managed to avoid Bomber Foster for almost a week, but the bloke was so determined to have Matty, that the inevitable was bound to happen. Yet he was "set-up" so well, that he was to come out of their meeting, far worse than he could ever have feared.

He was rinsing out his bucket one morning, when the deepest voice he had ever heard, boomed "Hey soft-cock, wash my fucker out while you're there."

Matty stopped rinsing and for a few seconds, just stood staring at the wall. But when nothing happened, he carried on rinsing. Then suddenly he felt a sharp pain in the left side of his back and, as he winced, he turned to face the most evil looking bloke he had ever clapped eyes on.

With his prison haircut almost making him seem bald, it gave his head a bull-like appearance and, his eyes were cold, dark and piercing. Yet they somehow matched the purple, horseshoe shaped scar on his left cheek.

His neck, arms and upper body, simply rippled with muscles. The bloke must have stood at least six-feet-six and weighed all of twenty-three stones, but as Matty continued looking him over, he almost burst out laughing when he saw how skinny the bloke's legs were. For they seemed so out of place to the rest of his body. It looked as if he had developed the top half, but neglected the bottom.

Then Matty turned, his eyes back to Bomber's face and he concluded there was no doubt he looked a hardman, but Matty did not fear him in the least and, when the bloke made no move to come at him, he simply turned and carried on rinsing his bucket.

The next thing he felt though, was his head being smacked against the wall, then everything went blank for a moment. This was then followed by different coloured lights, flashing across his eyes, accompanied by a blinding pain.

He shook his head to re-focus his eyes and felt blood running into them. Then as he wiped it away with the back of his hand, he turned to face Bomber, who by now, was standing with his hands on his hips, leering at Matty and goading him into making a move.

Which was exactly what he did. Like a raging animal he leapt straight at Bomber, who immediately threw his huge arms around Matty's waist and began squeezing with all his might.

Matty felt the breath go out of him as an excruciating pain shot down his spine. Then he suddenly felt himself blacking out and he knew if he didn't do something quick, the bloke would snap his back.

So he began punching downwards blindly, not knowing if his fists were connecting or not, then all of a sudden he felt blows raining down on the back of his head, but he only felt the first half dozen or so, for after that, he was out cold.

He hadn't realised it was a "set-up", if he had only taken time to look around the slopping-out room, he would have seen that there was only the two of them in there. Bomber's cronies had stood at the door, stopping everyone else from entering.

It had been Joe who had twigged what was happening, but by the time he had alerted the warders, it had been too late.

Now, as Matty came round, the only light that he could see was that coming from under the door, everything else was in total darkness, so it didn't take him long to work out that he was in solitary.

He tried to sit up but sharp pains kept shooting through his lungs, making him wince and his head was throbbing so badly, he could barely open his eyes. Then before he could stop himself, he began to spew, which made his lungs hurt even more as he wretched.

He lay still for a while after being sick, then he dragged himself up against a wall and sat, slumped forward, to relived the pain. At first only taking, shallow breaths, then slowly taking deeper ones as the pain eased.

As his mind cleared, he began asking himself why he had been put into solitary, after all, he didn't start the fight. Then he remembered something Joe had said about Governor Warren punishing anyone who got involved with violence.

"Still" he told himself, "If the Governor has any heart at all, he'll know how important it is for me to get out as soon as I can. If I explain about our Dotty, I'm sure he'll understand."

Governor Warren didn't see it that way at all though and, as Matty stood in front of him a few hours later, it was as much as he could do to stop himself from exploding, as the Governor told him "I will not tolerate fighting in my jail Glave, I couldn't care less if you started it or not, the fact remains, you took part in it and that's good enough for me."

All Matty could do was glare his contempt at the man, for he knew that if he was to say anything, it would be something nasty. Yet he did utter, "Fucking hell" when the Governor told him what his punishment would be.

"Two weeks in solitary confinement and the loss of two months remission." Then he added "It could have been worse Glave, I could have taken your other months remission off you too, but I'm going to keep that in reserve, just in case you step out of line again." He held Matty's glare for a few moments then asked sharply "Any questions?"

Matty slowly shook his head, for his pride would not let him explain about Dotty, but if the Governor could have read his murderous thoughts, he would have locked him up for life.

He waited until he was back in his cell, then he let his temper free. He began kicking and punching the walls, oblivious to the pain and bruises he was inflicting on himself and, at the top of his voice he began screaming, "FOSTER YOU SCAR-FACED BASTARD, I'LL KILL YOU WHEN I GET OUT OF HERE, I'LL TEAR YOUR FUCKING UGLY HEAD OFF YOUR FUCKING SHOULDERS, JUST YOU WAIT, I'LL HAVE MY FUCKING DAY WITH YOU."

Over and over, he kicked, punched and screamed, until finally he crumpled into a heap in the corner of the cell and with tear filled eyes, he whispered, "I'm sorry Dotty, honestly my love, I'm sorry."

The more he focused his thoughts on Bomber Foster though, the less he thought about Dotty and, as the days passed, his hate for the bloke began to fester.

He reckoned he had spotted a weakness in the big ugly bastard, so every day he practised a move he thought would 'do' him and, even though the cell wasn't big enough to practice the whole move, he still had room to work out the final part.

With the cell also being in darkness, he decided to go through the motions with his eyes closed and, to his surprise, he found that he could concentrate a lot better. So from then on, he would stand with his back against the cell door, count the first three steps off in his mind, then take off on the fourth and land the blow on the fifth.

He even tried taking off on different feet, but found that the right was best. Then he tried diving in at different heights, until he was finally satisfied, he had the move perfected. All that remained now, was to get Joe to arrange a meeting with Foster and sort the bastard out.

In his lust for revenge though little did Matty realise just how obsessed he had become with Bomber. He even took to calling his move "The Bomber Drop." For every time he practised it, he would finish by saying, "Now drop you bastard." Until it became automatic for him to say it.

Even when he wasn't practising, he would lie on his bunk chanting it, or he would sing in a silly high-pitched voice, "Bomber, Matty's coming for you, it won't be long now."

As the days passed, he became more delirious with exhaustion and rage and, if he could only have seen himself, he would surely have been ashamed. For this wasn't the gentle Matty any more. This was a ranting, raving lunatic, whose mind had sunk so low, he was no better than the likes of Bomber Foster, or even his brother Siddy. This wasn't the caring brother of a retarded sister; this was an animal.

He had often thought to himself what he would turn into, if he was to go any length of time without Dotty's calming influence, now, unknowingly he was finding out. For not only was he behaving like his brother, but also like his father. In other words, he was reverting to type.

The sight of him shook Joe when he was at last released back onto the wing. Even in the short time Matty had been away, Joe could see a big change in the lad.

It wasn't just the loss of weight, or the terrible state his hands were in either. There was an air of nastiness about him and, when he barked at Joe, "I want a meeting setting up with Foster and I want you to do the bastard today" he feared the worst. For Joe realised Matty had lost his sense of decency, something inside the lad had snapped, turning him into a bully.

Joe shook his head in despair as he looked at Matty lying on his bunk with his eyes closed, for he knew exactly how the lad would react when he told him what had happened to Bomber Foster. "I'm sorry Matty" he said calmly, "But I thought somebody would have told you, Foster was transferred to Leeds last week."

Then, just as Joe had feared, Matty exploded. "What the fuck do you mean" he raged, as he got up off his bunk and stood towering over Joe, "Transferred to Leeds. You're fucking lying Coalflax, you're just saying that to stop me getting at the bastard."

Joe thought he was going to be killed any minute, but it was Dicka who saved him, by telling Matty in a panic stricken voice, "He's not lying Matty, honest he's not. They shipped Foster out so you and him couldn't get at each other when you came out of solitary, honest Matty, that's the truth."

Matty stood glaring down at Joe for a few moments, then pushed him onto the floor. Suddenly he felt very weak, as if someone had pulled out a plug in him and all his emotions were draining away.

He threw himself back onto his bunk and lay face down, thinking what a total waste it had all been. All that pent up hate, all that craving for revenge didn't mean a thing now, now that the object of his anger had been taken from him, he felt deflated.

He also began to feel sorry for himself and, was sure that if Joe and Dicka hadn't been in the cell, he would have broke down and cried.

Nothing was ever to be the same again between them after that day, as Matty lost the will to communicate. Oh he said the odd word, but he never engaged either of them in conversation.

Whilst Joe and Dicka for their part, steered clear of him whenever they could. With all three of them now, counting off the days to Matty's release.

On the morning it came, he shook hands with the pair of them and mumbled something about meeting on the outside for a pint but Matty knew he was lying. For the only person from Durham jail, he wanted to bump into again, was a bloke with a horseshoe shaped scar on his left cheek and who answered to the name of Bomber.

CHAPTER FOUR

After the prison gate had closed behind him, Matty stood with his back against it and, for a few moments, sucked in lungfull's of cold, crisp, January air.

As he stood, he watched the soft, white flakes of snow slowly descending over everything and, for the first time in ages, as a sense of peace came over him, he smiled.

He looked down to his right and, through the snowflakes, he could just make out the River Wear, as it wound its way through the old racecourse and off through the town.

Then he slowly stretched out his hand and let some of the flakes fall gently onto it, but the minute they touched his palm they melted and, as the rivulets trickled down his wrist, he sighed "Just like tears of sadness." For the snowflake was still the most gentle, forlorn thing he had ever known, but this of course, brought his mind round to Dotty.

He had thought about her quite a lot lately and, as he smiled again, he heard himself say, "The gentlest snowflakes of them all."

He knew it wouldn't be long now before he saw her and, even though there was still a nagging doubt in the back of his mind, he felt sure she would recognise him. After all, he had an advantage over all the rest, for he was probably the only friend Dotty had ever had and this he felt, was the key to bringing her back to normality.

After soaking up the peace for a few minutes longer, he tucked his brown paper carrier bag under his left arm, pulled up his overcoat collar, then set off for the town centre to catch a bus back to Houghton.

He hadn't particularly wanted to go back there, but the problem was, he didn't have anywhere to go. For the only person he knew who would give him digs, was Big John.

If he could put him up for a couple of weeks, until he found a job and a place of his own, that would be a great help. Then he would get Dotty out of Ryburn and maybe pay somebody to look after her whilst he went to work. Just how he was going to do all this, was still a mystery, but he knew that somehow, he had to find a way.

Barely had he gone twenty yards down the road though, when he suddenly became aware of someone calling his name. He turned and looked over the road to the car-park and was quite surprised to see Bob Hunter, leaning on his open car door and shouting, "Come on Matty son, hurry up, I'm freezing my bloody balls off standing here."

Matty quickly crossed the road, then as he reached the car, he took Bob's outstretched hand and asked, "What in hell's name are you doing here then Bob?"

"I've come to take you home in style son" Bob told him, feeling full of himself. Then he stepped back and as he looked Matty up and down, added "I must say Matty, you haven't half filled out while you've been inside, it must have been all that good living you've been doing."

They both smiled as Matty replied "Aye, that's right Bob, but I don't think I'm going to miss it, do you?"

Then pointing to the car, Bob said, "Come on, get in and I'll take you for the best pint of beer in Durham and I bet you can use one too?"

Again they smiled, but as they pulled away from the prison, Bob noticed Matty's stern glare as he looked at the prison gates. "What's up son, sad to be leaving then?"

Matty shot him an angry glance, but when he saw that it was as much as Bob could do to stop himself from laughing, he knew he was having the piss taken out of him, so he simply replied "Bollocks."

Then for some reason they both burst out laughing and Matty felt himself relax, for even though he didn't really know Bob, he was glad he had been there to meet him.

After a bit of initial chit-chat, the journey through the town lapsed into silence, as Bob concentrated on his driving whilst Matty sat looking out of the window at all the different shops.

Then as they drove into the market square, memories of his childhood came flooding back to him as he remembered the times his father had taken the family through to the Durham Miners Gala, or as they used to call it, The Big Meeting.

He closed his eyes and instantly he could see all the different Lodge banners, fluttering in the breeze and, even now, he gasped. slightly at the array of colours. Then he saw and heard the people, dancing arm in arm, zigzagging across the road, singing and laughing as they did so.

Then, somewhere in the distance, he heard his favourite band and suddenly he felt himself come out in goosepimples, for in his mind he saw himself racing back along the parade until at last he found it, the Scotchie band. My, how he had loved the sound of those bagpipes and, he smiled to himself now as he recalled how he had told anyone who would listen, that they were his most favourite band of all.

"Here we are then" Bob said, startling Matty back to reality. Then bringing the car to a halt in The Five Bells car-park, added "Wait till you taste this pint son, as I said, it's the best in Durham."

As Matty got out of the car, he nodded and replied "Well I hope it's as good as you say Bob, cos it's a fair while since I've had a pint down this neck. Mind if it's that good, I reckon I'll be pissed on three of them."

As it was only half-eleven, there was only a handful of people in the place. Bob indicated to Matty to sit at one of the tables next to the window, whilst he went to the bar for the drinks.

When he had sat down, Matty looked around the place and was in awe of what he saw. He had never been into such a posh looking pub in his life.

For there was a carpet on the floor and brass and copper ornaments hanging everywhere. Each table had its own ashtray and beer mats, there were ornate lights hanging from the ceiling and the barman was even wearing a tie.

Then suddenly, he became aware of just how scruffy he must look. So he quickly tucked his scuffed boots under the chair and hoped no one had seen them. Then he took off his frayed cap and put it into his pocket, which only made him aware of how much he had out-grown his overcoat. He looked down then at his trousers and exclaimed, "For fucks sake!" when he saw they were at half-mast.

So when Bob arrived with the drinks, the first thing he was greeted with was, "What the hell did you bring me in here for Bob, are you trying to make me feel ashamed or something, I bet I look a right tramp to these blokes."

Taken aback by Matty's sudden outburst, Bob's first thought was to have a go at the ungrateful bastard, but when he saw that he was really upset, he tried to placate him, saying "Now. now Matty, pay no heed to these buggers, you are every bit as. good as any one of them. Ok, so you need some new clobber, but that doesn't make you any less of a person, now does it?"

Matty just sat staring at the floor stewing and still feeling ashamed. So Bob realised he had to do something quick, or the lad just might, up and walk out, so he decided to tell him of his plans.

"Do you fancy a job?" he asked as casually as he could, "Because I could use another pair of hands back at the Jolly's. Of course, there's accommodation goes with it too" he added smugly.

Bob had hit the nail on the head, for Matty glanced up at him and asked, with a puzzled look on his face, "What, you mean me live at the pub with you and Bella?"

"Well not exactly with me and Bella," he replied with a sigh of relief, "In the caravan, at the bottom of the pub yard."

"That old bloody thing!" Matty exclaimed, "I think you're either joking or taking the piss Bob, cos the last time I saw that, it was falling to bloody bits."

"It's not now though Matty" Bob enthused, "Big John, Bella and me have done it up and, if I say so myself, we've made a damn good job of it."

Bob sat expecting a quick reply, but he didn't get one. Instead Matty went back to staring at the floor. He wasn't in a mood this time though, he was actually thinking about living in the caravan, after all, he didn't have anywhere else to live, so inwardly, he was pleased with Bob's offer.

It took him a few minutes, but eventually he said, without looking up, "I suppose it wouldn't hurt to take a look."

Once again feeling full of himself and back in charge of the situation, Bob slapped Matty on the shoulder, saying "That's the spirit son. Now come on and cheer up and get that beer down your neck, after all, this is supposed to be a bloody celebration, isn't it?"

Matty looked up at him and smiled, "Aye, I suppose you're right." Then picking up his pint, he added sheepishly, "Sorry I was a bit sharp with you Bob."

"Awe, forget it son, it's understandable for you to be a bit edgy considering where you have been for the last year. Now let's lighten up and get some supping done."

For the next hour or so, that was exactly what they did, with Bob of course, doing most of the talking, asking endless questions about Matty's time inside.

Most of them he answered, but the one thing he never mentioned was his run-in with Bomber Foster. For he felt that was personal, something to sort out in the future if ever he came across the bloke again and, as much as he hated himself for thinking it, he hoped that one day he would.

As they talked, Matty had also realised Bob had never mentioned Dotty, so when a lull appeared in the conversation, as casually as he could, he asked, "Oh, by the way Bob, how's our Dotty doing, has anyone been to see her lately?"

This was the one subject Bob hadn't wanted Matty to get onto, but he knew that it was inevitable, so in a very serious voice, he replied, "I was in last week to see her son" then pausing to look down at the floor, continued, "I'm afraid it's not good news though Matty, the Doctor through at Ryburn thinks she's completely gone now. Oh they've tried all sorts of treatment but she never responded." Then as he looked up from the floor, he sighed heavily as he added, "I'm sorry son."

Matty felt himself begin to tremble with emotion, as all kinds of thoughts raced through his mind. He began blaming everyone he could think of for what had happened to Dotty.

Not just Siddy, but his mother, father and Bomber Foster, yet at the end of his internal raging he finally came back to blaming himself and, as Bob got up to go back to the bar, Matty felt himself filling up with tears, so he quickly took out his handkerchief and pretended to blow his nose, then turned to look out of the window in case anyone was watching him.

He was so racked with guilt, he kept saying, "Sorry Dotty my love" under his breath, over and over again and, it wasn't until Bob came back with the pints did he suddenly stop, spin round to face Bob and bark, "I'll get her out, you mark my fucking words if I don't."

Bob was taken totally by surprise by the look on Matty's face and by his venomous outburst. He knew he had to do something quick or the lad would explode, so putting the beer down on the table, he put his arm around Matty's shoulder and told him, "Of course you'll get her out son, once you've got yourself settled and into a routine, who knows, you might even meet a young lass and get hitched, then you'll have somebody to help you look after your Dotty, you'll see, just give it time."

He stood for a while longer, quietly hoping he had got through to Matty and, when the lad slowly nodded his head and looked up at him, Bob knew he had calmed him down again, but as he sat back in his chair, he thought, 'Thank Christ for that, the last thing I want him doing is losing his rag again and ending up back inside. After all, there's a lot of planning gone into this day, aye and a few quid too, so I don't want the silly sod ruining it now.'

Bob took a sip of his drink, but looked at Matty over the top of his glass as he did so and, seeing that there was only a hint of temper left in his eyes, he asked, "Are you hungry son?"

Food was the last thing on Matty's mind, but now at the mention of it, he suddenly realised, he was hungry, so as a reply, he nodded.

"Good." said Bob, feeling in control again, "Because Bella has cooked you something special, so we'll finish our drinks, then head back to Houghton, cos if we're late, she'll kick our bloody arses for us."

Even though he didn't feel like it, Matty heard himself chuckling at Bob's last statement, for the thought of Bella giving them both a good kick up the arse, somehow tickled him.

As they drove through a little place called Carville, then on to the Houghton road, Matty felt both depressed and apprehensive.

Depressed at the thought of going back to the Market Place and, apprehensive at what would be waiting for him when he goes there. For if there was one place he never wanted to see again, that was it.

Yet when he got out of the car and stood looking around at the houses, he suddenly felt a feeling of belonging. For although he hated the place, he had never really known anywhere else in his adult life.

He looked up towards their old house and smiled forlornly at it. It hadn't been much, but it had been their home and, with a heavy layer of snow covering all the houses, it didn't look the slum it really was.

Then, images of his father and Siddy shot into his mind and his thoughts suddenly turned bitter as he recalled the times his old man made him take on Siddy in the back yard. For it was there that his violent streak was born, it was there his vicious temper was put into him, as he had to furiously fight Siddy off or get another hammering and, it was there he was turned into the hard case he was today. Oh he hated the Market Place for the poverty it held, but he hated it more for the bad memories it held for him.

"Come on Matty son," Bob called as he got out of the car and headed for the steps leading to the front door of the Jolly's, "Let's get inside out of this bloody cold."

"Ave. I'm coming Bob" Matty called back, as he shook his head with sadness, but as he reached the steps, he stopped, for one more lingering look, then followed Bob in.

Climbing the stairs to the living quarters above the bar, Matty was still full of bitter thoughts of his father and Siddy, but he stopped abruptly when the most delicious smell came wafting down the stairs to meet him. He stood for a few moments sniffing in the gorgeous aroma, then Bob nudged him in the back and told him, "It's no good standing sniffing at the bloody thing Matty let's get up there and get the bugger eaten."

"Sorry Bob" he replied, a little embarrassed, "It's just that I haven't smelt grub like that for years, it smells bloody handsome."

"Aye" Bob told him proudly, as they carried on up the stairs, "If there's one thing Bella can cook, it's a bloody good steak."

The first thing they heard as they entered the living room, was Bella's voice, as she called, "Sit yourselves down lads, dinners nearly ready, oh and Bob, pour the lad a drink."

Bob didn't reply, he simply pointed to an arm chair by the fire, for Matty to sit on. He then opened a bottle of brown ale and poured them both a glass.

Matty was in awe as he sat looking around the room. Everything seemed clean and polished, the chair he sat in was so comfortable, he felt it wouldn't take long for him to nod off.

Bob watched him out of the corner of his eye and smiled as he asked, "Is it comfy enough for you Matty?"

Matty chuckled as he replied, "Comfy, bloody hell Bob, I think I've died and gone to heaven."

Bella appeared then from the kitchen and, it seemed as if Matty was looking at her for the first time, for she seemed to be so different to the woman who served his beer on a Friday night.

"There you are Matty son," Bella enthused.

"Get that down you, I bet you could do with a decent meal."

As Matty got up from the arm chair and sat down at the table, the smell was wonderful, he'd never had food like steak and all he could do, when he sat down, was sit and stare at it.

Bob slapped him on the shoulder saying, "Come on bonny lad, if you leave anything on your plate, Bella'll not be happy mind."

Matty ate his meal without saying a word, so engrossed in devouring his meal.

Bob and Bella decided not to engage him in conversation and just let the lad enjoy it.

Fifteen minutes later, as he put his knife and fork down on his plate and sat back, he looked at Bella and humbly said, "God Bella, I've never had grub like that in my life, it was bloody lovely, thank you."

But she didn't reply, she simply nodded and carried on eating her meal.

As she did so, Matty took a sly look at her. She looked about thirty-five or so and, although she seemed a bit on the plump side, he thought she looks quite attractive for an older woman.

The thing that hit him the most though, was how gentle natured she seemed. She had always given the impression of being the brassy sort of woman, but he realised he was wrong.

After the dinner dishes were cleared, Bella brought in two big platefuls of apple pie and custard, prompting Matty to exclaim, "If I eat that lass, I reckon I'll burst."

Both Bob and Bella chuckled, with Bob saying, "You'd better eat it son, or I'll tell you now, she'll kick your arse."

All three of them burst out laughing then, with Matty doing just as he was told by clearing his plate.

With the meal now finished and Bella busy washing-up, Bob and Matty sat in front of the fire enjoying a nice glass of beer.

Bob glanced across at him and noticed how heavy Matty's eyes looked.

"You ready for a kip son?" Bob asked him.

Matty nodded, saying, "Yes, that I am Bob, your missus has knackered me, she's a hell of a cook Bob, isn't she."

Bob chuckled as he replied, "She is that, that's one of the reasons I married her, not the only one mind, but one of the main reasons."

They sat in silence for a few minutes longer. Then Bob noticed Matty's eyes were closing, so standing up, he nudged the lad's leg, saying, "Come on son, let's get you down to the caravan and you can have a good sleep."

Matty had never been into the back yard of the pub before, oh he'd looked over the walls a few times, but hadn't taken much notice of the place.

As he closed the back door behind him, he noticed a small out building to his left and, when Bob saw him go up to the window and look inside it, he told him, "That's the scullery Matty, that's where you'll head for first thing in the morning to get the brew on, ready for me to come down. I have a mug of tea while I pick me horses out."

Matty shook his head and smiled as he asked, "And what time would sir like his tea to be served may I ask?"

Bob played along with him as he answered, "Oh about half seven will do me fine."

They both laughed, then carried on down to the caravan, which was about thirty yards further down the yard.

From the outside, it looked alright, it had been given a new coat of green paint and it had white floral curtains up at the windows.

There was supposed to be a step up to the door, but instead, someone had used an upside-down beer crate as a replacement.

As Bob watched Matty looking at it, he told him, "That's one of Big John's ideas, d'you like it?"

Then they both roared with laughter as Matty quipped, "Yes, that's got Big John written all over it."

Meanwhile, back up at the pub, Bella was almost finished doing the dishes.

She was very pleased with herself at how well the meal had gone down and was feeling full of hope for the future, for Bob may have had his plans for Matty, but so did Bella.

She had always been attracted to big hard men, hence the reason she married Bob, but things had gone stale of late as he seemed more content to get pissed on brandy every night, than pleasure her.

'But,' she thought, as she slowly began to rub her groin area, 'Now young Matty has come onto the scene, who knows what will happen.'

Matty too was thinking of the future and, as he went into the caravan and sat down on the bed, his thoughts were miles away.

What if things didn't work out at the pub, how would he manage for money? Where would he live? What about Dotty?

Lots of dark thoughts kept going around and around in his mind, after all, he knew very little of life, but had a feeling he was about to start learning lots of things he hadn't even thought about before and, told Bob so.

As Bob looked down at Matty staring at the floor, he almost felt sorry for the lad, but then he remembered what he had in store for him and dismissed his sentimental feelings by telling Matty, "Aye, I'm sure you will son, now get yourself a bit of kip, because I reckon an awful lot of beer is going to be drunk tonight."

Matty looked up at him and they both smiled. Then he nodded his agreement as he suddenly felt a wave of tiredness come over him and, as Bob was letting himself out of the caravan, Matty called, "See you at seven then."

As he sat in the silence on his own now, Matty looked around admiringly at his new home for a few moments. Then he flopped onto the bed, closed his eyes and began thinking of Dotty.

Then he quickly opened them again and looked once more at the velvet curtains and floral bedspread, contentedly telling himself, "Aye, I reckon she'll like her new home too." Then with peaceful thoughts filling his mind, he fell into a deep sleep.

It was probably the best sleep he had had in ages, but when he awoke it was pitch dark, so it took him a few moments to work out exactly where he was.

When finally it came to him, he sat bolt upright on the bed then began fumbling for his watch. Of course when he found it, he still couldn't see what time it was, so he then began groping around for the candle and box of matches, he had seen earlier on top of the set of drawers by the bed.

After finding the matches and striking one, he saw by its light that it was almost half-seven. "Christ!" he exclaimed, jumping off the bed, "I bet the blokes up in the bar think I'm a right dosser."

Now, feeling slightly flustered, he made his way into the kitchenette to give his face a swill, but he forgot to duck his head as he had done earlier, when Bob was showing him round, hence there was an almighty thud, as his head cracked against the panel, above the kitchenette doorway, almost knocking him flat on his back.

"For fuck's sake" he yelped, rubbing the top of his brow, then gingerly feeling his way towards the sink, where he leaned down and groped for the bucket of fresh water, then poured himself enough to have a good rinse.

Bending forward though, to scoop water up to his face, he promptly smacked his head again on the side of the draining board. "WHAT IN FUCK'S NAME" he bellowed, as once more, he rubbed the very same spot he had injured earlier.

Eventually, he did manage to have his wash, but then came the problem of finding the towel. He knew there was one in there somewhere, but could he as hell find it. So he groped his way back into the main room and dried himself on the bedspread. Then he felt his way to the table, picked up the two quid Bob had left him and, with relief, let himself out of the caravan.

As he walked up the pub-yard though, he thought 'It might look a nice place to live, but by Christ it's going to take some getting used to.'

The cheering and back slapping that greeted him as he walked into the bar, came as another surprise to Matty. For when he scanned the faces of the blokes who were there, most of them had only ever been nodding acquaintances. Oh there was the exception, like Big John and some of his work-mates, but in the main, most of them he didn't even know the names of.

What he wasn't to know of course, was that Bob had put on free grub and, had put the word out that there was also a free pint for anyone who turned up. With Big John also demanding a good turn out, it wasn't any wonder the place was full.

Yet there was another factor involved. For unknowingly Matty had rid the pub of its number one bully by hammering Siddy as he did and, even though no one mentioned it, they were all quietly grateful that they didn't have to put up with him anymore.

Just as he would have expected, it was Big John who gave him the warmest greeting, by flinging his huge arms around him and yelling, "BY GOD MATTY, IT'S GREAT TO HAVE YOU HOME AGAIN."

Matty was totally overwhelmed by it all and it took a few minutes to sink in, but he was home, for better or worse, he was back in the Market Place, back amongst his own kind again. Inwardly though, he didn't know whether to feel happy or sad about it, for he had often thought that the Market Place, was sometimes a prison of its own.

As the beer flowed though and different blokes came and had a chat with him, his spirits lifted and, by half-nine the party was in full swing. But suddenly the singing, the laughter and the rattle of dominoes petered out and, Matty, who was at the far end of the bar, turned to see what had happened to cause this.

He looked over the heads of the crowd towards the door and smiled to himself, when he spotted Sergeant Shilton, standing just inside the doorway.

It was obvious that everyone in the bar knew who he was and, had either become nervous or wary, when he had walked in.

But when the Sergeant made a beeline for Matty and began shaking his hand, they all gasped in unison for this was one sight they never thought they would see, a son of Jimmy Glave, shaking the hand of the most hated copper in Houghton-le-Spring.

After a few minutes though they got over the shock. Some sidled out in disgust, but most of them went back to supping their beer, occasionally keeping a weather eye on the Sergeant, who was totally aware of the hostile feelings towards him, but couldn't give a toss. For Matty was the only one that mattered, it was him and him alone he had come to see.

As Matty ordered him a pint, the Sergeant slyly looked him over and came to the conclusion he didn't look too bad considering where he'd been. But he did notice the scar tissue on his knuckles and jumped to the conclusion that the lad must have had a few set-to's whilst inside. Then when Matty turned to give him his drink, he noticed the bump on his brow, so smiling he asked, "What happened to your head Matty, did you fall down or something?"

Matty warily felt the bump, then chuckled as he replied, "No, I had a fight with a caravan." Then seeing the puzzled look on the Sergeant's face, he began to explain how kind Bob and Bella had been and how they had done it up for him to live in. "The only problem is though" he concluded, feeling the bump again, "It's a bit on the small side." To which, the Sergeant burst out laughing, attracting a few sideways glances as he did so.

When a lull appeared in the conversation, Matty excused himself and went out to the urinal, leaving the Sergeant standing on his own at the bar.

The Sergeant had been aware of Bob looking at him sideways for a while now, but when he looked directly at Bob, the bloke turned away. Inwardly the Sergeant smiled at this, for he had Bob Hunter down as a wrong 'un and his sly behaviour, only served to confirm this.

For little did Bob know, that when he first came to Houghton the Sergeant had delved into his background, which was something he did whenever a stranger came onto his patch, to run something like a pub and, he was fully aware of Bob's street-fighting escapades, but seeing as how the bloke had kept his nose clean up till now, he had never had cause to bother him. Now though. in the light of his kindness to young Matty, the Sergeant couldn't help thinking that things were not as straight-forward as they seemed to be.

When Matty returned, they chatted on for a while longer about the future and finding a job and, maybe settling down. Then the Sergeant finished his pint, shook Matty by the hand again as he wished him good luck, then made his way towards the door.

As he came level with Bob though, he stopped and beckoned him to him. A little nervous, Bob leaned over the bar and, putting on his best smile, said "Alright then Sergeant Shilton?" Then pointing with his thumb towards Matty added, "It's nice to see the lad back again, isn't it?"

The Sergeant stood about a foot from Bob's face and studied it for a few moments. Then told himself that this was one of the most insincere bastards he had ever clapped eyes on and, his reply left Bob in no doubt just what he thought of him. "Aye, it's all over for the lad now, all the bad times are hopefully behind him." Then he sternly glared deep into Bob's eyes, as he added "And I hope your motives for helping him are the right ones, because if they're not, you'll have me to deal with." Then without even giving Bob a chance to reply, he turned and walked out.

Aware that several customers had been watching the confrontation, Bob didn't react to the Sergeant's threat, but inwardly he was raging. For the one thing he didn't need, was a shithouse like Shilton cocking up his plan, but as his temper left him though and he began to think straight again, he reckoned he had found a solution to the problem. If he did manage to persuade Matty. to take up fighting, Houghton would have to be the one place where it never happened. For Bob concluded that, if they weren't on Shilton's patch, the bastard couldn't touch them.

By now it was getting on for closing time, so Bob decided to call last orders. Then after another twenty minutes he had the place cleared, apart from Matty, Big John, Bella and himself.

"At last" he said, pouring himself a large brandy, then coming round from behind the bar and plomping himself down on a stool he added, "Now maybe we can have a drink in peace, but I must say though Matty, I thought the lads did you proud."

"A bloody good do" slurred Big John, who was well on his way to being drunk.

"Aye it was that" Matty mused, as he reflected back on the night. "But I was a bit surprised to see Sergeant Shilton here though. I wonder how he knew I was coming out."

"I told him" slurred Big John again, "I saw him down town the other day, but he never said he was coming up though."

Then for a few moments there was a strained silence, as the three of them mulled over their thoughts of the Sergeant. One liking him, one grudgingly respecting him and, the other one loathing him.

Bella interrupted their thoughts though, by announcing that the party seemed to be over and she was heading for bed. If they wanted more drink, they could help themselves, which Big John promptly did.

"By the way" the big fella said, sitting down again to take his huge weight off his already aching feet, "What do you think of the caravan?"

"Oh it's fine Big John" Matty told him, then as his face broke into a grin, he added "Apart from the step that is."

"Cheeky young bugger" the big man retorted, "That's the best idea I've had in years." Which prompted a huge round of laughter.

Eventually though, it wasn't long before the conversation took on a more serious note. Matty had been half expecting it to anyway, for he knew that once the beer got hold of Big John, he would turn maudlin.

He also knew how uncomfortable it would make him feel, but he didn't show it, even when the big fella told him "I hope you didn't have anything of value left in the house Matty, cos your Siddy sent a couple of blokes through from Penshaw with a horse and cart and cleared the lot out. What they thought they couldn't sell they burnt, so if there was anything of yours you wanted, I doubt if you'll find it now."

Bob glanced at Matty, half expecting an angry outburst and was surprised to see the lad didn't even bat an eyelid. He just stood, staring down at the floor, as if his mind was a million miles away.

It was his poems he was actually thinking of, the few he had written and the book Frank had given him, but he knew there was no way he was going to mention this to these two. So picking up his glass, he smiled forlornly as he eventually replied "No big fella there's nothing left up there that I want and, the only thing of value that was ever in the place, is now in Ryburn Asylum."

Of course he knew fair well that his last comment would kill the night, but he was getting a bit fed up anyway and, when Bob asked him if he wanted a refill, he pretended to yawn, and said "No thanks Bob, not for me, I think I'll head off back down to the caravan." Then trying to leave on a lighter note, added "Some of us have to get up early for work you know."

Big John, who had not been aware of the fullness of Bob's offer, suddenly looked puzzled and asked "Work, what works that then Matty?"

Pointing to Bob as he headed towards the door, Matty told him "Ask my bloody bossman. I'm sure he'll tell you what it's all about. Now goodnight apiece." With Big John looking even more puzzled now, he left them.

As he reached the back door though, he stopped when he heard Big John roar with laughter and, he smiled to himself as he uttered "Aye that's right big fella, that's what I'm going to be, a bloody tea-boy."

Matty slept that night, but only fitfully. For one half of him couldn't wait for morning, whilst the other half was dreading it, as he knew fair well what he had to do, that was go through to Ryburn.

He hadn't mentioned it to anyone, but on the other hand why should he. Dotty was now his concern, all he could hope for, was that she recognised him. He felt sure she would, but always there was that nagging doubt at the back of his mind.

By the time Bob came down to the scullery the following morning at half-seven, Matty had already been there a good hour. "Sugar and milk?" he asked Bob, as he came in and sat down at the table opposite him.

"Aye, two sugars and a drop" then spreading his morning paper out on the table, added "Mind I must say, I didn't really expect to see you this bloody early."

"Well we did say half-seven" Matty reminded him, then hesitated, as if to say something else but couldn't find the words.

Bob spotted this, so asked "Something on your mind Matty?"

It took him a few seconds to answer, but he did, telling him "There is actually Bob, I was wondering if it would be alright to start work tomorrow. Y'see I've got a few things that need sorting out and I may as well get them sorted now as later."

Bob didn't reply, he pretended to carry on reading his paper, but he was really thinking, 'I bet he's off to see the lass, aye and I bet he tries to bring her back here, but he's in for one hell of a shock. Still, as he says himself, it's best to sort it now rather than later. At least this way, I'll be able to settle him down quicker.' So with a knowing smile, he finally told him "Of course you can have the day off son and, as far as tomorrow's concerned, you can forget that too, for Sunday is my lazy day, so you needn't bother to get up early, ok?"

Slightly relieved that there wasn't going to be any hassle. he got up from the table and began to put on his overcoat and cap "Cheers Bob" he said, as he then headed towards the door.

"How're you fixed for money?" Bob called.

Matty turned and pulled out the two pound notes Bob had given him "I'm alright Bob, I've still got this" then with a puzzled look added "But how I still come to have it, is a bloody mystery though, considering how much ale was supped last night."

Then as he closed the scullery door behind him, Bob sat listening to his footsteps as he walked off and with a wry smile, uttered "That's because I paid for the bastard, but I'll get it all back one day young Matty, you see if I don't."

On the bus ride through to Ryburn, Matty wondered what he must have looked like to the rest of the passengers. What, with the state of his clothes and holding a bunch of daffodils in his hand, he reckoned he must have looked a strange sight indeed. 'But still' he thought, looking down at the flowers and smiling, 'I know someone who will be pleased to see me.'

Forty minutes later, nervous and confused, he stood around the reception area of the asylum not knowing what to do with himself and, his frustration was just beginning to get to him, when a young lass came up and asked "Can 'I help you sir?"

For a few moments his awkwardness took him over again, as it had often done whenever he was confronted by a pretty female and, this one was so clean looking and so neat and tidy, he was totally transfixed by her.

But after rebuking himself though for being so bloody stupid, he replied "Er, yes luv, I've come to see my sister Dotty, I mean Dorothy, I'm her brother, Matthew."

"And what would your sister's surname be sir?" she asked, as she looked him up and down and with a hint of impatience in her voice.

With a look of dire confusion on his face, at being asked such a stupid question, Matty replied indignantly "Well Glave, the same as mine."

Her face almost broke into a smile at Matty's simple reply, but she stopped herself and putting on an air of authority, told him to take a seat whilst she went to find matron.

Sitting down on one of the four chairs, just inside the doorway, he watched her as she walked off down a long corridor. "Stupid cow" he uttered, "I hope she isn't looking after our Dotty. She might be a good looker, but by Christ, she's a stuck up little bugger."

As he waited for her to return, he took off his cap and stuffed it in his pocket then generally tried to smarten himself up. He tried re-arranging the flowers, but they always seemed to fall back into their original position.

Then he realised just how badly he was sweating from his nervousness, so he rubbed his hands down the side of his coat in an effort to dry them, but ten seconds later, they were just as damp. For being so close to Dotty now, was beginning to get to him, the moment he had been looking forward to and the moment he had been dreading for so long, was almost here. He kept telling himself, over and over, that he had nothing to worry about, Dotty would recognise him, but then that nagging voice at the back of his head, was always there, asking "Will she?"

After what seemed an hour, but was really no more than ten minutes, the receptionist returned, but as she clip-clopped back along the corridor, it wasn't her who took Matty's eye, but the woman she was with.

She was a tall, stout, round faced woman of about forty and was wearing a spotlessly clean, dark blue uniform and a white nurse's hat, but the thing that stood out most about her, was her walk. It was more like a march, as if she was in a parade or something.

Matty stood as they approached him, but wasn't sure if he should salute her or not, for she seemed so military. Yet when she spoke, there wasn't the slightest thing military about her voice, as she said in the softest tones Matty had ever heard "Hello Mister Glave, I'm matron Ashcroft, I'm told you wish to see your sister Dorothy."

He fumbled for his words again as he stuttered "Aye, I mean yes, that's right, I... I've been working down south and this is the first chance I've had to get back and see her."

She studied him for a moment, for she knew he was lying but she couldn't help feeling sorry for him. He looked so pathetic, standing there with his disarranged bunch of daffodils that her heart went out to him.

She knew the background to Dorothy's case so she was fully aware of where Matty had been, but so as not to embarrass him, she didn't let on she knew as she told him "Ok then Mister Glave, you can see her, but I hope you are aware that Dorothy won't recognise you."

Matty felt a twinge of anger then and replied sharply "But she might."

Matron Ashcroft looked into his eyes and could see the deep hurt in them. She was aware of his devotion to his retarded sister, so she realised that no matter what he was told, he would never believe anything anyone told him, until he saw her for himself.

"Come on then Mister Glave" she told him, turning towards the long corridor again, "I'll take you to her, but please, don't get your hopes up too high."

They walked along the corridor for about thirty yards, then it opened out into a ward. There were six beds along the inside wall and another six by the windows.

He scanned each bed for Dotty, but couldn't recognise her on any of them. Then the matron pointed to the farthest bed on the window side and whispered "There she is, at the end by the window" then turning to him, added "Now if you want me, I'll just be here and, please Mister Glave, for your own good, don't stay too long."

He knew she was a kindly woman and that she meant well, so as he smiled at her, he assured her, "Don't worry matron, I'll be alright."

Then he walked slowly through the ward, trying his best not to look at some of the wretched souls on the other beds. But it was difficult, for there were some terrible sights and was glad when he finally reached Dotty.

She was sitting on the side of the bed, staring out of the window and, as he came round to face her, he felt the tears well up inside of him as he saw how terrible she looked. For she was no more than a bag of bones and her once, beautiful flowing hair, had been shaven off. Her creamy coloured skin was now white and pithy and her big, twinkling brown eyes, were empty and sunken.

He knelt down in front of her and stretched out his hand with the flowers in it, then whispered gently, "Hello Dotty my little darling, it's Matty I've come to see you and look" he added, nodding towards the flowers, "I've brought you some daffs, your favourites. Nice eh Dotty, nice eh."

But there was no response just a sad, empty stare, as she continued to look out of the window.

He felt the tears welling up again, so he stood up, put the flowers down on the bed and blew his nose. Then he sat down beside her and cuddled her to him and, as he slowly began to rock her back and forth, he told her, "My poor little darling, all you ever wanted was love and look what's happened to you, you end up all on your own in a place like this, a prisoner of your own mind. At least I got out of my prison, but you my angel, are locked in yours forever. Yet your only crime, was to be a Snowflake." Then he hugged her tightly to him and, as the tears rolled freely down his cheeks, he added, "It's so sad our Dotty, so sad."

For the following ten minutes or so, he sat gently rocking her again, remembering some of the lovely times they had had together walking the old moor, collecting wild flowers and watching out for different birds or animals, like rabbits or foxes. He could still hear her childlike laughter whenever they spotted one and, he smiled forlornly at the memory of it.

But his smile vanished suddenly when he remembered the night of the rape, then as the image of Siddy shot into his mind, he closed his eyes tightly and hissed, "I should have killed you, you bastard."

It was then the matron touched his arm saying, "Come on Mister Glave, I think you had better go now."

He stood up and looked down into Dotty's eyes again. Then, in one last desperate attempt pleaded, "Please Dotty, please my darling, say Matty's name, come on, you can say it." For a split second he thought he saw her eyes flicker, but it was only his imagination. So he hugged her once more and told her how much he loved her, then kissing her on the forehead, told her "I've got to go now Dotty, but I promise I'll come again and remember, Matty will always love you, so ta-ra my little Snowflake." Then with one last lingering look, he left her.

The matron, who had stood watching those last painful moments, was as near to tears as Matty was. She had seen some heart rendering sights in her time, but the sight of this big, hard looking bloke, cuddling his frail retarded sister, really got to her and, as they reached the reception area once again, she told him sympathetically "I'm sorry you had to go through that Mister Glave, but at least you now know what the situation is and, as for coming again, I wouldn't advise it. You see, Dorothy doesn't know you, but you still know her and all you will be doing is tearing your heart out every time you come. It's best you leave her for me to look after, I'll see she is well cared for I promise, and if you leave me your address, I'll write to you if ever there is a change in her condition."

Matty hated every word she was saying, for he knew in his heart of hearts the woman was right. Maybe one day in the future, when he felt strong enough to handle it, he'd come again, but right now, all he wanted to do, was find somewhere, where he could release his emotions.

Outside of the Asylum, as he walked down towards the main gate, he spotted an old garden shed. He went in and closed the door behind him, then crouched down on his haunches and cried like a baby.

He felt so sad, so alone and so scared of the future. For he knew that now there were no Snowflakes left, no gentle influences to calm him, there was every chance he could turn wild, or revert to types like his father or brother.

He had felt it whilst in prison, after his set-to with Bomber Foster and, if he hadn't had Dotty to turn his thoughts back to, he knew he would probably have snapped altogether.

How long he sat sobbing for, he didn't know, for Dotty's pitiful image kept coming into his mind, but finally the tears dried. So after chastising himself for being so bloody soft, he pulled himself together and left the shed.

On his return to Houghton though, he decided not to go straight back to the Jolly's, instead, he decided to take a stroll to a place called Miller's Hill.

Before his friend Frank had died, this used to be Matty's. favourite spot, but it must have been three years since he was last here. He had passed it often enough on his way to work, but he had never bothered to go up the hill, for he knew how emotionally painful it would have been.

But now, as he sat once again crouched down on his haunches, he felt drained of all emotion and, oblivious to the cold and sleet, he began picking out various spots on the outskirts of the town, where he used to take Dotty flower picking.

He could barely make some of them out, but he knew they were there. The Seven Sisters Wood, the old moors, Warden Law Hill and of course, the Pasty Burns. Wonderful memories came flooding back to him as he smiled forlornly at each one of them.

Then, as he looked down to his right, his smile suddenly disappeared, as his eyes fell upon The Market Place. He sat glaring at it for a few minutes, with nothing but hateful thoughts running through his mind, for it was that place which held most of his worst memories.

Then slowly he turned his head directly down to his left and a sudden chill ran through him, for this was the place he dreaded looking at most and, as he leaned over to look down the cliff face, they had nicknamed the Queen's Steps, once again he could see Frank's broken, twisted frail body lying at the bottom.

The general theory had been, that since he had worn irons on his legs as a result of having polio, he had somehow tripped and fallen over the edge, but Matty knew differently though. He knew Frank had tried to climb down the Queen's Steps that day he had left him on the hill, after they had had a tiff. Now as he sat, with his eyes riveted to the spot where Frank had been found dead, he cast his mind back to the very first time he met his gentle, crippled friend.

It had just been after Matty's sixteenth birthday, in the summer of forty-six. He had been on his way up to the hill with Dotty one Sunday afternoon, when he came across what looked like two kids, aged about ten or eleven, whacking another kid of the same age with sticks. He had left Dotty and chased them, shouting "Get away you little buggers, leave the lad alone."

Then when he had reached the kid who was being beaten, he had been shocked to see that he wasn't a kid at all, in fact, if anything, he had looked older than Matty was.

As he helped the lad pick up his pieces of drawing paper, that were strewn about the ground, he asked "Are you alright then young 'un?"

To which the lad replied "Aye, I'm ok." Then wiping the tears from his eyes, he began to help Matty pick up the papers.

"The little sods want their arses kicking" he remembered saying, but he also remembered how shocked he had been at Frank's reply.

"It's not really their fault" he had said, "It's obvious somebody has taught them to take the micky out of cripples, otherwise they wouldn't have known how to do it in the first place." Then as he tucked the pieces of paper under his arm and turned to walk up the hill, he'd added "Besides, it's all I've come to expect living in a place like this."

Matty had not been aware that the lad was a cripple, but as he watched him walk off stiff legged, he shook his head in amazement at the lack of anger in the lad. For he knew that if it had been him they had attacked, he would have taken the sticks off them and wrapped them around their necks.

Then he remembered going back to get Dotty and taking her by the hand, they had followed the lad up the hill. He was having such difficulty in walking though, that it wasn't long before they caught up with him. Then as they had come level with him, Matty had asked "Do you want a hand?"

A faint smile crossed his lips now as he remembered Frank's curt reply. "Why" he had retorted, "D' you think because I'm a cripple, I can't manage or something?"

Matty remembered feeling a bit put out at Frank's reply, so he hurried on past him, dragging Dotty behind him. But when he was about three quarters of the way up the hill, he stopped and looked round to see how Frank was doing. What he saw was probably one of the bravest things Matty was ever to see, for Frank had been on his hands and knees and, was slowly working his way up the hill. It was then that Matty's heart had gone out to the lad, so he had told Dotty to sit down and wait for him, then he had gone back to help him.

Matty had shook his head in dismay when he had seen how much sweat was coming out of him. Then, as he had picked him up, kicking and protesting, he remembered saying "For Christ sake shut up you bloody fool and don't be so bloody awkward."

By the time, they had reached the top though, Frank's temper had quietened some and, after putting him down, they began to chat like two old friends, which over the next two years, was exactly what they became.

Although Frank had indeed turned out to be older than Matty by two years, he was a very weak person, Matty reckoned he could have weighed no more than four stones, so everywhere they went, Matty would carry him.

His body might have been weak, but there had been nothing wrong with his mind, for Matty would sit in awe at Frank's wonderful theories on life and how marvellous nature was. He seemed to know the habits and lifestyle of every creature Matty could name and his drawings were ever so good. But it was Frank's gentle wisdom that had fascinated him most, he seemed to have an answer to every problem Matty had. Even his aversion to cockroaches was explained away, by Frank telling him that everything on this earth belonged here, otherwise it wouldn't have been put on the earth to start with and, just because we didn't like something, was really not a reason for wanting to kill it.

Matty smiled to himself now, as he thought of the hundreds of cockroaches he must have killed since Frank had talked to him about them, for if there was still one thing he couldn't stand, it was those little shiny black bastards and as he thought about them, he suddenly felt himself shiver.

Then he turned his mind to the first time Frank had mentioned poetry to him and he remembered how embarrassed he had been, for he had felt such a sissy when Frank had asked, "Do you read any poetry Matty?"

"No" he had replied sheepishly, "That's not my sort of thing, I don't go in for all that."

Then he recalled the bollocking Frank had given him and he smiled again to himself, for if there was one thing that would now remain with him forever, it was his love of poetry.

Frank had also taken to Dotty and called her his little dove. He would also draw lots of pictures of flowers for her, which had delighted her to such as point, that Matty had sometimes felt a twinge of jealousy, but never once had he shown it.

As time had passed and they had become closer, they then began to open up to each other and Matty smiled yet again, as he recalled the first time he had told Frank how he likened gentle beings like him and Dotty, to a Snowflake. At first he thought that Frank might laugh at him, but he should have known better, for instead of laughing, Frank had thought it a beautiful idea.

Now, he shook his head in disbelief, as he also recalled Frank telling him, he also had the qualities of a Snowflake. "Some fucking Snowflake I turned out to be" he uttered as he wiped the sleet from his eyes and cast his mind back over the last twelve months.

Then as his mood turned to one of bitterness and anger, he closed his eyes tight and hissed, "Why Frank, why you stupid sod, why?" For he was remembering the reason, he thought Frank had died.

Matty had told him one afternoon, whilst up on the hill, that just for one day, he wished he could have been him, for one day, to see the world as he saw it. But Frank had retorted, "Aye and for one day Matty, I wish I could be you. For one day I would like to be free of these bloody irons and be able to skip and run, but most of all, to be able to climb the Queen's Steps as good as you can."

For some reason, Matty had been shocked at Frank's reply, not so much at what he had said, but the bitter way in which he had said it and, Matty remembered telling him angrily, "Don't talk so bloody stupid Frank, ok so I'm a good climber and I'm strong, but does that make me something special, you may have more goodness in your little toe, than I have in my whole body, if anything, you are the one who is special Frank, you and the likes of our Dotty." Then to emphasise his annoyance, he had raised his voice as he added, "So let's have no more shit like that off you, alright?"

They had sat in silence then, both deep in their own thoughts. Matty had been so shocked at Frank's admission, that it visibly showed. So Frank decided it was best not to provoke him any further as Matty's outburst had actually frightened him.

Half-an-hour had passed and the feeling between them had become so strained that Matty decided to call it a day. He then made some feeble excuse, about having to get home because his tea would be ready, but Frank had told him that he wanted to stay up the hill a little longer, so still in a bit of a huff, Matty had got up and left. As he had walked down the hill though, he remembered, how guilty he had felt at leaving Frank to make his own way down.

There had been no way of knowing though, that that was to be the last time he would see his friend, for on the following Tuesday, he had overheard two blokes talking at the pit, about a crippled lad that had been found dead at the bottom of the cliff, by the side of Miller's Hill.

Now he shuddered, as he remembered the shock and then the panic that had gone through him. Then he remembered how he had frantically looked for Frank's house, for although he had known the street he had lived in, he hadn't known the number.

When eventually he had found the house and Frank's mother had indeed confirmed it had been him, Matty had been devastated. He ran up Miller's Hill and looked down over the cliff side and, even now, he could still see himself crying his heart out and shouting "Why Frank, why?"

It had taken a long time to get over Frank's death, for Matty could not help blaming himself. If Frank had not tried to be like him by climbing down the Queen's Steps, he knew the lad would not have died. He also felt that if he had not left him alone that day, he would still be with him.

How long Matty had been sitting on the hill he didn't know, but at last the cold was beginning to get to him and he suddenly realised just how wet he was. So he stood up, took one last lingering look at the spot where Frank had died, then slowly began walking back down the hill.

As he did so though, he felt a sudden change come over him. For with finally accepting that he had lost Dotty, he came to realise that there was no room in this cold, hard world for such things as Snowflakes. If he was to survive, from now on there was only one person he would look out for, that would be himself.

Then, as he reached the bottom, he stopped and looked back up the hill. "All gone now" he told himself, as he recalled some of the wonderful memories he had of the place, "Aye, and no more Snowflakes either" he added, shaking his head sadly.

As he turned to walk away though, a sudden chill ran through him, as a very familiar voice whispered from behind him, "But you are wrong there Matty, there's still one Snowflake left."

Without even stopping to look round, he replied "Piss-off Frank."

CHAPTER FIVE

That heavy aura of sadness which Matty seemed to have carried with him for so long, slowly began to evaporate in the following weeks, as he threw himself into his work at the pub.

Not only did he carry out the everyday tasks, such as re-stacking shelves, changing barrels and helping out behind the bar, he also white-washed all the outer buildings at the back of the pub. Places like the bottle shed, the scullery and the urinal. He would have done the wall too if Bob hadn't stopped him.

"Still" Bob told himself one day, as he stood watching Matty, "Not a bad return for two quid a week really, it would have cost a sight more than that if I'd hired some bugger to do it."

Bob knew two quid wasn't a lot to be paying Matty, but he didn't want the lad having too much money in his pocket, he wanted to keep him short so when the time came to approach him about fighting, he wanted money to be the big persuader.

For an idea was beginning to formulate in his brain, it would take a bit of setting up and more than a touch of luck, but he felt that if things went as he planned, he could have Matty fighting within a month.

He had told Bella what he had in store for Matty but no one else. He had also given her a bollocking for spoiling him with silly presents, like shirts, socks and vests. For as he told her, how could the lad be wanting for things, if she was continually giving the buggers to him.

Yet Bob did not have the slightest idea what Bella's motive was for giving Matty the presents, but she had decided, that if it was alright for Bob to use the lad for his own ends, then she would too and, just like Bob, she was playing Matty along until the right opportunity presented itself.

She cooked him his favourite meals, made sure his clothes were washed and insisted he bath twice a week. But as there were no facilities down the caravan for bathing, it meant he had to use the bath in the living quarters. Which he did whenever he thought Bob and Bella had gone out for the night, or were working down in the bar. He felt so relaxed, he even took to leaving the bathroom door ajar sometimes, which meant he was totally unaware of the pair of lusting eyes watching every move he made.

For as he had come to trust Bella, there was no reason for him to doubt her motives either. When she ruffled his now growing hair, or squeezed his bum, not once did he think it was anything other than a friendly gesture, it never occurred to him that she was actually flirting, for as he looked upon her as a motherly figure, that was all he thought she was being.

He would sometimes catch her talking to the customers about him, telling them how well he was doing and how well he had settled down. This of course would embarrass him, but he knew she only meant well so he never pulled her up about it.

Matty had also become very popular in the bar, which surprised him, it seemed as though some of the blokes were only coming in to see him. But the truth was, they knew they would be able to drink in peace, without any bother, for if trouble did start, they knew Matty would sort it instantly, Bob had also noticed how popular the lad had become by the takings. Little did Matty know that the extra trade he was bringing in, more than paid for his keep and wages put together. Yet Bob never let him know this, after all, he wanted the lad to be beholding to him as long as possible.

Another thing that had surprised Matty, were the different characters who used the place. For only ever having been in the pub on a Friday night, with the likes of Big John and his workmates, he never got to see who came in the other nights and, some of them he took to in a big way. People like Geordie Ridley, Meggie Lenn and Donny Dobbin were great folk and he knew that whenever any of them came in, he would be in for a good laugh.

Geordie for instance, had a false right hand, which for some reason or another, he disguised by wearing a pair of black leather gloves and, if you were someone who did not know this, you could be easily fooled into thinking he had two good hands. So quite often, when strangers came into the bar, Matty would chuckle to himself whenever he saw Geordie sidle up to one of them, for he knew fair well what would come next, an arm wrestling contest.

Of course Geordie would always insist on using his right arm and as his hand was only strapped on by an elasticated band, the minute his opponent exerted the slightest pressure, the hand would spring backwards, giving the impression it had been snapped off at the wrist. This coupled with Geordie falling to the floor and writhing about, screaming like a stuck pig, often sent his opponent flying out of the door, thinking he had done some terrible damage to Geordie's arm.

Someone always went after them though and explained the situation, then with everyone having good laugh, Matty would stand them both a pint and as far as he was concerned it was money well spent.

Meggie had been another he had become fond of, but he still blushed with embarrassment every time he recalled the first night he had met her, out in the men's urinal.

It had been the week after he had come out of jail, on the Saturday night and as he was still feeling pretty miserable with himself, he hadn't really taken much notice of what was going on around him, so he didn't see Meggie come in. Yet when she came and stood next to him and began fucking this and fucking that, Matty had thought what a foul mouth the bloke had had, for he was totally unaware that Meggie was a woman. But seeing as how she was dressed and spoke like a man, it was understandable.

About nine-thirty though, Matty was to find out the truth the hard way.

He had just got into the urinal and was standing relieving himself, when in walked Meggie She undid her trousers, squatted down and began to do the same. As Matty stood there watching her, he was dumbstruck and, when she stood up again, re-buttoned her trousers and asked him was he alright, he didn't know where to put his face, he was so embarrassed.

When he had walked back into the bar a few moments later though and saw how everyone was in hysterics, he realised then that something was amiss and after Big John explained it to him, he couldn't help but laugh too.

For it turned out she was a farmer, her father had wanted a son but as Meggie was all he was to get, he had decided to turn her into a lad and now, apart from certain parts of her anatomy, she was male through and through.

The bloke who provided most laughs though, was without doubt Donny Dobbin. Some nights he would have Matty laughing so much, tears ran down his cheeks, for there was no telling what he would get up to next.

One night he came into the bar with a pig's head under his right arm and asked for two pints, one for him and one for his mate, pig face. Then he would stand there talking to the pig's head about football, the weather and anything else he could think of. He would even ask if anyone fancied a double hand at dominoes or darts, but the funniest part of it had been closing time, for he had refused a last pint, saying him and his mate had a date with a couple of sows'

Then there was the time he came back from the urinal with a sausage sticking out of his fly, giving the impression he hadn't put himself away properly and, as it was an extra large sausage, many a bloke's eyes widened in amazement at what they thought was his manhood.

Although Matty hadn't realised it, it was having people like these around him that had got him through those first hurt filled few weeks. Oh he still had trouble sleeping at night, for Dotty's empty, sad eyes still haunted him and, most nights he would hear her sobbing, somewhere in the darkness, but he had found that taking a good swig of brandy before he went to bed, often helped him get through the night, so he took to keeping a bottle by the side of the bed.

He had tried several times to go back to Ryburn, but at the last minute he had decided against it. For matron Ashcroft's words kept coming back to him and he knew she was right., Dotty would never know who he was, but he would always know her, therefore, he would be the only one to suffer.

Besides, after his visit to Miller's Hill, he had promised himself that he would be stronger now, he wouldn't let his mind drift into thoughts of such things as Snowflakes or poetry. He knew that if he was to make anything of himself, he would have to be tougher and not let life walk all over him. He had no one to look out for now and no one to plan a future for but himself, exactly what sort of future he would have, he didn't know yet, but he was determined to have one.

He also felt that his violent days were behind him, yet after his fifth week of working at the Jolly's, he was to almost kill a bloke. The temper he thought he had such good control of, was to suddenly flare up and once again, it was to be because of Dotty.

Friday as usual, was a busy night and, as Matty pulled a round of six pints, he called along the bar to Bob "Looks like we're in for another heavy session boss."

"Aye, we are that" Bob replied, equally as busy.

A few minutes later though he stopped serving and called Big John over to him "Give Matty a hand for half-an-hour will you big fella, I've got to pop out on a bit of business."

As Big John came behind the bar Matty smiled to himself as he thought 'Aye, the pressure must be getting too much for Bob again.' For whenever they got very busy, Matty had come to notice how Bob suddenly had some business to attend to. 'Still!' he thought, smiling to himself again, 'It's his pub and he's paying the wages, so I suppose he can do what the hell he likes.'

Three quarters of an hours later though, Bob came back but didn't go behind the bar as he normally did, instead he stood at the other side and asked Matty to pour him a large brandy. Being so busy, Matty didn't notice Bob's hand shake as he put the glass to his lips. Besides, three customers had just walked in, so he headed off down the bar to serve them.

"What'll it be lads" he asked in his customary cheery voice.

"Two bitters and a large whisky" the taller of the three told him, throwing a pound note onto the bar.

As he pulled the pints, Matty gave the big 'un the once over out of the corner of his eye. He looked a mean bastard and, by the scars on his face, he looked as though he'd been in a few battles too.

He poured the whisky then went to the till for the change, but as he was handing it back, the big bloke suddenly grabbed him by the fingers and with a sneer, asked "Are you that hardman Matty Glave I've been hearing so much about?"

Matty's first thought was to jump over the bar and nut the bastard, but common-sense held him back. Instead he wrenched his fingers free and stood glaring at the bloke, who in return, stood leering at him.

Then, after about twenty seconds, the bloke said "I was talking to your brother Siddy the other day, he tells me you're not a bad scrapper, in fact he reckons you're that good, you could even give me a hiding, is that right?"

The warning bells began to ring in Matty's head as he felt himself begin to shake with temper, but again he held himself in check as he replied "Sorry mate, but I think you've got the wrong bloke, I don't consider myself a hardman, besides, I don't even know who you are."

"You don't fucking well know who I am son?" the bloke asked, then raising his voice in indignation said, "I'm Fighter Martin, one of the hardest blokes you'll ever fucking meet and if you don't believe me, let's go out the back and I'll take you on for twenty-five quid."

Matty was doing all he could to keep hold of himself, he knew he wasn't scared of the bloke, but he knew he didn't want to fight him either. So as casually as he could, he told him "No mate, I don't want to be scrapping for money, as far as I'm concerned my fighting days are over."

There were a few shocked murmurs then, as the blokes standing around them looked at each other in bewilderment, for they couldn't believe this soft-cock was the same person who had almost killed his bother a year ago in that very same bar.

Bob, who had been watching the confrontation in silence, came down the bar to where they were and asked "What's up Matty, got trouble?"

Without taking his eyes off Fighter Martin, Matty replied "Not really Bob, this bloke wants to fight me for twenty-five quid, that's all."

"Well" Bob said hesitantly, "If you want to take him on son, I'll stand the money, at least it'll be better than letting the bloke belittle you."

Matty shot Bob an angry glance, then looked around the bar at the expectant faces. The atmosphere was electric and he could feel it in every bone in his body. He knew what they all wanted him to do, for he could feel them silently willing him to do it. But he was to disappoint them though, for he turned away and began walking up to the far end of the bar, giving Bob an emphatic "No fucking chance" as he did so.

It was then Fighter Martin either played his trump card, or was to say the silliest thing in his life, as he called after Matty "If you'll not fight me, how about letting me fuck your daft sister then, I hear she's a good shag."

Matty stopped dead in his tracks, he felt rage surging through him, then in one movement, he turned and leapt onto the bar. But Bob had anticipated this and jumped between them, at the same time, he called for Big John and a couple of other blokes to grab Matty and hold him down.

This they managed to do but only just, as Bob hollered to him "Steady Matty son, not in here, if you want to take the bloke on, get out in the back-yard and do it, you've already smashed my bloody pub up once, for fucks sake don't do it again."

After a few minutes of fierce struggling Matty realised he couldn't break free, so he nodded to Bob to indicate he would do as he asked, but all the while, waiting for one of the blokes holding him to ease their grip just a little.

That didn't happen though, as Bob told those holding him down to keep a firm grip on him, then turning to Fighter Martin, he yelled "Out the back now, I'll bring the lad out in a minute."

It was not only Fighter and his two mates who went out, but the whole bar went too and it wasn't until they had all gone did Bob start talking to Matty in a calmer manner, telling him "Now calm down son, this bloke is a trained fighter, so it is no good just rushing at him in temper, stop for a minute and think about what you are going to do, alright?"

Trying to sound as though he was in control of himself again, Matty nodded as he replied "Aye, ok Bob, now let me get up."

Not quite convinced the lad was as calm as he pretended to be, Bob told the blokes holding Matty to keep him pinned down for a few minutes longer, then when he was sure he wouldn't explode, Bob said cautiously, "Right lads, let him loose."

They all stood back together and took a couple of steps away from him, fearing he might lash out at one of them, but he didn't, he simply headed for the door and went straight out to the back-yard.

Fighter, was by now stripped to the waist and in a boxer's crouched stance, was flexing his muscles and warming up. Matty didn't need to warm up though, the lad was on fire.

As soon as he caught sight of Fighter, he rushed straight at him and drove his right boot into the bloke's balls, lifting him a good two feet off the ground. Then he grabbed him by the hair and pulled his head, firstly onto his left knee, then onto his right. As he hit him with his right knee though, he let go of his hair, sending the bloke backwards and slamming against the scullery wall.

It had only taken seconds, but the yard was already sprayed with Fighter's blood, the bloke hadn't a clue what was happening to him, for it was happening so fast. He might have been a hard man, but so was Matty and the difference was, Matty was twenty years younger.

As Fighter stood, slumped against the wall, barely able to stand, Matty went for him again. This time he drove his boot into Fighter's belly, forcing an involuntary "Whoosh" from the bloke as his body doubled-up and he crashed to the ground.

Matty stood over him with a demented leer distorting his face, as he pondered on what part of Fighter's anatomy he would go for next, for the lad was completely gone by now, he was so hyped up with rage, all he wanted to do was inflict as much pain as he could on the bloke.

Although Fighter was beaten, this didn't seem to bother Matty as he began stamping on the bloke's already smashed face with his boot, splattering the freshly white-washed walls of the scullery with specks of blood.

Bob had seen enough by now, so he hollered to Big John and a few others to grab hold of Matty. Then he unlocked the scullery door and barked "Get him in there Big John and clean him up" then he added empathetically, "And for fucks sake try and calm him down."

He then turned to the crowd of onlookers and once again, at the top of his voice, he hollered "Come on now lads, the fun's over, so let's be having you all back in the bar."

As they ambled back inside, discussing the merits of the hiding and comparing it with the one Matty had given Siddy, Bob told Fighter's two mates to pick him up and follow him down to the gate at the bottom of the yard.

Meanwhile, Big John had managed to get Matty into the scullery and was washing him down, for he was covered in blood, yet none of it was his. So Big John could only conclude, that Fighter must have taken a right hammering.

He had too. His nose and cheekbones were shattered, his balls and stomach were swollen and were already turning black and blue, and blood was still gushing from the wound on the back of his head, where he had hit the wall.

Yet none of this mattered to Bob, for all he could think of was how well Matty had done and, as Fighter's two mates dragged him through the now unlocked gate, Bob stuffed twenty-five quid into Fighter's coat pocket, which was draped around his shoulders. Then as they were walking away, he called "Get him sorted out lads and when he comes round, tell him I said thanks."

As he walked back up the pub yard, Bob rubbed his hands with glee, for another part of his plan had worked. It had been a stroke of luck bumping into Fighter, the week before in Durham, for he was just what Bob had been looking for, a street-fighter who was a bit past it, but who was desperate enough to want to earn a few quid.

Of course he hadn't told Fighter how good Matty was, or why he wanted him to take the lad on. He had also told him that Matty might be a bit reluctant to fight and if he was, the only way to provoke him, would be to insult his daft sister.

'And my God' he thought now, as he walked into the scullery, 'It worked a bloody treat.'

Big John was rinsing out the cloth he had used to wipe Matty down and, as Bob came into the scullery, he shot him an angry glance, for he suspected there was more to the fight then met the eye, he also suspected that somewhere along the line, Bob knew more about it than he was letting on he knew.

Bob ignored him though and went straight over to Matty, who was sitting slumped in a chair by the table, feeling subdued, as he always did after losing his rag.

Putting an arm around his shoulder and trying to sound fatherly, Bob said "It's all over now son, I've just seen the bastard off the premises and by the looks of him, I don't think we'll be seeing him again."

Matty didn't react, he just sat staring at the floor. Big John did though, as he asked Bob accusingly "One of your mates from Durham was he?"

"What the fuck do you mean by that" Bob retorted, "I've never seen the fucking bloke in my life."

Big John stood square to Bob now glaring at him, for he couldn't help feeling that something was amiss. He knew most of the hard men in the area, but he had never heard of Fighter Martin, so it was obvious he was from one of the towns such as Sunderland, Newcastle or Durham and, seeing as how Bob often went to Durham to see his landlord pals, Big John assumed there was a connection.

Bob sensed trouble, so trying to bluff his way out of it, he said "It's bloody obvious who set this bugger up isn't it? Dear brother Siddy. He wanted to get his own back on Matty for the hiding he gave him, so he went out and hired that useless twat to do it."

"Bollocks" said Big John, as he threw the cloth into the sink, "Where would the likes of Siddy get twenty-five quid?" Then he stormed out of the scullery, leaving a deathly silence behind him.

Bob let Matty stew in his thoughts for a while, then slapping him on the shoulder, said "Come on son, snap out of it, let's go into the bar and have a drink."

Matty didn't react straight off, his mind was still full of Fighter's vile words, but eventually he slowly looked up at

Bob. Then slowly shaking his head, he replied hoarsely. "No thanks Bob, I think I'll just go down to the caravan and try to get my head down, besides, the mood I'm in, I don't think I would be very good company right now."

As he ambled off down the yard, Bob watched him for a moment and actually felt a twinge of guilt. He dismissed this though by telling himself, it was for the good, for not only would he benefit by what he had planned for the future, but so would Matty. He had convinced himself that all that had happened was simply meant to be. It was as if destiny had conspired to throw him and Matty together.

For every bad thing that had happened to the lad, had turned out to be a good thing for Bob. Matty's mother dying, the lass being put away, losing the house and having nowhere to go when he came out of jail, had all helped to manoeuvre him towards Bob. He had had to do a bit of planning along the way of course, like showing up at court, visiting the lad in jail, preparing the caravan and persuading him to live at the Jolly's. Then he had set up the fight with Fighter Martin, just to find out if the lad still had his vicious streak and, now that was proved beyond all doubt, he felt the time was right to execute the final part of his plan. So later that night, after closing time, he decided to pop down to the caravan and pay Matty a visit.

The caravan appeared to be in darkness as he rapped on the door, but when Matty called, "Who is it?", Bob simply opened the door and walked in.

"I've brought a bottle of brandy and a couple of glasses" he. said, sitting down at the table, then lighting the lamp. "There's a few things I'd like to talk to you about Matty, so I thought I'd bring something along to wet our whistles."

Matty, who had been lying face down on the bed, turned over and looked at him with a puzzled expression. "Is it important then?" he asked curiously.

Bob lit a cigar, then tilted his head back and exhaled the smoke, letting it drift slowly to the roof, "Aye, I think you could say that" he said casually, "But first, come over here to the table, I've got something for you."

Still puzzled as to what the bloke was up to, Matty got off the bed and sat in the chair opposite Bob, who by now was leaning forward again, filling two tot glasses of brandy.

"Well" Matty said, a hint of impatience in his voice.

As a reply, Bob took five, white five pound notes out of his waistcoat pocket and laid them on the table in front of Matty, then put one of the brandy's on top of the fivers saying, "That my son, is your winnings."

Utterly bewildered now, Matty shook his head slowly as he looked at the money. Then looking up at Bob said, "But I didn't fight him for money, I did it for the vile things he said about our Dotty."

"Aye, I know you did son" Bob told him, then chuckling, "But he was the one who came around here shouting his bloody mouth off, so why not make the bastard pay for it."

Matty sat staring at the money, he had never seen so much of it at once, but what he couldn't take in, was the fact that it was his. "What the hell am I going to do with all that?" he asked. Then, as his guilty conscience pricked him, he shoved the money back towards Bob and shaking his head, he said adamantly, "Sorry Bob, but I just couldn't take it."

Bob ignored him and took a swig of brandy, but out of the corner of his eye he glanced at Matty, hoping he would do the same, but the lad didn't he just sat staring at the money.

It was time for a new approach, so Bob asked him casually, "Ever had a woman, sexually I mean?"

The question had taken Matty completely by surprise and he felt a bit miffed at being asked it, which showed in his reply. "What the fuck's it got to do with you, if I have or I haven't Bob?"

"Now, now" Bob said defensively, "I'm not trying to pry, it's just that I've never seen you with a lass and I wondered if you bothered with them, that's all."

Matty was still angry though, "What are you trying to say Bob" he hissed, "D'you think I'm a homo or something?"

Bob burst into laughter and rocked back in his chair so much he almost fell off it as he replied, "No you silly sod, I don't think you're one of them." Then he laughed so much, tears began running down his cheeks.

It took Bob a little while to get over his laughing bout, but Matty sat patiently waiting for him to pull himself together. He was still miffed, but now it was being laughed at, that was doing it. He had even thought about smacking Bob one, but on the other hand, the bloke had been good to him and maybe there was a point to his question.

"Had a good laugh then?" he asked Bob sternly, when he had finally settled down again.

Wiping the tears from his eyes with the backs of his hands, Bob uttered "Would you believe it, a bloody homo of all things."

He poured himself another glass of brandy, then took on a more serious note, as he told Matty, "Look son, it's only your welfare I'm concerned about, nothing else. If you haven't been with a woman, it's obvious you must have your reasons, but I must say, that by the time I was your age, I'd shagged at least a dozen and enjoyed myself with a few more besides that. It's the sort of thing any healthy young bloke wants to do and I'm sure you are no different Matty, so if you've got a problem, maybe I can help."

Matty continued to glare at him, but his anger was abating. He concluded that maybe Bob was trying to help, so he broke his glare and as he looked down at the floor, he whispered "If you really want to know, no I haven't been with a woman."

Bob slapped him gently on the shoulder, "That's ok son, there's nothing to be ashamed about in that" he told him in his fatherly voice, "The problem is though, what are we going to do about it?"

A strained silence developed then, as Bob tried to work out what to say next. He knew he couldn't rush the situation, but he also felt that he had Matty just about where he wanted him. So draining his glass and pouring himself another, he began to tell Matty of his times as a street-fighter.

He told him of all the money he had had through his hands, the women he had had, the nice clothes he had worn, the drinking and the gambling, the popularity. He told him how people stepped aside whenever he had walked into a bar and how husbands would get jealous of him because their wives would give him the come-on, then there had been the feeling of power, of knowing there was only one top-dog and that was you.

By the time Bob was finished, four brandies later, Matty was in awe of the man, for he had never associated the things Bob had been on about with street-fighting. He thought it was only two blokes kicking the shit out of each other in a back-alley, for a few quid.

"Is that how you came to have the pub then, you bought it with your fighting money?" he asked enthusiastically.

"Aye, that's right" Bob said, nodding casually and feeling full of himself.

"But how long did it take you to get that much money though, Bob?" again full of enthusiasm.

"Oh, it took a few years, mind I spent a lot on the way of course, but by the time Joula Lowery caved my ribs in and finished me, I had enough put by to call it a day, and start my own business."

"Was this Lowery bloke good then Bob?" Matty asked curiously.

"He was that, bloody good in fact" then looking Matty straight in the eye, he added "But he wasn't as good as you son and if he was around today, I'd willingly bet a hundred pound you'd take him."

"What, me!" Matty exclaimed, "You mean me take on a street-fighter for money. No fucking chance Bob, it's one thing smacking somebody if they've insulted you or your family, but I couldn't fight a bloke simply for money." Then becoming rather subdued, he added "Besides, if the truth were known, I'm sick of violence."

Bob let him stew in his own thoughts for a few minutes, then asked "What else are you good at Matty, besides fighting? What else can you do that will give you a future. Surely you don't intend working behind my bar for the rest of your life and I'm sure digging ditches or hewing coal won't bring you in a fortune, but I'll tell you what son, fighting for a living will. With the talent you've got Matty, it would only take two or three years and you would be able to pack it in, get a little business, maybe a pub even, then find a young lass, settle down and have a family. Besides, after a few fights, if you decide you are not happy with it, you can always stop, but for Christ sake Matty, at least give it a try."

As he got no response, Bob carried on, "Anyway, what sort of bloke do you think you'd be fighting, only shite like Fighter Martin or your Siddy. You'd only be taking on blokes who wanted to kick the shit out of you, not decent ordinary blokes, so what do you say, give it a go eh, and see what happens?"

Matty's mind was in turmoil, for he knew that inwardly he didn't want to fight for money, but as Bob had been talking, he had been looking at the fivers on the table and working out how long he would have to work at the Jolly's to earn that much. "Twelve and a half weeks" he told himself, "That's how long, twelve and a half bloody weeks to notch up what I earned in two bloody minutes. My god, you talk about easy money and, as Bob says, I can always pack it in if I don't like it."

Then his next statement was like music to Bob's ears, as he asked "How would I go about getting fights though Bob, if I decide to have a go that is?"

Barely able to contain himself, Bob told him "Oh, you leave all that to me son, I'll do all the arranging, you just concentrate on keeping yourself fit."

"But what about the money?"

"That again, is my department" Bob told him. Then he went into detail of how they would split the winnings down the middle and, if there was a chance to get a few side bets on, he would share them with Matty too.

There were other things Bob felt he should discuss with Matty, like his doubts about Big John and that twat Shilton, but he reckoned that enough had been done for tonight. Besides, he had drank most of the brandy and it was beginning to get to him.

So he stood up and grabbing the table to stop himself from wobbling too much, said "Well young fella, I think we can say you have a future now. I've got a feeling in my water that things are about to go your way for a change." Then pointing to the money on the table, he added "And tomorrow morning I want you to take that, get down the high street and buy yourself some new clobber, for who knows, it might even change your luck with the lasses."

He walked to the door, then stopped and turned to look at Matty. "I know it's going against your nature son" he told him gently, "But you've got to remember, now you've only yourself to look out for and I think it's time you started to do that." Then as he left, he winked at Matty and said "Goodnight champ."

As he walked back up the yard, Bob smiled to himself, for he felt that at long last he had won. At least the hardest part was over with, all he had to do now was sort out a few minor problems then things would be under way.

Of course he had omitted to tell Matty about the bad side of street-fighting. Things like blokes being maimed or even killed, or blokes ending up like Fighter Martin, who would probably end up punch-drunk and taking on blokes for the price of a pint. For he didn't think any of these things would apply to Matty. After all, the lad was no drinker and apart from when he lost his rag, he seemed level headed enough, the sort who would save his money and do something with it. "And besides" he told himself, "He's always got me to look out for him" then he chuckled out loud at the thought of that.

Meanwhile, Matty hadn't moved a muscle since Bob had left him, for he was still transfixed by the money on the table and the thought of how little he had to do to get it. He hadn't agreed to fight for a living, but on the other hand, he didn't say he wouldn't either. Yet in the light of what Bob had told him about making a future for himself, he suddenly found himself day dreaming about what might be.

He imagined himself in that smart grey suit he had seen in Burtons window, walking down the high street and the lasses he passed, turning their heads to look at him. Then he saw himself stroll into the local dance hall with a bunch of mates and everyone pointing at him, saying, "Aye, that's Matty Glave, the best street-scrapper in the North and he's a nice bloke too."

Oh how he fantasised, he sat there for a good hour thinking wonderful thoughts of himself, in fact he was so happy, he was bursting to tell someone and that was when his dreaming ended. For the truth of it was, he had no one, No Dotty, no Frank, not even the rabbit. He had no one close enough to share his joy with and, as he went over and sat on the bed, he suddenly felt very lonely. For it was only now did he realise, just how much he missed his gentle friends.

He lay back on the bed and closed his eyes, he was tired, but sleep wouldn't come to him, as a thousand thoughts raced through his mind, with most of them being guilty ones. For he knew that if he did take up fighting for a living, he would be betraying his Snowflakes.

Finally though, sleep did come, but as he drifted off, he was completely unaware of the tears rolling slowly down his cheeks.

Yet he only went from one torment to another, as he suddenly heard Dotty's gentle sobbing, somewhere in the darkness, then her childlike voice calling "Matty, Matty, come and get me Matty, please come and get me."

Then another voice began calling his name and it didn't take him long to realise that it was Frank. So he began calling back, "Frank, Dotty, where are you, I can't see you, where are you?"

Then suddenly they appeared. Frank and Dotty were sitting cross-legged on the ground and with one hand they were stroking Billy the Buck, but with the other, they were beckoning Matty to them.

As he walked towards them though, they kept moving the same distance away from him. When he stopped, when he moved, they did. Until finally, in frustration, he turned and walked away from them, but when he turned again to look back, they were gone.

Then a replay of all he had gone through the previous year, flashed through his mind. Every character's face was distorted and every sound was echoed. Then when he couldn't take any more of it, he began screaming, "Stop it, for god's sake stop it." Even when he woke, covered head to toe in sweat, he still found himself saying it.

He spent the remainder of the night sitting on the caravan doorstep and by first light, he had made up his mind what he was going to do, he was going to fight.

For Frank, Dotty and the rabbit were all gone now and, as he had told himself on the hill that day, there was no time now for Snowflakes. Life, he had decided, was too short. If someone wanted something they had to go out and get it, they had to take life by the scruff of the neck and live it and, that was exactly what he intended to do.

By the time Bob got down to the scullery, Matty already had a pot of tea poured out for him. "Morning boss" he said cheerily, then noticing Bob cringe at the sound of his voice, shouted "And how's your fucking head this morning then?"

"For Christ's sake Matty" Bob told him, putting his hands over his ears, "You've got a voice like a bloody foghorn."

Matty burst out laughing as Bob sat down at the table and buried his head in his hands, then groaned from behind them, "Get me a couple of Aspros out of the cupboard, will you son."

Two pots of tea and two more Aspros later though, his head began to clear. He didn't normally get as drunk as that, but last night had been a special occasion and, by the look on Matty's face, a successful one too.

Before Bob could say anything though, Matty announced "I've decided Bob, I'm going to give the fighting game a try. So whenever you'd like to fix one up, I'm ready."

"Wow" Bob told him, putting up his hand in a steadying gesture; "It's not as easy as that Matty, there's a lot of things to be organised and I'll have to work out a training programme to get you into shape."

"Me, out of shape" Matty laughed, then standing up and posing like a body-builder, added "You'll not see many around here who look as fit as I do."

"But you're not fighting anybody from around here you silly sod" Bob retorted, "If you want to fight for good money, you'll have to take on young, strong, fit lads. Lads who think like you, that they are the best, so it won't do you any harm to sweat for a few weeks."

Matty stopped clowning around then and inwardly had to admit that Bob was right. Although he wasn't in bad shape, he knew he was nowhere near as fit as he had been in prison, when he did the training sessions with Officer Hughes. So again, full of enthusiasm, he asked "Ok then Bob, what do you want me to do first?"

Without even looking up from his paper, Bob replied "Piss-off down to the high street and spend some of that money that's burning a hole in your pocket, at least I'll get five minutes bloody peace."

So off Matty went and, when he reached the high street, he was like a kid let loose in a toy shop. He bought the suit from Burtons, but there was still enough left for shoes, sweatshirts and a jumper and, as he walked back to the Jolly's, he stopped to count how much he had in his pocket and was pleasantly surprised to find he still had two quid and a bit of small change.

He couldn't wait to dress up and show Bob and Bella how smart he looked, but he was to be a little disappointed when he presented himself to them, up in the living quarters.

Bob looked him up and down, then uttered "Mmmm, not bad." But Bella actually laughed, as she told him "Aye, they are nice Matty, but you don't wear a red jumper on top of a green sweatshirt, then put a grey suit on top of that. You need a nice white shirt and a red tie to go with your suit." Then seeing the disappointed look on his face, she added "I'll tell you what, I'm going shopping later, you can come with me and we'll see what we can do to smarten you up."

"The only problem with that is though Bella, I've spent most of my money now" he said.

To which she replied, "Awe, that's ok Matty, you can have a little pressy from me."

Which prompted Bob to utter, "For Christ's sake" as he set off down the stairs to open up the bar.

With Matty and Bella out of the way that afternoon, it gave Bob the chance to catch Big John on his own, after closing time. For Bob hadn't forgotten the big man's outburst the previous night and, if he was to be a key part of Bob's team, there were one or two things to be sorted out.

So just after half-three, as Big John drained his last pint, Bob asked him to stay behind, as he wanted a word with him. Of course Big John knew what it would be about and he was still a bit upset with Bob, for he still felt he had set Matty up. But when Bob calmly pulled him a pint and asked him to sit down at one of the tables with him, he dropped his guard a little.

"Is it about last night then?" he asked firmly.

Bob took a sip of his drink first, then put the glass down on the table before he answered. "It's partly about that" he told him, "But there is something else I want to put to you. I don't think you are going to like it much, but on the other hand, there's not really a lot you can do about it" he fumbled then, for the last few words, for he knew this could make the big man flip, but finally, he got them out. "Young Matty has decided he wants to be a street-fighter and he wants me to handle him."

Big John slammed his pint glass down onto the table and barked, "You must be fucking joking, the kid's not cut out for that game" then with venom in his voice, added, "Unless of course, you've persuaded him he is."

"Not at all" Bob lied, "We simply had a chat last night about his future. All I did was point out various options to the lad, he's the one who decided on the fight game, not me."

Big John sat glaring at him, not knowing whether to believe him or not. After a few minutes of thought though, he came to the conclusion about one thing Bob was right on, even if he did object to it, there was bugger all he could do about it. So knowing Bob knew this, he asked, "So what do you expect me to do about it then?"

"Well I'd like you to join my team, that's what."

"What fucking team?" the big man growled.

"The back-up team I'm putting together for Matty. I need you and may be a couple of more blokes to look after him when the fight's over, calm him down, that sort of thing and, I'll need somebody to watch his back, in case anybody takes a sly dig at him."

"Of course" he continued, "There's money in it for you, I thought maybe three quid a fight. I'm not going to force you though Big John, if you want in, well that's fine, but if not that's ok too, just as long as you don't go saying anything silly to Matty, like trying to talk him out of fighting."

Big John thought for a while longer before answering. He didn't like it one bit. But seeing as how it was Matty's choice and in view of the money Bob was offering, maybe it wouldn't turn out as bad as he first thought it might. Besides, he would always be there to make sure nothing too serious happened to the lad. So with this in mind, he told Bob, "Ok, count me in."

"Good" Bob said, sounding pleased with himself, then adding in a more serious tone, "But I want no more shows of temper like last night mind, if you are in, just remember who the gaffer is, alright?"

Big John didn't reply though, he just sat staring at Bob for a few moments longer, then slowly got up and left leaving Bob to chuckle at his victory, when he noticed the bloke hadn't. even finished his pint.

As Bob had expected though, Big John fell into line. Especially when he realised how keen Matty was to take up fighting. He even helped with the training, well, the exercising bits and the weight-lifting. The five mile run Bob had mapped out for Matty, he could do himself, for Bob had insisted he did it every day, come hail, rain or shine.

Matty did it too and he enjoyed it. He also enjoyed the extra grub Bella was feeding him and the extra attention she was paying him. She would even pop down the yard sometimes just to watch him train, or so she said. What she was really doing though, was fantasising about him as she watched and, with each passing day, she was becoming hornier and hornier, but for the moment, the only person to benefit from this was Bob, for she was in his trousers, any chance she got.

Bob had also contacted Cuddy Wheeler, his ex-cuts man and, he too had agreed to join them. So when Big John told him, he had recruited a couple of tasty lads from Hetton-le-Hole, to help him with Matty, Bob felt that everything was in place, all he needed to do now was fix up a fight.

This he did with ease, as nobody had ever heard of Matty, his name wasn't feared. So the following Friday morning, just as Matty got back from his run and was working out what exercises to do, Bob stopped him.

"Don't bother with that today" he called as he walked down the yard towards him. "I want you to go up to our place and have a bath, then come back down to the caravan and try and get a few hours kip."

Matty looked at him puzzled, "Why?" he asked, "I don't feel ill or anything."

Bob shook his head in mock exasperation, then told him with a chuckle, "I know that you silly sod, but you my son, are going fighting tonight."

CHAPTER SIX

As much as he had tried, Matty didn't sleep a wink that afternoon. Nor could he eat the fillet steak Bella had cooked for him as a special treat. Bob, of course, had simply put this down to nerves and had assured him that once the punches began flying, he would settle down and give a good account of himself.

It wasn't fear of his opponent that was making Matty nervous, but the thought that he might show himself up. For try as he may, he could not recall hitting a bloke without feeling anger, so how the hell was he expected to walk up to someone and begin kicking the shit out of him, if he felt no malice towards him.

Unknown to Matty though, Bob had also had the same fears but he reckoned he had an answer to the problem. Yet the one person he didn't want to find out what it was, was Matty.

As they had sat chatting that afternoon, when he came up for the meal he never ate. Bob told Matty all the details of the fight and he had listened intently.

He was to fight a lad by the name of Clapper Greenaway, in a field backing on to a pub called The Red Lion, in the village of Lumley, about five miles from Houghton. The purse would be fifty pounds, which meant Matty was in for another twenty-five quid pay-day if he won and jokingly Bob told him, "Try and make it last a bit longer than the last twenty-five."

Then Bob set about telling Matty as much as he could about his opponent, which he remarked cockily, was the sign of a good handler. He told him that although Clapper wasn't as big as Matty by about two stones and a few inches, he was lightning with his fists, especially his right. So he warned Matty, that for the first five minutes or so, to keep away from it and keep veering to the bloke's left.

He also told him that the lad was good and hard, he had had four fights so far and won them all and seeing as he was only twenty, that was bloody good going, as Bob had also heard, two of his opponents had been seasoned fighters.

Then Bob had gone on to explain about being searched for weapons and how he would have his hands checked for knuckle-dusters or rings, but Bob had burst out laughing when Matty had asked about the rules, for as he told him, "There was only one fucking rule and that was to win and, you did that by being the only one left standing."

Now, as Matty threw on his coat and headed off up to the bar, to be introduced to the rest of the team, he suddenly thought of his father and wondered if he would be proud of him. "After all" he told himself, as he felt a twinge of anger run through him, "He was the twat who taught me to fight." For Somewhere in the back of Matty's mind, he was still resentful at being what his father had turned him into.

"That's what I like to see, punctuality" Bob told him as he walked into the bar dead on seven o' clock. Then turning to the bunch of blokes gathered around him, said, "Gentlemen, here he is, the future street-fighting champ of the North, Matty Glave."

Matty actually felt a bit embarrassed when Bob introduced him, firstly to the lads from Hetton, Billy and Stef, then to the cuts man, Cuddy Wheeler.

He shook hands with the Hetton lads, but as Cuddy only gave him a slight nod of the head and didn't even offer his hand, Matty took an instant dislike to him. There was also something shifty about the bloke, something that told Matty never to trust him. But as Bob had told him Cuddy was the best cuts man he had ever seen, Matty decided to say nothing.

As the fight was set for eight, Bob decided it was time to be on their way. So with Bella giving Matty a kiss for good luck and the blokes in the bar giving him a resounding cheer, they set off for Lumley.

Bob, Matty, Big John and Cuddy occupied the first car, whilst Billy, Stef and a few of the Jolly's regulars, filled the second car. Quite a lot of blokes wanted to go with them, but Bob had insisted on taking only a small party, for he wanted to be sure everything went as planned, as he too, didn't want to make a fool of himself by being involved in a cock-up.

To appease those who didn't travel though, he had agreed to try and get a bet on Matty for them. As they were mostly five and ten shilling bets, Bob didn't mind, for he had already decided that the lion's share of the side betting, would be his.

Twenty minutes later as they drove into Lumley and pulled up outside The Red Lion, Bob told everyone to stay in the car whilst he went inside to sort things out.

Matty could feel the sweat on his palms, so he slyly rubbed his hands down the side of his trousers and hoped no one had seen him. Big John had though, so in an attempt to calm the lad, he tried to strike up a conversation with Cuddy and hoped Matty would join in, but when Cuddy turned out to be a man of few words and Matty obviously not in the mood for chitchat. the big man gave up and went back to sitting in silence.

After what seemed like an hour, but had only been ten minutes, Bob came back out of the pub and climbed into the car. "There's a road at the side of the pub" he told them, "We can get round to the field that way." Then slapping Matty's leg, added, "And the money's down lad, fifty notes to the winner, now how does that grab you Matty my son?"

Matty glanced sideways at Bob and smiled. Then slowly nodding his approval said, "Not bad Bob, not bad at all."

What Bob had omitted to tell him was the fact that he had also laid another twenty in side bets, which more than covered his whole lay-out for the night.

Clapper Greenaway was already in the field when they got there and, as Matty jumped over the fence, the first thing that greeted him was the bloke's voice, as he mockingly called, "Let's see how high you fucking well jump when I've finished with you, you cocky bastard."

Although waiting to react, Malty didn't. Instead, he stripped off his shirt and began flexing his muscles in an attempt to warm up, also hoping that he might intimidate Clapper with his size, but to his annoyance, the bloke never looked at him once.

Bob gave him some last minute instructions and once again reminded him to keep away from Clapper's right hand. Then some bloke cane over to him and searched him, then checked his hands for rings or knuckle-dusters. As a sign that he was satisfied Matty was clean, he grunted, gave a quick nod of the head, then ambled over to Clapper and went through the same procedure all over again.

The atmosphere was building by now as the crowd sensed that the fight was about to get underway. There was a lot of shouting and cheering going on as different blokes voiced their encouragement, it was mostly for the Lumley lad, but Matty did recognise one or two voices calling his name. Then, above the din, a booming voice shouted, "RIGHT LADS, STAND BACK AND LET THEM GET AT IT."

The crowd gradually quietened in expectation and edged slowly backwards, leaving Matty and Clapper isolated inside the human ring. They stood about ten feet apart and were by now, facing each other.

Matty, still not knowing quite what to do with himself, put up his fists in a boxer's pose, then just stood, staring at his opponent, who by now had also put up his fists and was moving them in a circular fashion, as he began to edge his way to Matty's left.

Thinking the bloke was trying to line him up with the right and remembering Bob's warning about it, Matty began edging the other way, only to be smacked flush on the nose, by a left cross he never even saw coming.

He reeled back, but didn't lose his balance. He was stunned for a second, but not long enough to give Clapper any advantage and, as they both began edging to the right, Matty quickly wiped the blood away from his eyes, telling himself as he did so, "For fuck's sake Bob, if his left is that good, god help me if he hits me with his bloody right."

Clapper didn't though, instead he split Matty's right eye-brow, but again it was the left he did it with.

That second punch was enough though, enough to get Matty in the temper Bob had hoped it would and, as Clapper stood goading Matty to come at him, there was no doubt in Bob's mind that, that was exactly what Matty would do.

"Fuck all this silly boxing business" he raged to himself, then went steaming in at Clapper, with arms and feet spinning like a windmill, sending the bloke reeling backwards into a bunch of his own supporters.

The difference between the two fighters showed itself now, for where Clapper stood back after he had hit Matty, Matty didn't. He grabbed the lad by the hair with both hands and bent him forward, then holding his head about two feet from the ground, proceeded to kick him in the face six times in as many seconds. Then he flung him to the ground and began stamping on his head.

Bob looked quickly across at Clapper's handler, waiting for the nod, which would be the signal that his man had had enough and when it came, Big John and the Hetton lads jumped on Matty and pinned him to the ground, with Big John telling him, "Steady Matty son it's all over now, come on now ease up son, ease up."

It took a good five minutes for them to subdue him, but when they did, Cuddy was straight there with his little wooden box. He cleaned Matty's nose up and found it was only badly bruised, but his eye needed stitching so he immediately went to work with the cat-gut and needle.

As Bob went over to collect his winnings and the purse money from Clapper's handler, he looked down and saw what Matty had done and wasn't surprised in the least to see that Clapper's face was in one hell of a mess for the lad had taken a good kicking by any standards, which had prompted his handler to tell Bob as he handed him the money, "Some fucking animal you've got there mate, where do you keep him, in a fucking cage?"

Bob chuckled, as he jokingly told him, "No mate, in a caravan." Then he went back to his own lads, waving the money above his head, as he did so.

The welcome Matty received when they got back to the Jolly's was tremendous. Even bigger than when he had come out of jail, with the difference being of course, he had put money into some of their pockets and looked like putting quite a bit more into them in the future.

Bella had put a 'spread' on, which meant it wasn't long before the place took on a party atmosphere, with blokes whooping and hollering at being associated with a winner, for that was how they viewed Matty now.

Bella had been first to greet him, by flinging her arms around his neck and planting a big sloppy kiss on his lips, but Matty being too caught up in the euphoria, didn't take much notice of her and it was just as well Bob didn't see her either, for the kiss was certainly far from being motherly.

To celebrate the victory Bob ordered the team double brandy's, but as the night wore on, they went back to the drink they liked best, which was beer. Matty didn't though and neither did Bob, so by midnight when Bella decided it was time to call it a day, they were both sitting slumped in the corner, leaning against each other and out for the count.

After Big John helped her clear the place, she stood with her elbow on the bar and shaking her head, said to him, "Would you look at those two then, they don't look so bloody hard now do they Big John?"

Big John chuckled as he looked at them, then replied "Aye, you're right there Bella lass, I reckon neither of them could fight their way out of a paper bag at the minute."

They stood for a while longer watching them, but unknown to each other, they were both thinking about Matty.

Seeing him so vulnerable now, it got Big John to thinking about when Matty had been a lad. What a gentle kid he had been and not even a bad thought in him. Always polite and cheerful, never cheeky like his brother and always glad to see him, whenever Big John visited the house.

Then he suddenly thought of Jimmy and wondered just what he would have made of tonight's events. Then a flash of Matty stamping on Clapper Greenaway's head came into his mind and he curled his lip with disdain as he thought, 'Aye, I reckon Jimmy would have been proud of that bit at least.'

Bella was thinking something entirely different though, she was thinking of a way she could get Matty to herself and, just like her scheming husband, she came up with something.

"Before you go Big John" she said casually, could you give me a hand with these two please, because I don't think I'll be able to move them on my own, do you?"

So firstly, after a bit of huffing and puffing, they managed to get Bob up the stairs and onto the bed, where they left him then went back down to sort Matty out.

Being two and a half stone heavier though, the lad took a bit of shifting, but eventually, with a lot more huffing and puffing this time, they got him down to the caravan and also flung him on his bed.

"Bloody hell" Bella exclaimed, as she wiped the sweat from her brow, "The bugger must weigh a ton Big John."

"And the bloody rest" he retorted, his chest wheezing and heaving up and down with the effort.

They both sat on the edge of the bed for a few minutes until they got their breath back, then Bella said "Right big fella, I can manage from here, you go and get yourself away home and I'1 1 see you in the morning no doubt."

Then as Big John got up, Bella began to undo Matty's boot laces, but as he was going out of the door, she called "Oh by the way Big John, can you drop the latch on the front door for me please?"

"No problem" he replied, then closed the door behind him.

Bella watched him walk up the yard and into the back door, then barely breathing, she waited for a few minutes to be sure he had gone.

Then, when she felt it was safe, she lit the candle by the bed and stood looking down at Matty. 'At last' she thought, as she let her eyes drift slowly over his muscle filled body, starting off at the face, then working her way down to the bulge between his legs.

Without taking her eyes off the bulge, she slowly sat down on the bed beside Matty, totally transfixed with lust, her mind racing at the thought of what was hidden inside of his trousers. For being so close to the one thing she desired most, was driving her mad.

She had glimpsed at it a few times when she had spied on him in the bathroom, but when she had known she could not touch it. Now was different though, with Matty deep in his drunken stupor, now she could take a chance and as she put her hand gently over the bulge, then began to slowly rub it up and down, she moaned with sheer pleasure.

Even through his trousers she could feel how big it was and the more she rubbed, the hornier she became, until finally she could stand it no longer. So very gently she undid his belt, then slowly loosened his trouser buttons. At the sight of his pubic hair she began to shake with excitement and when his penis finally came into view, she almost climaxed at the sight of it.

She sat for a few moments, her mouth watering in anticipation, then she bent her head forward and lightly kissed the end of it, letting her tongue flick in and out of the slit. Then she took him fully in her mouth and began working her head back and forth until gradually, even though Matty was spark out to the world, it began to stiffen.

When it was good and hard, she stopped sucking and sat back for a moment to look at it, then involuntarily gasped at what she saw. "Oh my god" she moaned, "What a magnificent sight it must be nine inches at least." Then thinking she might wake him, she put her hand to her mouth and sat holding her breath for a few moments watching to see if he would stir.

When he didn't move though, she picked up the candle and held it nearer his body to give herself a better look at his glorious prick. As she held the candle over him though, a drop of hot wax fell onto his lower stomach, making him wince in his sleep.

This frightened Bella and once again she held her breath in case he woke up, but when he didn't, she quickly redid the buttons on his trousers and fastened his belt. Then she blew out the candle and tip-toed over to the caravan door, when she stopped and turned to look back at him. She couldn't see him but she could still feel him in her mouth and at the memory of it, she whispered "Yes Matty my lad, you are without doubt... The Cock of the North."

The following morning when Matty woke, it wasn't just the inside of his head that was throbbing, his nose and right eye throbbed too.

"Christ!" he exclaimed, as he tried to raise his head off the pillow, then yelped out loud when he touched his right eye and even louder when he touched his nose.

He lay back again to ease the pain in his head and tried to focus his eyes on something in the caravan, as everything was just a blur at the moment. He blinked his eyes a few times and gradually his vision began to clear. "Thank god for that" he sighed, "For a minute. I thought I'd gone bloody blind."

Then, as he rubbed his hand across his lower stomach, he winced as it touched the blister that had been left by the candle wax. "Bloody hell" he said out loud, "I might have won the fight, but I bet Clapper feels a lot better than I do this morning."

After several more minutes of moaning and groaning, he finally managed to get himself up into a sitting position on the side of the bed. Then completely forgetting about the blister on his stomach, he proceeded to scratch it. "For fuck's sake" he yelped this time, looking down at the blister, then added, "I don't know how the hell Clapper did that, but it's bloody well annoying me."

The blister was the last of his worries though, for as he tried to stand up, he keeled over sideways and went crashing into the table and chairs, sending them flying against the caravan wall.

He rolled over and lay flat on his back, wondering what the hell was wrong with him, for never having been drunk on brandy before, Matty didn't realise he had a hangover. This coupled with his injuries was the reason he was in such a state, but with a lot of effort and a few more curses, he finally managed to stand up and grope his way into the kitchenette,

After swilling his face and inspecting his facial injuries in the little mirror that hung on the wall, he threw on a shirt and gingerly let himself out of the caravan, then very slowly walked up to the scullery.

By the time he reached it, he thought he had walked half-a-mile then he staggered in the open door and slumped down on the chair opposite Bob.

As he sat with his head in his hands groaning, Bob chuckled to himself, then as an act of revenge, yelled "AND HOW'S YOUR FUCKING HEAD THIS MORNING THEN MATTY?"

Matty cringed and put his hands over his ears, croaking "For fuck's sake Bob, have a bit of sympathy will you."

Bob didn't hear him though, for he was too busy laughing. But when he stopped, he went to the cupboard and got Matty some Aspros, then filling a glass with water said, "Here, take these, they'll shift it for you."

Within half-an-hour the Aspros began to take effect, but Matty was still puzzled as to why he felt so bad. "I can only remember Clapper hitting me a couple of times" he said, "So why the hell do I feel so rotten Bob?"

Bob laughed again. "You silly bugger" he called him, "It's the brandy that's making you feel like that, you'll be feeling your injuries but it's the hangover that's giving you most trouble. I had a bit of a head myself this morning when I got up, but I'm fine now" then with a chuckle in his voice he added, "Mind I'll tell you what though Matty son, if you carry on performing like you did at Lumley last night, you're going to have to get used to having hangovers."

"So you think I did alright then?" Matty asked, cheering up a little at Bob's compliment.

"Aye, you did that son" then chuckling added, "Once you got started that was."

Matty twigged there was something amiss, so leaning over the table and putting his face about six inches from Bob's, he asked suspiciously, "Was his right really his best punch?"

Bob leaned back away from Matty's face and chuckled again, "It worked didn't it" he told him, almost laughing now.

"You sly bastard" Matty said, feigning to slap Bob's head with the back of his hand, then bursting into laughter himself.

"Well at least you now know what will happen to you, if you don't get stuck in from the start" Bob told him as he poured another mug of tea each for them.

"Aye, I think you can say the lessons learnt" Matty replied, as he once again felt his nose and eye and winced as he did so.

It turned out to be a lesson well learnt too. For Matty came to view the fight game as a business, simply a way of putting money in his pockets. Oh he still had the occasional doubt if it was right or not and he still had the bad dream with Dotty and Frank beckoning him to them, but he reasoned that with time, both of these things would fade from his mind.

By the time spring had passed and summer came, he no longer had the doubt in his mind, but he still had the dream sometimes. He found though, that by getting drunk, he could even wipe that out of his memory, so most nights, that was what he did.

As he only drank brandy now, he suffered many a hangover too, but by July the third, his twenty-second birthday, he had also become used to them. For not only did he get drunk with the new bunch of friends he had acquired, he had also to celebrate six more victories.

The first four had been for fifty pounds, but the last two had been for a hundred. Which meant Bob was moving him up into a bigger league, taking him to places like Sunderland and Newcastle.

Of course, Bob knew these lads would be a lot harder than the likes of Clapper Greenaway, but he also knew that Matty was improving. In fact it was getting harder for Big John and the lads to pull him off, which scared Big John a little, for he could see the day coming when Matty might easily kill someone.

It wasn't only in his fighting that Big John had seen a change in the lad, for his general manner had changed too. He had become cocky and arrogant, almost bordering on being a bully. It was as if the lad was reverting to type, for Big John could see traits of Matty's father coming out in him and, what was worse, traits of brother Siddy too.

By now, he had also become the centre of attraction wherever he went and he loved it. He was often seen in various parts of the town with his so called new friends, who were really only hangers-on, blokes who would borrow a quid till Friday, but would forget when Friday came, to pay him back.

This didn't bother Matty though for whenever he saw his pockets getting empty, he would simply ask Bob to get him another fight.

Yet his spending had bothered Bob, for since the fighting had started, he reckoned that Matty hadn't saved a penny and he wondered if it had anything to do with the lad having too much time on his hands. For with him doing so well, Bob had agreed to Matty not working behind the bar anymore.

The lad still did his training and kept himself in good shape, but when the training was over, he was off with his mates somewhere and often didn't come back till after closing time.

Bob also knew he was gambling as he had seen him a few times at the local dog-track, but what he didn't know was that Matty had also taken to playing cards in the back room of Willie Holts snooker hall, where drink was served to the privileged customers, of which Matty was one.

This meant that not only was he squandering his money on gambling, but also on booze and if he ran out of money, Willie would let him run up a slate, knowing full well that the next time Matty fought, he would be in the very next day with more money to spend.

He would sometimes buy Bella little presents too, like ear-rings or a scarf, telling her they were in appreciation for what she had done for him, but Bella of course, misconstrued his gestures, by telling herself it was because he fancied her. For since that night in the caravan when he was drunk, she had fantasized that Matty was really aware of what she had been doing to him, but had been too shy to acknowledge it.

This of course, couldn't have been further from the truth. Matty was still oblivious as to what happened that night and still looked on Bella as a mother figure. Oh he was enough of a man to notice her ample breasts and shapely bum and, for her age she wasn't a bad looker, but as he had told Ray Purvis, one of his new mates one night as they stood at the Jolly's, even the thought of shagging her would make him sick.

Ray had laughed at him, for he knew Matty was hopeless with women and had chided him by saying "I reckon shagging any lass would make you sick Matty."

For since they had become friends, Ray had fixed Matty up several times, but the following day when he had asked how Matty had done, it had always been the same answer, either she wasn't his type or it was her wrong week. Even when Ray had fixed him up with one of the biggest bags in Houghton, who he knew was a sure thing, Matty had told him the next day that he didn't get anywhere with her.

He hadn't either, but not because she didn't want to, but because of his old problems like being shy and awkward. For although having money in his pockets and wearing nice clothes had improved his confidence a lot, with lasses it was the same old Matty and the only sexual relief he got, was when he relieved himself, alone at night in the caravan.

Someone else who was to see a change in him, was Sergeant Shilton and he didn't like what he saw one day as he drove along the high street.

He came across Matty looking in Burtons window, so he pulled up, got out of the car and walked up behind him, then slapped him on the shoulder, saying "That's a bit expensive for a barman to be buying isn't it?" referring to the sports jacket Matty was looking at in the window.

Stung at being referred to as a barman, Matty swung round sharply but when he saw who it was, his face changed instantly into a smile. "Alright then Sergeant" he beamed, taking his right hand out of his pocket, then shaking hands with him. "Long time no see, how are you keeping these days?"

"Fine" the Sergeant replied, slyly looking Matty up and down, then nodding to the sports jacket, added smiling "But I wish I could afford gear like that."

"Awe, I'm only looking" Matty lied, "There's no harm in dreaming is there Sergeant?"

Sergeant Shilton knew he was lying and felt a twinge of anger, for he could see by the clothes Matty was wearing that he could afford the sports jacket and, he knew fair well where the money was coming from too.

He's heard all about the lad's exploits on the grapevine, but as he never fought in Houghton the Sergeant had decided to turn a blind eye to it. After all, the kid didn't have anything else going for him, life had given him a fair kicking too, so as long as nothing serious ever happened to him, the Sergeant had thought 'What the hell, let him get on with it.'

He was shocked by Matty's manner though. There was a brashness about him, as though he was advertising the fact he was a hardman, which made the Sergeant wonder if there was any gentleness left in the lad.

He also wondered if he thought of Snowflakes anymore, or read poetry. For he certainly seemed a different bloke to the one he had had the heart to heart with, that night in the cells.

The Sergeant scanned his face and saw the scar above his right eye, but apart from that, his face was relatively free from any disfigurement fighters normally had, like broken noses or cauliflower ears, so maybe he isn't doing too bad. Yet it still irked the Sergeant to think that Matty had chosen to fight for a living instead of getting a proper job and settling down somewhere.

Then the Sergeant tried broaching other subjects, like did he ever see his sister or brother now, was he courting or what were his plans for the future. But as Matty only gave him staccato type answers, he thought 'What the fuck, it's like talking to a brick wall.'

What he didn't know though, was that Bob had primed Matty for just this occasion, by warning him to say nothing to the Sergeant that would make him suspicious and, if he did meet him, not to be too friendly with the bastard either.

On both accounts Matty had succeeded, but as the Sergeant left him and got back into his car, little did Matty know, of the anger and frustration the man was feeling, for he couldn't help but feel that in some way he had let Matty down.

Then as he drove off the Sergeant looked back in his rear-view mirror and he smiled to himself as he saw the lad going into the shop. "Can't afford it my arse" he uttered. Then his face distorted into a scowl as Bob Hunter's image came into his mind, he smacked the steering wheel with his right fist and growled, "I know one thing for sure though, if anything bad does happen to the lad, I know whose door I'll be fucking knocking on."

Matty for his part, was unperturbed by his meeting with the Sergeant, for he had far more important things on his mind at the moment. Ray had told him that he was fixing him up with a cracking lass from Rainton, called Jean Turner and she was a good thing.

Ray was fixed up with her mate Carol and they were to meet them that night at the Welfare Hall dance. He had assured Matty that Jean was the best of the two, but Matty had heard all that before. Because for some reason Ray always ended up with the good looking one, whilst Matty invariably ended up with the wallflower.

Tonight though, he felt things could be different, hence the reason for buying the sports jacket. If this Jean Turner was all Ray said she was, he wanted to look his best and if she was as hot as Ray had made out, with any luck, he just might get his end away.

Yet Jean Turner turned out to be no different to all the other lasses Ray had raved on about. She was short and dumpy, with a fat round face that was covered with too much make-up. Her hair was blonde with black roots showing through and she had a beauty spot painted on the left side of her mouth, which she had somehow managed to smudge.

Which didn't surprise Matty really, for she could talk the hind legs off a donkey and, as Matty wasn't one for dancing, whilst Ray and Carol were on the dance floor, he had to sit and suffer her incessant chatter for most of the night.

By the time the dance finished at eleven o'clock, Matty felt he knew every member of her family and just about everyone who lived in Rainton, plus all her workmates at Horner's Sweet factory.

Matty thought that with the dance finishing he would be rid of her, but he was wrong. For Ray and Carol had disappeared, which meant he was lumbered with the task of walking Jean home, as the last bus to Rainton, which was three miles away, had left an hour earlier.

He didn't really mind though, for it was a warm summer night and as there was nothing else to do but go back to the caravan, he felt the walk might at least help him to sleep, because with thinking he was having this cracking date, he hadn't drunk too much.

What she had been talking about between leaving Houghton and reaching the bottom of Rainton Hill, about half-a-mile from the village, Matty had no idea, for he had managed to switch himself off, thus reducing her jabbering to a distant drone, but as they walked up the hill, she did say something that caught his attention.

"Aye, that's right" she rattled, answering herself, "I told him straight, it's either me or Sunderland bloody football team."

Matty looked at her puzzled, for he hadn't a clue what she had been talking about. So he asked her to repeat it.

"I said I was engaged once, but I finished with him because of Sunderland football team. Some weekends I never saw the bugger cos he was always pissing off to the match with his mates, so I gave him an ultimatum, I said it was either me or bloody football."

Matty waited for a few moments to hear what came next, but as she didn't say anything, he asked "Well, what happened then?"

"What happened then" she exploded, "What happened then, the bastard went to the match the following week, so I told him to piss-off."

It was as much as Matty could do to suppress his laughter, but inside he was chuckling away to himself. For he knew that if he had had the choice of listening to her rattle or watching Sunderland play, it would be Sunderland every time.

When they reached Rainton he was still chuckling to himself, but when she led him into an alley, "For a snog" as she said, his chuckling soon stopped, for the last thing he fancied was kissing her.

In the alley, she put her handbag down on the ground, then as she opened her coat, she warned him "Now don't think because I was engaged mind, I'm easy, because I'm not. I'll let you try your hand but that's all, ok?"

'You must be fucking joking' Matty thought. 'The quicker I get away from you lass the bloody better.'

Then an idea came to him. "I'm sorry lass" he said, taking a step back from her, "But I'm dying to go to the lav."

"That's ok" she told him, pointing to the end of the alley, "You can go along there for a wee, nobody'll see you."

It was then Marty played his trump card, for as he broke wind, he replied "But it's not a wee I want though."

His planned worked. She buttoned up her coat, picked up her handbag and stormed off down the alley, shouting as she went "You dirty Houghton bastard, piss-off back where you belong."

A couple of minutes later, as he jogged back down Rainton Hill, Matty burst out laughing as he recalled her tale about being engaged. Then through his laughter he began singing the Sunderland football chant at the top of his voice. "SUND-ERLAND. SUND-ER-LAND, HOWAY THE LADS, HOWAY THE LADS" and was still singing it when he reached Houghton.

That summer was probably the most carefree time Matty was ever to know. With no one to look out for, plus his new life-style and plenty of money in his pockets, with no shortage of friends to help him spend it, every day was to be looked forward to with a touch of excitement. Yet his lack of a sex life inwardly bothered him. Oh it was alright joking about it with Ray and the lads, but as a young, fit, healthy, red-blooded male he knew something special was missing from his life.

He'd even had chats with Bob about it, but with advice like, "Just stick it up them" or "Slap it in their hands" he considered Bob a bit crude, he felt that there must be more to it than that.

What Matty didn't realise though, was that he was actually looking to fall in love, for he longed, not only to have sex with a lass, but to kiss her and cuddle up to her. To caress her and also to protect her, to love and be loved. He didn't want just any old slag, he yearned for a lover, someone who would always be there for him no matter what. Someone to fall asleep with and wake up to. Someone he could make a home with, but especially, someone to bear him children.

Yet by the time the summer sun began to weaken and autumn came along, Matty's life was to take another dramatic turn. Bob had bought some tickets for a buffet dance at The Swan Hotel, in Chester-le-Street and at Bella's insistence, he got one for Matty too.

As it was on a Thursday night, which was usually dull, Matty agreed to go. It wasn't his sort of thing but Bella had made such a fuss about him going with them, he decided that all things being equal, why not.

Come the night of the dance though he began to have doubts about going, as he was up in the living-quarters getting ready. For Bella fussed over him like a mother hen, brushing down his suit, straightening his tie and trimming his hair to perfection, until in the end he felt more like a dummy in Burtons window than a man.

Finally, when she was satisfied, she had him looking just how she wanted him, she stood back to admire her handy work "My" she said, with pride in her voice, "You do look something special Matty, even if I say so myself, I bet you'll be turning a few heads tonight my lad."

Matty looked at himself in the mirror and had to admit he had never looked so smart. Even Bob was pleased at how he looked and commented, "A bit different to the day you came out of jail, wouldn't you say Matty? Remember how disgusted you were with your appearance that day, eh?"

Matty's mind flashed back to the Five Bells, where Bob had taken him on the morning of his release and he remembered it very clearly. The scuffed boots, the coat and trousers that were too short for him and the frayed cap.

Oh yes he remembered that day well and as he looked himself up and down in the mirror once more, he silently vowed that he would never look as scruffy as that again, no matter what.

Then he turned and looked at Bella, then at Bob and nodding his head, slowly said "Aye, I reckon between the two of you, you've done a bloody good job."

"Awe away with you Matty" Bella replied, then began fussing with her own hair to hide her embarrassment, as Bob picked up the paper and pretended to be reading it, so he could hide his.

An hour later though, all thoughts of embarrassment were forgotten as they walked into the ballroom of The Swan Hotel, where a huge bloke with a mass of ginger hair came bounding towards them.

"Tot my old mucker" Bob called to him, then shook him vigorously by the hand when he reached them.

Then the bloke greeted Bella with a kiss on the cheek, then turned to Matty saying in a thick Irish brogue, "So this is the young fella you were telling me about then Bob?" Then he stood back a pace and began looking Matty up and down. Then shaking his head, he continued, "And I must say Bob, he looks every bit the power-house you said he was and I'd be proud to shake the lad's hand" which he did.

With the greetings over, Tot led them through a maze of tables to one he had been keeping for them.

As they walked in single file behind them, Bob couldn't help but notice the puzzled look on Matty's face. So stopping for a moment and letting Tot and Bella carry on, said to Matty "It's alright son, the bloke's harmless. I know he seems a bit overpowering when you first meet him, but he's a good 'un really, and he's been a damn good mate to me over the years."

"That's who he is" Matty laughed, "I thought for a minute he was a bouncer or something."

Bob had mentioned Tot to Matty several times, for he too was a pub owner and was one of the blokes Bob met on a Tuesday for a game of cards, through at Durham, but he'd never told him how big the bloke was, or what a mass of hair he had and, as Matty glanced over Bob's shoulder to look at Tot again, he thought 'I bet he must weigh twenty-odd stone and with his hair sticking up like it is, I bet he's the best part of seven feet too.'

Bob assured him though that Tot was a pussycat. For despite his size the bloke had never been a fighter. Oh he could handle himself alright, but there was no way he was in Matty's class. "So" Bob warned him, "If he gets a bit loud, don't go losing your bloody rag with him, cos remember, he's a mate of mine."

As Matty and Bob reached the table, he heard Bella pronounce "Arr, here he is Annie, the young lad I was telling you about, the one whose living with us." Then turning to Matty she said "Matty, this is Annie O'Rourke, Tot's wife."

Matty took the soft, limp hand she offered and smiled at her. He would dearly like to have said something to her, but as usual he just dried up, then stood there like a dummy feeling awkward.

"Come on Matty" Bella told him, "Sit yourself down" for she could sense his awkwardness. Then when he'd sat, she leaned over to him and whispered "Now try and relax."

Bella's fussing though, only served to make him feel more awkward, but Bob came to the rescue by asking Matty to go to the bar with him, which he did willingly.

As Bob ordered the drinks, Matty stood leaning on the bar looking around the place and was surprised to see just how posh it was, much posher than The Five Bells had been and it was full of posh looking people too.

Then as he glanced back towards the table, he saw Annie looking at him. She gave him a faint smile then turned her head away, then so did he. But when he looked at her again, again she was looking at him. So he smiled at her, but this time she just turned her head away.

In his awkwardness, Matty hadn't really taken much notice of Annie, but now, sitting again at the table, he kept glancing at her out of the corner of his eye and was shocked to see just how beautiful she was.

She had long, jet black hair, with a silken sheen to it and her face was dark with rosy cheeks. Her eyes seemed to be almost as black as her hair and her lips were red and full.

Her voice had the same Irish brogue as her husband's and when she laughed it had a beautiful lilt to it which seemed to captivate Matty and put him almost in a trance. Which hadn't gone unnoticed by Bella, whose eyes were beginning to turn the same colour as Annie's dress, emerald green.

As the night wore on though, Annie seemed to be ignoring Matty and as most of the conversation was about pubs and old times, he decided to excuse himself and go outside for some fresh air.

As he leaned on the car-park fence overlooking the River Wear, he took in a few deep breaths and smiled to himself as he saw the reflection of the moon in the river. 'What a beautiful night' he thought, 'Ideal for romance.' Then he chuckled to himself as he said out loud "It's just a pity I've no bugger to share it with."

Then suddenly he felt something touch his arm and when he glanced sideways to see what it was, he got the shock of his life to see Annie standing next to him.

"Hello big fella" she cooed, "D' you mind if I join you?"

"Aye, yes, of course not" he stuttered all at once, then silently cursed himself for sounding so stupid.

They stood side by side in silence for a few moments taking in the tranquil view. Then Annie slowly turned towards him, reached up on her tip-toes and kissed him lightly on the cheek.

With pleasant surprise Matty turned to face her and for a few moments they held each other's eyes. Then slowly putting his arms around her, he lifted her up towards him and kissed her fully on the lips for what seemed an eternity.

When finally they did break the kiss, he held her to him and gently caressed her hair, moaning contentedly as he did so.

For at that moment, Matty had fallen in love. He felt that all the waiting was suddenly over, this was the moment he had suffered so many frustrations for, he felt that here and now, was the beginning of his life.

He kissed her again, but as he did so he felt her hand drift down between his legs and begin to caress his already aroused penis. Slowly she worked her hand back and forth until finally she felt him shudder with relief, then she broke the kiss and huskily whispered in his ear, "Is that what you wanted my darling?"

He nodded slightly and moaned, but didn't really want to move, he just wanted to stand there, holding her and smelling her forever. He didn't even want to open his eyes, in case by some chance he would find he was only dreaming, but eventually, he did.

Then she suddenly eased herself from him and began straightening her dress. As she did so, Matty stood looking at her and smiling, thinking how small she was, for she must only have been five feet tall, yet her body was well proportioned, she had all the bumps in the right places. Even though she must have been about Bella's age, they looked worlds apart. Whereas Bella was plump, Annie was curvaceous with skin that was like silk to touch. Bella was thirty-five and seemed it, but Annie was more like a young lass, frisky and gay,

Finally satisfied that everything was back in order, she asked with a touch of alarm in her voice, "How long do you think we've been out here Matty, because Tot might get suspicious?"

"Only about ten minutes" he told her, putting his hand gently under her chin and lifting her face up towards his.

But she pulled away from him again, saying "No Matty please, I've got to get back. I'm only supposed to be at the lav and ten minutes is an awful long time for a piddle."

Then, as she fussed with her hair she said, "I'll tell you what though, come over to our place next Tuesday afternoon about closing time, Tot'll be off to Durham to play cards with some of his mates and he won't be back till six, so" she added coyly, "We'll have a few hours together to do what comes naturally, ok big fella?"

He nodded and gave her a knowing smile, then a thought suddenly struck him, 'But I don't know where your place is though Annie.'

"Sorry my darling" she said apologetically, "I thought you knew, we have a pub at Gilesgate, The King's Head, d' you know it?"

He took hold of her again and smiling down at her, said softly, "I haven't a clue where it is, but by Tuesday I'll certainly find out."

She quickly gave him a peck on the cheek, then turned and hurried back into the dance, leaving him sniffing the air and pretending she was still with him. Then he looked up at the moon and smiled as he whispered to it, "And to think, only ten minutes ago I thought I had no one to share you with."

He felt so calm, so at ease with himself as he kept reflecting back on what had happened to him. He couldn't believe that such a beautiful woman could fancy him and as he remembered the climax she had given him, he felt a stirring in his loins once more.

For another ten minutes or so he wallowed in his pleasurable memories of Annie, then ambled back into the dance hall. As he did so, he told himself that nothing could shatter his feeling of happiness, tonight he felt like a king and no one was going to spoil it, but alas, he was wrong.

For as he made his way towards the table, he could see only Bella sitting there and the look on her face was like thunder as she greeted him with, "And what the hell do you think you've been up to?"

He sensed there was obviously something amiss, so as he sat down, he tried to look hurt at her tirade as he asked, "What do you mean Bella, I've just been out to the lav, then outside for some fresh air."

With her voice slightly raised now, she stormed back at him, "Aye, I bet you've been out bloody side, with fucking Annie."

Bella's language took Matty by surprise, for he had never heard her say 'fucking' before, which led him to believe that she must really be upset with him.

Which she was, but not because he had gone outside with a married woman who was a friend of theirs, but because she was seething with jealousy. She had brought Matty tonight to show him off to Annie, but it had all backfired on her.

Trying his best to calm her, he said, "Aye, I did see her outside, but I was only talking to her though, nothing like you're implying went on."

"Bollocks Matty" she retorted, "When Annie came back in here, she had guilt written all over her face, it was as much as Bob could do to stop Tot landing her one."

Matty's mood suddenly changed at the thought of Tot hitting Annie. Now he glared at Bella, who had instantly spotted the change in his mood and, when he growled "Where are they now?" she felt a sudden tremble of fear run through her.

Softening her tone, she replied, "Bob's taken them through to the lounge to try and calm Tot down."

Just as Matty was about to get up, Bob returned to the table. Disdainfully he looked down at Matty and shook his head, then he sat down and half turned his back to him and pretended to be watching the couples on the dance floor.

"Well" Bella asked impatiently, "What's happened to them then?"

Bob didn't even look round as he replied, "They've decided to call it a night."

"And did he smack her?" Matty asked sharply.

Bob still didn't turn to face him, but over his shoulder he said, "No he didn't, but I'll tell you what, I wouldn't have blamed him if he had."

"But we didn't do bugger all" Matty snapped at him, "All we did was have a chat."

Then Bella, who by now was getting a little courage back, asked, "So how come your bloody trousers are in such a mess?"

Matty looked down and cringed at the damp patch just below his belt and to the left of his fly. As his trousers were light grey, the dark stain stood out a mile and he began cursing himself for being so bloody stupid as to have not seen it before. Then trying to lie his way out of it, said "Oh that, I had an accident when I went to the lav, that's all."

"Huh" Bella retorted, then hissed, "A man doesn't piss himself that high up in his trousers, I know."

Matty could have argued on but he knew he was beaten, so he decided just to stew in silence. Five minutes later though Bob suggested that they too call it a night and as it turned into such a disaster, Matty and Bella both agreed.

He thought the journey home would be a bad one, but it wasn't that bad at all. For Bella had calmed down by now and was trying to explain to Matty why it was wrong to have anything to do with Annie. Seemingly she had had an affair before, which had almost crippled Tot for the man was devoted to her. He had forgiven her though, but only if she promised never to do it again, which she had. "Then this happens" she concluded, "And you of all people Matty, had to be involved."

"Ok, ok mother" he told her smiling, "You win, I'll have nothing more to do with Annie O' bloody Rourke, now can we please change the subject."

CHAPTER SEVEN

Matty had lied through his teeth though, for at five-to-three the following Tuesday afternoon, he stood at the bar of The King's Head in Gilesgate and ordered a glass of brandy.

Annie treated him just like a normal customer, but by a quarter-past-three she had the place cleared and the front door bolted. Then she walked back behind the bar and opened the door up to the living quarters. She stopped for a moment and turned to look at Matty, then with the index finger of her right hand, she beckoned him to follow her.

Neither spoke as they climbed the stairs, but when she showed him into the living room, he grabbed her and pulled her to him, saying "Paradise at last." Then he kissed her hungrily on the lips.

Although she enjoyed his kisses, they were not what Annie was after. So breaking free from him, she told him to make himself comfortable whilst she got herself ready for him.

She had only been gone seconds though, when he suddenly realised how much he was sweating, for over the past few days he had thought of nothing else but this moment and he was a bundle of nerves about it. Kissing and cuddling were one thing, but sex was something else and he wondered if he would end up making a fool of himself, or if Annie would laugh at his feeble attempts to satisfy her, for after all, he was still a virgin.

Then she called to him from somewhere along the landing, "Matty my darling, come and see what Annie's got for you."

He stood up and wiped his sweaty palms down the sides of his trousers, then walked slowly to the door he thought her voice had come from. But he was wrong and, it wasn't until he had tried the third door, that he finally found her.

She was on top of the bed, lying on the quilt completely naked. It was a sight he had never seen before and it showed in the way he just stood there, gawking at her and drooling from the mouth.

"Come on Matty my love" she cooed, patting the bed next to her, "We can't do much with you over there and me here now, can we?"

He began to walk towards the bed, but he didn't feel as though he was walking, it was more like a floating feeling, with his eyes never once leaving her body. Then suddenly, he found himself sitting on the bed beside her.

He sat staring at her and when he didn't make any attempt to take off his clothes, she reached between his legs and began to rhythmically knead his penis, gasping out loud though when she felt how big and hard it already was. Then with excitement in her voice, she asked, "Is my hand the only thing you're going to put that lump of mutton in darling?" Then coyly she told him, "Now come on, take your pants off and let Annie see what she's getting."

But he still didn't move, nor did he say anything, it was as if he was paralysed. All he could do was stare at her beautiful brown nipples and the mound of her thick, black pubic hair.

Annie sensed that something was wrong. 'Could he be shy' she wondered, 'Or maybe even a pervert. Maybe he just likes being wanked. Or could it be.' Then she burst into laughter, at the thought that had just come to her.

It took her a minute or two to get over her giggling fit, then she asked him the question that had made her laugh so much. "Matty my darling, have you been with a woman before, I mean, have you had sex with one?"

At first he was going to lie, but he knew it would only backfire on him, so he sullenly looked at the floor and slowly shook his head.

Again Annie burst into laughter, but this time it was louder than ever and she was so far gone with it, that she didn't notice Matty's face turn into a scowl as his mood changed to one of anger.

He stood up and began mimicking her laughter. "Ha ha fucking ha" he raged. "So the big tosser hasn't had his leg over yet, how fucking funny, ha ha ha."

Realising how much she had upset him, Annie jumped off the bed and threw herself at him, flinging her arms around his neck and pleading, "No Matty darling, no, you've got it all wrong, I'm not laughing at you, I'm laughing because I can't believe my luck. Which woman wouldn't laugh with joy if she was to come across a twenty-two year old virgin, especially one who is hung like a stallion. No my beauty, Annie isn't laughing at you at all." Then as she began to slowly caress the back of his neck, she felt the tension drain from him.

For the next two hours or so, Annie set about teaching Matty how to do all the things she had ever wanted a man to do to her. She taught him how to oral her whilst squeezing her nipples, she taught him how to take her in the best positions for deep penetration which she loved, as she liked to feel a man right inside of her and she was in sexual heaven when he rammed her hard, for Annie had a lust for pain.

She was no ordinary woman, she was perverted and, took great pleasure in abusing her young, naive, sex toy. She showed him no love, for she felt none, all she had eyes for, was what hung between his legs. Every time it went limp after he had climaxed, she would quickly coax it to stiffen again, then she would carry on satisfying her warped needs.

Matty, for his part, didn't know any different, for never having had sex before, he simply assumed that this was what couples did. Some of the things she wanted him to do seemed strange, like Annie having to feel pain before she could climax but he told himself, that if that's what it took to satisfy his woman, then that was what he'd do.

He had also forgotten to take any protection with him, but in the end this was not a problem, for Annie seemed to have an endless supply of nodders in the drawer by the side of the bed.

Which was just as well really, for when he looked down at the floor as he dressed later, he counted five used ones. "Not bad for a lad" he told himself smugly.

When he had finished dressing, she led him back down the stairs and through a passage to the back door. He just wanted to stand there kissing her but she kept telling him to go, as Tot might turn up at any time. She knew she was lying of course, for Tot wouldn't be home for at least another hour, but she wanted to tidy up the bedroom and have a bath before he got in, as she didn't want to go through another night of jealousy like she had on the night of the dance.

When they had got home that night, he had slapped her, but when Matty had asked if Tot had hit her, she had lied, for she didn't want to spoil the little scene she had going with him. She reckoned that if they were discreet, they could keep the affair going for a little longer yet.

Later, as she lay in the bath, she chuckled at Matty's naivety and she laughed out loud when she recalled him saying he loved her. Then shaking her head and smiling lustfully, she thought 'No Matty my big beautiful prick, there is no such thing as love.' Then stroking herself between the legs, she said out loud, "There's only fucking, deep, painful fucking and, once I've had my fill of you, you'll go the same way as the rest." For Annie didn't like her affairs to last too long, hence the reason she had been caught the one time she had.

As she began to masturbate herself with vigour, she cast her mind back over all the lovers she had had since marrying Tot. There must have been at least a dozen and, as she brought herself to a climax, she pictured them all in her mind, with their pricks standing proudly at the ready, to hump her till she screamed with painful pleasure.

Yet as Matty got off the bus as it arrived back in Houghton half-an-hour later, he was on cloud nine. He was so full of happiness, he feared he might burst and as he walked towards The Lamb Inn for a celebration drink, he actually found himself singing.

Then later as he walked into The Jolly's, Bob was totally confused by how calm and serene he was. He's never known the lad talk so gently, when he asked for a brandy and inquired as to what sort of day he's had. It was as if the hardman had been taken out of him and had been replaced by a priest or somebody. He certainly didn't sound like the brutal streetfighter he was.

For a good half hour Bob puzzled as to what could have brought on such a change in the lad, then suddenly it hit him. 'Of course' he told himself, 'That's where the bastard has been, through at Gilesgate to see Annie. Aye and I bet he's shagged her too, the sly, useless twat.'

Bob didn't show his anger though, for he felt it best not to let on he knew, after all, he was a fit, horny young bloke and if Annie was offering it on a plate, you couldn't really blame the lad. But as he sat watching Matty out of the corner of his eye, he thought 'I only hope no fucking trouble flares up though and I hope it doesn't interfere with his bloody fighting, because that would put the kybosh on things for sure.'

Bob needn't have worried on that score though, for as Matty lay on his bed that night, he was already planning his future with Annie and part of his plans, was to put some money together so they could go off somewhere and start afresh, but to do that, he needed at least six more fights to get the amount he felt would be required.

He felt so full of joy that he barely slept and by the time Bob came down to the scullery the next morning, Matty had already finished his run and was into his weight training.

"Morning Bob" he called when he first caught sight of him, "Isn't it just grand to be alive."

Bob chuckled as he told himself 'Not if Tot O'Rourke was to catch you Matty.' Then out loud to Matty he said, "Aye, it's a fine morning son, but these September mornings have a bit of a chill to them, so when you're finished, put some warm clothes on, the last thing we want is you catching a bloody cold."

But catching a cold was far from Matty's mind, the future was all he could think about and all he was to think about for the next five weeks. Yet whenever he had tried to discuss it with Annie, she would instantly try and change the subject, but being so naive, he simply put it down to her feeling sorry for Tot, as quite often she had said what a good, kind man he was and how she would hate to have to hurt him.

So Matty decided to give her time to find the right moment to tell him and in the meantime, he would carry on loving her as he had, with his dream of the future, his constant companion.

As it was only a Tuesday that he ever visited Annie, he had plenty of time on his hands, but he didn't spend it with Ray and the lads, for since he had fallen for Annie, he looked on them as rather immature. Neither did he spend his time drinking and gambling, for he was determined to save every penny he could. Instead, he went for long walks over the old moor, pretending Annie was with him, having long, loving conversations. Or he would simply put in some extra training, after all, it wasn't only the fighting he had to keep fit for now, but to satisfy his woman too.

Yet on his sixth visit to Gilesgate, Matty's whole world was to come tumbling down, as fate emerged once more from the wings, to deal him yet another crippling blow.

Annie had been as receptive as ever that afternoon, but when Matty wanted to take her for a third time, she said, "Sorry lover, but there are only two nodders left in the drawer and Tot will need them himself when he comes home tonight."

At first Matty laughed, for he thought that Annie was joking, but when he noticed the serious look on her face, he stopped and asked her, "You're kidding me aren't you, you don't really have sex with him still, do you?"

"Of course I do Matty" she told him, a little confused at his question. "After all, he is still my husband and that means he still has a right to fuck me."

"A right to fuck you" Matty replied, with anger in his voice now. Then as he leapt off the bed his voice rose as he repeated it again, "A right to fuck you, you must be fucking joking. You are my woman now and he has no rights at all as far as I'm concerned."

He stood by the side of the bed, towering over her, his face distorted now with anger at the thought of what Tot and her did after he left, he closed his eyes and pictured him humping her doggy-style, just as she had taught Matty to hump her and he almost screamed with rage.

He began to dress quickly, for he felt that if he was to stay any longer he might do something he would regret, but she began pleading with him to stay and talk about it.

"Talk" he barked at her, "What do you think I've been doing for the past six weeks. I've talked alright, talked about our future, but it seems that while I was talking, you were fucking him behind my back."

"Please Matty no, it's not like that at all, I'm married to Tot, so therefore I'm obliged to let him fuck me, please can you not see that?"

But Matty was too far gone with jealousy and when he was finally dressed, he looked down at her and shook his head with distain, then very quietly he told her, "I live in Houghton, you live in Gilesgate, just make sure our paths never cross again, for only god alone knows what I might do to you if we ever bump into each other."

Then he set off towards the door, but Annie ran after him and jumped on his back, pleading, "Please Matty, please don't go darling, please don't go."

"He bent forward sharply and sent her flying over his right shoulder and crashing against the door, where she fell to the floor, holding her back and wailing like a demented animal.

At first he felt regret at what he'd done, but when he pictured her and Tot having sex again, he simply put his foot under her body and pushed her away from the door. Then as he rushed down the stairs, the words, "Fuck-meat, nothing but fuck-meat" kept swirling around in his head.

Again in his naivety, Matty had kept himself pure for Annie, for he was her man. So why couldn't she keep herself pure for him, after all, he was the one she said she loved, not Tot. She said it was only sympathy that she felt for him, but it was obvious the cow had lied and, it was obvious that he had only been using Matty for sex.

Now, as he sat by the roadside, about four miles from Houghton, he wallowed in self-pity. His emotions swayed from sadness to pure hatred. Sadness for himself and hatred for people like Annie O'Rourke, people he felt had used him for their own ends.

For at the end of the day, he felt that no one really gave a toss for him. All anyone wanted him for, was to make money out of him or use his body, he as a person didn't matter, he was merely an implement for others to use whenever they felt like it.

An hour passed, then two and it wasn't until he realised it was turning dark, did he look at his watch. It was six-thirty, the pubs would have been open half-an-hour by now. So with a heavy heart he stood up, stuck out his chest, uttered, "Fuck 'em all" then headed off to drown his sorrows.

As had always been the case with Matty, once the self-pity had passed, anger took over and, as the drink flowed his mood blackened. When someone accidentally bumped into him, he backhanded the bloke straight across the face. He had no idea who it was and didn't care either, for at that moment, everyone in Matty's world was a shit-house. "The only decent human being left" he told himself, "Was in Ryburn Asylum and she may as well be dead."

By the time he had made his way back to the Jolly's, he was mortal drunk, but also in a fierce temper and again Bob was to get a shock as Matty stood leaning against the bar, stiff armed to support himself and growled "A large brandy" then he thumped the bar and added, "Now."

Bob had seen Matty drunk on many occasions, but never like this. He knew something drastic must have happened to him and the only person he could put that down to was Annie. 'I bet she's blown him out' he thought, as he poured Matty his brandy. Then as he put the glass on the bar, he told him, "Have this one on me son, then get yourself away down to the caravan, I reckon a good sleep would probably do you the power of good."

Matty picked up the glass, then sneered at Bob, "Who the hell do you think you're telling what to do, just stick to serving drinks and fixing up fights, because that's all you are fucking good for."

Bob was stung by Matty's comments but didn't retaliate, mainly because he didn't want to get his head knocked off, but also because he didn't want the place smashing up again. So as calmly as he could, he said "Ok Matty it's obvious you've had a bad day, but please, try not to let whatever it is, get you down too much."

Matty glared at him, then poured his drink down his throat, threw the glass across the bar and said, "Cut the fucking bullshit Hunter and give me a refill."

Bob hesitated, but more scared than ever now, did exactly as Matty asked.

Watching all this from the far end of the bar was Big John and, as he looked at Matty over the top of his glass, he thought 'My god, it's finally happened, he's turned into the same sort of bullying bastard his father and brother were, with the only difference being, he's capable of causing a lot more damage than either of them.'

He put his glass on the bar and walked down to where Matty was standing. "Come on Matty son" he said, taking hold of Matty's left arm, "Let's get you to bed, you look totally knackered."

Then Matty did something even he never thought he would do, he swung his right fist straight into Big John's face, sending him reeling backwards over a table, then crashing to the floor.

The whole bar, which was already stunned into silence by Matty's attitude, gasped in unison at the sight of Big John being dropped, for he was by far the biggest bloke in the area and no one had ever seen him on his back, as no one had ever been big enough to do it.

Big John wasn't knocked out, but he was stunned for a few seconds. He shook his head to clear his vision, then looked up at Matty, who by now had gone back to drinking his brandy and was totally ignoring the big man.

As he wiped the blood from his nose, Big John said, "I suppose you think that was clever, do you son?"

Matty still ignored him and slammed his glass down on the bar and demanded Bob pour him another.

"No Matty" Bob replied, "You're getting no fucking more and you can do what the hell you like about it."

Matty stood glowering at him, his face distorted with hate for the man, then he said sarcastically, "You mean you are not going to use the fucking cricket bat on me Bob like you did last time, or is the difference now, that I'm facing you and you haven't got the fucking guts to use it?"

Bob was scared stiff, but he had to stand his ground in front of the other customers so glaring back at Matty, he told him "I've no intention of using the cricket bat Matty, so you can knock the shit out of me if you like, but you had no cause to hit Big John like you did. That bloke has been good to you, he was always there when you needed him and just look how you've paid him back for that."

By now Big John was back on his feet and although he was angry, he was also feeling pity for Matty. He knew the lad hadn't just turned like he had, for at that moment he was no different to his father or brother, who both used to turn nasty in drink. No, Matty had been made to turn nasty, firstly by his father, then by Bob, for he still felt that Matty had been set up by him, Bob had planned it all, from that first fight with Fighter Martin through to where he was now, probably the most brutal fighter on the circuit.

Oh there had been other factors involved, like the rape of his sister and her having to be put in Ryburn, his mother dying, then prison. The lad having no one but Bob Hunter waiting for him when he came out, which was why the caravan had been done up and then there had been his so called mates, who had only wanted him for his money.

Big John was well aware that Matty wasn't the brightest of lads, he knew the kid could be easily led and that's what had happened, so at the end of the day, he felt it wasn't really Matty's fault that he had punched him.

The big man then wiped his face with his handkerchief, examined the blood on it for a moment, then putting it back in his pocket said calmly, "Aye Matty, you are a hard lad, but I'll tell you something son, you are nothing but a fucking bully. Far worse than either your brother or father were and I fear you are going to turn even more nastier. Thankfully though, I'll not be there to see it, because you and me are finished."

Then Big John edged over to where Bob was standing and as he added, "But it hasn't all been your fault son" he let go with his right fist, landing it smack on Bob's left eye, sending him crashing back against the shelf with glasses and bottles of spirits on it.

Bob fell to the floor with a shower of glass falling after him, but he wasn't aware of it though, for he was knocked out cold.

Then as Matty stood laughing at the spectacle, Big John shook his head in disgust, then walked out of the bar and out of Matty's life forever.

When he awoke the following morning, Matty had a stinking hangover and his mood was foul, for he was still full of bitterness towards Annie.

He staggered up to the scullery for some aspros, but when he saw Bob sitting at the table with a huge black-eye, he chuckled as he asked, "Who gave you that fucker Bob, me?"

Bob scowled at him, "No you drunken piss-pot, but it was because of you."

As Matty could only remember the forepart of the night, he had no recollection at all of what had happened when he had got back to the Jolly's, so shaking his head in confusion, he asked "What the hell do you mean because of me?"

Then Bob proceeded to tell him what had happened and concluded by telling him that Big John was finished with him.

Matty sat in silence for a few minutes, feeling a twinge of guilt at having hit the big fella. But then his thoughts turned back to Annie and he told himself, "Fuck 'em, fuck the lot of them." Then he stood up sharply sending his chair crashing back against the wall and glaring at Bob, said out loud "And fuck you too" and went storming out of the scullery.

Bob poured himself another pot of tea and began wondering if it wasn't time to pack the fighting in, for everything had begun to turn sour now and with the state Matty was in, there was no telling what he might do to somebody and the last thing Bob wanted to be involved with, was bloody murder.

For that was what the lad was quite capable of, but even more so now, now he had lost all sense of reason, which Bob felt sure he had. The trouble was though, how in hell's name would he tell Matty, for he knew he had come to rely on the money.

Also of course, if Bob did put an end to the fighting, Matty would be of no use to him anymore, so he would have to tell him to leave, which he knew would upset Bella, because she had become quite fond of him. But if it had to be, then it had to be.

For the moment though, Bob decided to let things ride, which would give him time to work out exactly what to do, but in the meantime, his only hope was that Matty kept a hold of himself and did nothing stupid.

But little did Bob know what a bad state Matty's mind was really in. Life had kicked him yet one more time and it wouldn't take much to send him over the top completely.

Bob had voiced his fears to Bella, but she seemed to have taken it well. Yet that afternoon, when he went off to the local dog-track, she went down to the caravan.

Matty heard the rap on the door, but ignored it, thinking it was Bob. But when he saw the handle turn and Bella walk in, he was a little surprised.

She sat down on the edge of the bed and smiled at him. "Now young Matty" she said gently, "What's this Bob's been telling me about you turning nasty."

Matty lay still and slightly shook his head, then took another swig of brandy before replying, "I don't know what you mean Bella, I can't recall being nasty to anybody."

Then she began stroking his left arm, which surprised Matty again, for it certainly wasn't a motherly type gesture at all and, when he looked into her eyes, they were filled with lust.

Matty was shocked at what he saw, but not as shocked as he was when he suddenly felt his penis twitch. "Christ" he said to himself, as he looked down at the bulge between his legs getting bigger, "Don't tell me you fancy fucking her."

As she continued to stroke his arm, she said "You' do look in a bit of a mess Matty, I bet you haven't washed or shaved today, have you?"

Again, he just shook his head slightly.

"I'll tell you what then" she told him, unable to control the touch of excitement in her voice, "Why don't you come up to our place and have a good bath and a shave, in the meantime, I'll cook you a nice meal." Then standing up and smacking him on the side of the leg, she added "Come on now, shift your arse."

They walked up to the pub together, then when they reached the living quarters, he went into the bathroom, whilst she went into the kitchen.

As a course of habit, Matty left the bathroom door ajar, never thinking for a minute that Bella would spy on him, but when he had got out of the bath and was clearing the steam off the bathroom mirror so he could shave, he suddenly got a glimpse of Bella, watching him through the open door.

His first instinct was to turn on her, but when he felt his penis twitch again and he looked down to see it was semi-erect, he decided to carry on shaving. In fact he even turned towards the door slightly, so she could have a better view of him.

By the time he was finished shaving, his penis was fully erect and he was actually feeling as randy as hell. So he took a step back, on the pretext of giving himself a fuller view of his face, but with his left hand he accidentally knocked the door open and when he turned sharply to look at Bella, he was both disgusted and excited at what he saw.

Bella was leaning against the wall with her right hand up her skirt and between her legs, whilst her face was distorted with self-pleasure.

"Oh my god!" she exclaimed in shock, as she quickly removed her hand from between her legs and slyly wiped it on her skirt.

Matty looked at her sternly, then his face turned into a smile as he asked, "What's all this then Bella" then looking down at his penis he added, "D' you fancy it then?"

She stood with her mouth open, still in shock at being caught spying on him, but when he indicated with his head towards his penis, she smiled with relief as she realised what he wanted her to do.

She dropped down on her knees and took it in her right hand, then slowly she began to lick the end of it. She raised it a little and slid her tongue all the way down it to his balls. Then she slid it back up again and took him fully in her mouth, moaning with pleasure as she did so.

She could see that she was about to bring him off so she stopped sucking and stood up. Then, still holding him by the penis, she led him through to the bedroom.

As Bella told him she was infertile, there was no need for nodders, which excited Matty even more, for he had never 'ridden' bareback before and did he enjoy it.

He humped Bella in every position Annie had taught him, which surprised her some, for she had always that he would be a novice and, he also surprised her by the roughness of his humping and several times she had had to ask him to ease up because he was hurting her so much.

Yet Matty didn't give a toss, she wanted fucking so he would fuck her, but it would be his way, rough and painful, just like Annie had taught him.

By half-five she had had enough, besides Bob would be back shortly and she didn't want him to catch them. She reckoned things would be ok with Matty now, now he had her to take his aggression out of, 'And my god' she thought, 'Am I going to enjoy letting him.'

Over the following month or so Matty did change, but alas it was for the worse. By the beginning of December, he had become more bitter and twisted than ever. He still had his sex sessions with Bella and others besides, for since Annie, he had required a need for it, yet it was always a hurtful sort of sex, never any gentleness or love attached to it.

During that period, Bob had managed to get him a couple of fights in which he had almost killed his opponents, worrying Bob even more that something fatal might happen.

Matty also got hit more in those fights than he had ever done before. For he was drinking very heavily these days and hardly ever bothered to train. He spent most of his time in a drunken stupor, lying on his bed in the caravan, wallowing in self-pity and only speaking to people when it was necessary.

So one morning when Bob picked up the post off the floor by the front door, he was surprised to see a letter addressed to Matty, because as long as Matty had lived with them, he had never received one before and, as he didn't see much of Matty these days, he simply pushed it under the caravan door.

Matty never saw the letter though, for he accidentally kicked it under the bed and it wasn't till almost two weeks later did he find it.

As he was feeling under the bed for a brandy bottle that might still have a drop left in, his hand suddenly touched something and, when he pulled it out, was as surprised as Bob had been to see it was a letter.

He looked at it curiously for a few moments, then opened it, firstly, looking at the signature on the bottom, it was from Matron Ashcroft. Then, as he read the letter, he began to tremble, not with drink, but with emotion, as he read,

>Dear Mr Glave,
>
>It is with great sadness that I have to inform you, that your sister Dorothy passed away at six-thirty this morning.
>
>If you wish her to have a private funeral, could you please contact me immediately, but if you do not, we will be holding a service for her on Thursday, at ten o'clock in the asylum chapel, then we will bury her in the chapel grounds.

Yours in sorrow

Matron Ashcroft.

Matty crumpled the letter up in his fist as he screamed at the top of his voice, "NO, NO, NO" he kept yelling, "NO SHE CAN'T HAVE DIED, NO SHE CAN'T." Then he fell onto the bed and cried his heart out.

He cried on for an hour or so, then a horrible thought suddenly struck him, what day was it. For in his drunken stupor he had completely lost all track of time.

Hurriedly he unfolded the letter and looked at the date on top, it read Saturday 2nd December 1950. He had no calendar, so he had no way of knowing what today's date was. Then he looked at his watch and saw it was only just gone eight, Bob would be still up in the scullery reading his morning paper. So almost tearing the handle off the caravan door, he dashed off up the yard.

Bob was still there and he was still reading his paper, but Matty didn't say a word, he just grabbed it out of his hands and looked at the date on it, it was Wednesday 15th December.

"Fucking Jesus!" he exclaimed angrily, throwing the paper to the ground, then turning to glare at Bob. "When did this fucker come?" he barked, holding up the letter.

Bob was both confused and scared, for he hadn't the faintest idea what Matty was on about. "Wha-, what's up with you Matty?" he stuttered, "What the fuck have I done wrong now?"

Matty leaned across the table, putting his head right next to Bob's and shoving the letter in his face, he hissed through clenched teeth, "This bastard, that's what I'm on about, this letter, when did it come?"

Bob leaned backwards away from Matty's head, for he knew how lethal it was but all the while trying to think when the letter had come. Then luckily he remembered and with relief he told him, "A week gone Monday, aye that was it, a week gone Monday" then trying to sound concerned, added, "Was it bad news then ' Matty?"

Matty continued to glare at him, but he could just see himself grabbing Bob by the hair and banging his head off the table. But he didn't, for it was then a sense of guilt came over him as his thoughts turned to Dotty. So instead of hitting Bob, he simply walked back down to the caravan and wallowed in yet more self-pity.

Matty had scared the life out of Bob and as he sat in the scullery putting the paper together again, he finally decided that he had had enough of the lad. "Aye" he told himself shaking his head, "It's time he went." for Bob knew it would only be a matter of time before Matty turned on him.

'I'll give him till after Christmas' he thought, 'That's only a couple of weeks away and I don't want to upset Bella by chucking him out with that just round the corner. No I'll wait till the year turn's, then get rid of the shit-house.'

If Bob could have seen inside of Matty's head though, he wouldn't have waited that long, because Dotty's death was that one remaining thing, which was to finally send Matty over the edge.

By the time Christmas Eve came Matty had virtually become a recluse. He wouldn't even open the caravan door to Bella, which upset her so much, even Bob began to be a little suspicious as to what her motives were, for crying so much.

Matty did leave the caravan over the Christmas period, but only because his hunger drove him to it, yet he never went out through the pub. Instead, he would jump the wall and go down town for pies or fish and chips, then he would return the same way.

Come New Years Eve though, he was forced to go up to the pub, for it was a bitterly cold night and he had run out of paraffin for his heater. So he decided to go up to the bar and sit in front of the fire to warm himself through.

As it was early and with it being such a cold night, there were very few people in there, but those who were, he simply ignored as he picked up his brandy, then went and sat on a stool by the fire.

He hadn't even spoken to Bob; all he had done was throw some money onto the bar and nod towards the brandy bottle. He had also ignored Bella when she had asked how he was, in fact, he didn't even look at her. Which puzzled Bob, for he had been thinking something entirely different about the two of them.

Then a few minutes later the door opened, but as Matty was sitting with his back to it, he didn't see who came in. But when he heard a female voice break into laughter, he suddenly felt himself begin to shake with rage.

For it was Annie O'Rourke. She and Tot had popped over from Gilesgate, to have a New Years drink with Bob and Bella before things got too busy.

Now either they hadn't seen him, or they had chose to ignore him, for not once did they acknowledge him, but on the other hand, he was doing his best to ignore them also. Yet the more Annie laughed, the louder it seemed to become, until in the end he couldn't stand it any longer. For he was convinced she was laughing at him.

Then his temper snapped and he stood up, threw his glass into the fire and went storming over to her. "So what do you find so fucking funny this time, you Irish cow?" he barked, "Eh, what's so fucking funny then?"

By now he was towering over her and for all the world, Bob thought he was going to land her one. But Tot grabbed Matty's arm, half spinning him towards him, saying, "Don't you talk to my wife like that you bastard." But before Tot could say anything else, Matty nutted him fully in the face, then grabbed him by the hair and drove the bloke's head down onto the bar.

Tot was out cold and didn't feel the two kicks Matty gave him as he fell to the floor, nor was he to see the back-hander Matty gave his wife, sending her thudding against the wall, cracking her head against it, then crumbling in a heap on the floor.

It had all happened so suddenly, Bob and Bella didn't have a chance of stopping him, but now, as Bob watched Matty smugly surveying his handy work, he reached under the bar for the cricket bat.

"Don't even think about the bastard" Matty growled at him, spotting what he was up to, "Cos I'll break both your fucking arms if you as much as touch that cricket bat."

Bob stopped dead in his tracks, then put both of his hands back on top of the bar where Matty could see them. But his nerve hadn't deserted him altogether, as he nervously told Matty to get out or he would call the cops.

Matty's first instinct was to go for Bob, but then Bella chirped up, pleading, "Please Matty don't, please for my sake, besides" she added, looking at Tot and Annie's bloodied bodies, lying on the floor, "Don't you think you've done enough damage for one night?"

Matty looked at her, then at Bob, then down at Tot and Annie, who was by now sitting with her head in her hands whimpering like a dog. Then he looked back at Bella and Bob and burst out laughing like some demented maniac. Then he calmly walked over to the door, opened it and as he left, he called back, "Fuck the sodding lot of you."

He had no idea where he was heading, but after leaving the Jolly's, Matty's mind was in such turmoil he didn't care where he went, he just walked and walked, until finally the cold got the better of him and he decided to look for a pub.

He found one called The Colliers Rest, which told him he must be on the far side of town and it was a pub he had never been into before, but that didn't matter, for as he had no coat with him and his teeth were beginning to chatter with the cold, he thought, 'Fuck it, any hole will do.'

Surprisingly, there were quite a few people in the place and, as he pushed his way, to the bar, he spotted one or two decent shags amongst them too.

Gruffly, he asked the barman for a large brandy and a bottle to take out, for he certainly had no intentions of going back to the Jolly's tonight, so wherever he slept, he'd need a comforter with him.

"Sorry sir" the barman told him politely as he served Matty his glass of brandy, "But we don't sell spirits by the bottle."

Matty glowered at him, then through clenched teeth he hissed, "I want a fucking bottle, now."

The barman instantly shot off along the bar and said something to a bloke Matty presumed was the Landlord, for he certainly looked the Bob Hunter type, which meant Matty took an instant dislike to him.

Then he walked up the bar towards Matty and said, looking him up and down, "I'm sorry but I can't sell you a bottle of brandy mate, with it being New Year and all, I haven't got that much left myself."

"Bull-shit" Matty barked, "Give me a bottle or I'll smash your fucking pub up, alright" then sarcastically he added, "Mate."

Matty was a fearsome sight at the best of times, but his scruffy unshaven appearance made him look even more frightening and, when the Landlord looked into his mad, glaring eyes, he decided for the sake of peace, to back down and give Matty his bottle.

With that settled, Matty went back to his bitter thoughts of Annie, but it wasn't long after that he heard another voice from his past he seemed to recognise and again, it was one that filled him full of loathing for the person it belonged to.

He looked over the heads of the crowd to the far end of the bar and, yes it was him. He had the same black, greasy, slicked down hair with its raggy ends and he chuckled to himself as he thought, 'Well fuck me, who would have thought I would have bumped into that bastard after all this time' then he chuckled out loud as he added, 'It must be my night for settling old scores.'

He picked up his bottle of brandy and stuffed it in his trouser pocket, then pushed his way through the crowd to the far end of the bar, where eventually he found himself standing directly behind the bloke.

Then, as he stood looking at him for a few moments, he shook his head with disgust, but then he noticed the walking stick he was leaning on and again he chuckled to himself thinking, 'Well, at least he didn't get away with it altogether.'

Then he gently tapped the bloke on the shoulder and, as he turned, Matty nutted him, at the same time, saying quite calmly, "Happy New Year our Siddy."

Siddy dropped to the floor in a heap, snapping his walking stick as he fell. But Matty had only stunned him and, as Siddy climbed up onto his knees, he glared up at Matty with as much hate in his eyes for his brother, as Matty had for him.

As the pub fell into a deathly silence, neither of them moved a muscle for about thirty seconds or so. Then Matty told him, "She's dead you know, our Dotty. She died in Ryburn the other week." Then he seemed to drift off, as if he was recalling some fond memory of her, but it was only for an instant. For as his face distorted into the most grotesque leer, he growled, "And it was you who killed her, you bastard." Then he kicked Siddy viciously in the face, causing his head to jerk back so violently, it appeared to become detached from his neck.

Matty then spat on Siddy, uttering "You useless pile of shite" as he did so. Then he turned and headed for the door, but he didn't have to push his way through the crowd this time, as a corridor of fear opened up before him.

His mood was as black as thunder now, as he came out of the pub and began staggering around the town, swigging the brandy as he went, oblivious to the people pointing at him and laughing at the spectacle he was making of himself.

Then after an hour or so, the cold once again began to penetrate his anger and he decided to look for some sort of shelter from it.

So he staggered on a little longer, then came to the Welfare sports ground, where he remembered seeing a pavilion once. So he jumped the fence and began looking for it, but as it was so dark, it took him a while to find it. Eventually though, he did, but it was locked. So putting his shoulder to the door, he burst it open, stumbled, then fell flat on his face.

He lay there for a moment, then remembered the brandy bottle. "Oh no!" he exclaimed, as he felt his trouser pocket, then sighed with relief when he found it wasn't broken.

Then he got onto his knees and began groping around in the dark for something to sit on, which turned out to be a pile of old goal nets someone had thrown into a corner. Then he took the brandy out of his pocket, huddled up and, as he put the bottle to his lips, he uttered, "Fuck the lot of them."

Yet the more he thought about the events of the night, the more twisted his thinking became, until finally, in his drunken stupor, he fell asleep.

It could have been the drink addling his brain, but it was more likely bumping into Siddy again, that once more triggered off all the bad memories Matty had carried these last two years or so, culminating once again in his dream of the Snowflakes.

He hadn't had the dream for ages, but there they were just as he had seen them all the previous times, Frank and Dotty sitting cross-legged on the ground, stroking Billy The Buck with one hand and beckoning him to them with the other.

But again, as had happened so many times before, the moment he walked towards them, they would simply move the same distance away again. Until finally, once more in frustration and anger, he turned away from them.

As the night wore on though, thanks to the brandy he drifted into a deep sleep, but only to wake again a few hours later shivering profusely with the cold and the sound of his rattling teeth, almost deafening him.

"Christ" he said out loud, as he stiffly stood up and leaned against the wall, "Where in god's name am I?" For he had no recollection of how he came to be in the pavilion.

As it was still dark, he had to grope his way around until he found the door, then he staggered through the grounds until he found the fence, which he promptly jumped over, thinking, 'How the hell did I get in there?'

Then, as he made his way back to the Jolly's, he tried to piece the events of the night together. He remembered quite clearly what had happened at the Jolly's but could only vaguely recall bumping into Siddy. What happened after that was a mystery, he couldn't even remember having the dream, but on the other hand, he never remembered it on the other occasions he had had it either.

When he reached the Jolly's, he climbed over the wall and let himself into the caravan. Then he kicked off his boots and jumped into bed fully clothed, where he lay for a while shivering, until his body heat slowly began to warm up the bed and, with the coming of the warmth, he finally dozed off to sleep.

CHAPTER EIGHT

Later that afternoon Matty was awoken by a tremendous thumping on the caravan door and Bob hollering, "Matty, come on I know you're in there, so open the bloody door, come on, open up."

Matty lifted his throbbing head off the pillow and angrily groaned, "What the fuck..." Then jumped out of bed and threw the door open, saying "Is it necessary to hammer the door like that, you simple twat?"

As Bob brushed past him he said, just as angry as Matty was, "I've been knocking for ten fucking minutes, I thought you were dead."

Then Bob plomped himself down on one of the chairs by the table, whilst Matty went back and sat on the side of the bed, scratching his head and asking, "Well, what the fuck do you want then?"

Bob hesitated for a moment, but he had come this far and he knew he couldn't back down now. So as calmly as he could, he told Matty, "Tot's in a bad way, he had to have an operation last night to rebuild his face, by all accounts you made a right fucking mess of him."

"Then of course there's Annie. You managed to crack her jaw into the bargain as well. So all in all, you've done a fair bit of damage Matty."

When Bob had finished speaking, Matty glanced at him sideways, shrugged his shoulders, then asked, "So?"

"So" Bob repeated, letting his temper get the better of him as he mimicked Matty's non caring attitude, "So that's it Matty, it's all over, the fighting, everything, completely finished with" then Bob steeled himself as he added, "And I want you out of the caravan as well."

It was Matty's turn to let his temper go this time, as he glared at Bob now and growled, "You bastard, you mean you're throwing me out."

"If you like" Bob replied defiantly, then he stood up and edged towards the door.

Matty chuckled sarcastically as he watched him preparing himself for a quick getaway and he asked, "But what if I don't want to leave Bob, eh, what will you do then?"

"That's easy" Bob told him, standing in the doorway now, "I'll burn the fucking caravan to the ground." Then he slammed the door behind him and walked quickly off up the yard before Matty had a chance to move.

'Well, well' Matty thought, shaking his head in disbelief, 'Who would have thought that then, the bastard wants me out.'

Another time, he would have gone after Bob and belted him, but now, with his head still throbbing and his body aching all over, he simply said, "Fuck it." Then climbed back into bed, curled up and went to sleep.

When he woke up four-hours later, he felt much better. The effects of the brandy were wearing off and he didn't seem to ache so much. Then he suddenly remembered his visit from Bob and what he had said. "The twat" he uttered, when he recalled the bit about Bob telling him to get out.

He lay for a while longer with his eyes closed, but he wasn't sleeping. He was trying to figure out what to do, but his mind was so confused, he didn't know where to start.

Then he reached over to the drawers by the side of the bed and took out his money and counted it. There was seven pounds, four shillings and nine pence. "Fucking hell" he said, shaking his head in disgust, "Seven quid, is that all I've got to show for what I've been through." Then turning on himself he said, "That, is a fucking disgrace Matty Glave."

He sat for a while looking at it. He knew he wouldn't get far on it, so the answer was, he would try and get a fight somewhere. But the only trouble with that was, where the hell did he start. For he had always left that side of things to Bob.

"If only" he told himself, "If only Bob would fix me one more fight, I'd have enough money then to square my debts and piss off somewhere, out of the way of the lot of them."

The problem was though, getting Bob to fix the fight and, for the next hour or so, he concentrated his thoughts on how he could get Bob to change his mind.

Then like a flash it came to him. "Of course" he said excitedly. "That's who will do it for me, Bella, my wonderful, cock-happy Bella."

He looked at his watch, it had just gone half-three. If Bob was going out anywhere, he's be going about now. So Matty waited ten minutes, then went up to the pub.

He went straight up stairs and into the living room, where he found Bella sewing some curtains. "Hello lass" he said cheerily "Is Bob about?"

She was still in a mood with him for what he had done the previous night, so huffily she replied, "No he isn't, he's gone through to Sunderland General to see Tot and he'll not be back till sixish."

Matty could tell by her tone that she wasn't feeling too friendly towards him, but he persevered. "Did he mention anything to you about chucking me out?" he asked, sounding sorry for himself.

"Aye, he did that" she told him, never once taking her eyes off her sewing, "He said if you weren't gone by Saturday, he was burning the caravan down."

'Saturday' Matty thought, 'He never said anything about Saturday. I thought he meant I had to be out today and, seeing as it is only Tuesday, I've got a bit of a breathing space.'

Then he knelt down by Bella's chair and putting his hand on her knee, asked, "Did he also tell you he won't get me anymore fights?"

"Aye" she answered again, determined not to look at him, but fully aware of his hand on her knee.

"But if I'm to leave lass, I've got to have another fight to put some bloody money in my pocket." Then changing his tone to one of self-pity, he said "You see lass, I'm bloody skint, all I've got in the world, is seven quid and that won't get me far now, will it?"

She stopped sewing and looked at him. He looked a right mess. His hair was tousled, he hadn't shaved for what looked like days, his clothes were dirty and he stunk of sweat. But she knew that no matter how he looked, she would always fancy him, but more especially, what he carried between his legs.

"I'll tell you what" she said, her tone softening, I've got twenty pounds put away, you can have that."

Matty shook his head as he replied, "Even that's not enough Bella, I need at least a ton. Y' see I owe Willie Holt forty and I'll need a bit behind me till I can set up somewhere. So, the only answer is for Bob to get me a fight." Then as he began to stroke her leg, he added "Will you help me lass, will you have a word with Bob for me, eh?"

She smiled at him, then sighing, she told him, "Ok Matty, I'll have a word but I can't promise anything mind, because I know Bob was awfully upset about what you did last night, but I'll try."

"Cheers Bella" he said, winking at her and slapping her leg gently. Then looking at his watch, asked, "What time did Bob say he would be back, sixish?"

"Aye" she replied, nodding.

"Well it's only four now" he told her, then with a sly grin on his face and indicating towards the bedroom with his head, asked, "Do you fancy a bit then?"

She did and, as she put her sewing down on the floor, she stood up and said, "Of course I do you horny sod" then walking out of the living room door, she added "Follow me and I'll show you just how much."

They had barely started though, when Bella stopped suddenly and cried, "Oh my god."

Thinking he was hurting her too much again, Matty also stopped and asked, "What the hell is wrong now?"

"There's a car just pulled up outside" she told him, panic in her voice, "And I'm sure it sounded like Bob's."

Then she quickly jumped off the bed, telling Matty to pick up his clothes and get into the bathroom, whilst she hurriedly put on her skirt and jumper and stuffed her underclothes under the bed. Then she dashed back into the living room and picked up her sewing again.

She only just made it by seconds and, as Bob walked through the living room door, he could see that she still looked flustered.

But she didn't give him a chance to say anything, as she quickly asked, trying to sound surprised, "What are you doing back so early?"

"I've had trouble with the car" he told her, still a bit puzzled at her appearance. Then showing her his dirty hands, added, "I'll just pop through to the bathroom and give these a scrub, I'll be back in a minute."

With sheer panic in her voice now she called after him, "No Bob, you can't go in there, Matty's having a bath."

"Matty!" he exclaimed, turning to face her. "What's he doing up here?"

"He came up just after you left and asked could he have a bath. That's all." But he knew by the look on her face, that something was wrong.

Then he sat down in the arm-chair behind the door and looked at her suspiciously. He could see something was up with her, so he asked, "Has he been saying something he shouldn't?"

"No" she replied as evenly as she could, then added, "Well he did mention something about you getting one last fight because he was skint, but that's all."

Bob continued to look at her suspiciously, then he heard Matty walk along the landing and off down the stairs. So he promptly got up and went into the bathroom.

However, it wasn't until he had washed his hands and was then drying them, that he felt there was something odd about the bathroom and at first he couldn't quite figure what. Then suddenly it hit him.

There was no steam on the mirror and the room itself had a chill to it. Then he bent down, and felt the bath, it was cold and dry, as if it hadn't even been used and, touching the towels, he found that they were also dry.

"That bastard hasn't had a bath" he told himself, confused. "So what in hell's name had he been doing up here?" Then it dawned on him and, as a horrible thought crossed his mind, he shot back into the living room.

Bella's flustered appearance had been a dead giveaway but he had been too thick to see it. Now though, he wanted the truth and, as he sat back down in the arm-chair, he barked, "Come here."

Bella sensed that he had discovered something, but trying to sound offended asked, "What do you mean, come here?"

Bob's face was like thunder, as he barked again, "Just what I mean, come over here and stand in front of me" then he growled, "Now!"

So apprehensively she got up and went over to him, then gasped with shock as firstly he lifted up her skirt with his left hand, shook his head in disgust when he saw she was not wearing knickers, then put his right hand between her legs.

As he did so, his eyes never left hers and, as he felt the telling dampness, he hissed through clenched teeth, "Just as I fucking well thought." Then he reached up and smacked her across the face, sending her spinning backwards and falling onto the settee.

But before she could even scream, he was on her again, slapping her as hard as he could, over and over and calling her all the filthy names he could think of.

As Matty had decided to give Bella a couple of days to work on Bob, he didn't go back up to the pub until Thursday afternoon. But when he put his head around the kitchen door, expecting to see Bella, he got a bit of a shock, for it was Bob who was in there, drying some dishes and putting them into the cupboard.

"Alright Bob" he said, trying to hide his disappointment. "Er is Bella around anywhere?"

It was an effort to suppress his anger, but Bob managed it as he answered calmly, "No she isn't Matty, her mother has been taken ill in Redcar and she's popped down there for a few days to look after her."

"Mmmm" Matty uttered in reply, unable to hide his disappointment this time.

Which prompted Bob to ask, "Why, was there something you wanted to see her about?"

"Nothing of importance" Matty lied, "I was just hungry that's all" then cheekily he added "You haven't cooked any grub, have you Bob?"

'Well the cocky bastard' Bob thought, as he struggled now to hold his temper, 'He shags my wife, then expects me to cook for him,' but outwardly he managed to ignore Matty's question.

Instead, he threw the tea-towel onto the draining board and brushed past him, but as he got to the door he turned and, making believe he had just remembered it, said "Oh by the way, I've managed to fix up a fight for you, but I hope you've been keeping in shape, because it's tomorrow night, down in Darlington." Then the tone of Bob's voice changed, as he added "But come Saturday morning though Matty, I want you to pack your things and get out. The fight should put a ton or so in your pocket and I'd like you to use it to get as far away from here as possible, alright?"

Matty felt the hackles on the back of his neck rise, but he didn't react, he simply nodded and glared contemptuously back at Bob as he did so.

"Fair enough then" Bob told him, turning again to go out of the kitchen door, "I'll see you in the bar tomorrow night about seven." Then he was off along the landing and down the stairs.

Matty stood for a few moments looking at the now empty doorway where Bob had been standing and, shrugging his shoulders thought, 'Bollocks to you, you tosser' then began rummaging through the cupboards for something to eat.

As Bob had gone down the stairs though, he had been thinking the same sort of thing about him, for now he felt nothing but hatred towards the lad and, all things being equal, tomorrow night he would get his comeuppance.

For Bob had lied, Bella hadn't gone to see her sick mother in Redcar, he had taken her to his sister's in Darlington, to keep her out of the way until Matty cleared off.

But whilst he was down there, he had also decided to visit his old handler, Barny Finch, in the hope that he could help him solve his problem of how to get revenge on Matty.

"Of course I'll help" Barny had told him, as he took a sip from the double whiskey Bob had just bought him, but studying the bloke over the rim of his glass and feeling a bit disgusted as he did so.

For Barny Finch was a hard man, who had lived in the world of hard men for most of his life. Firstly as a fighter, then as a handler and, the one thing that sickened him most, was a fighter who had lost his nerve, as had been the case with Bob.

Oh he'd been a good 'un once, he'd beaten some tough lads too. But after Joula Lowrey had caved his ribs in, he'd lost his taste for fighting.

Barny knew it happened to blokes sometimes, but he didn't like it and, if he hadn't had such a good relationship with Bob, he would have told him to piss-off and do his own dirty work, but as it was him, he agreed to help sort out the wife shagger.

"Is that bloke of yours as good as you said Barny?" Bob had asked.

Only to be told "Bloke, he's no fucking bloke, he's pure fucking animal. He's already killed one lad, aye and maimed a few more besides. But if they keep wanting to take him on, I'll keep letting the silly bastards."

"Good" Bob had said, nodding his head with satisfaction, "Because as I told you when I first took Matty on, it'll need somebody exceptional to beat him, cos he's capable of being a killer too."

Then they reminisced about old times, also how well they had both done out of their fighters since they had last talked. For when Bob had rang Barny in the beginning and asked his advice on how to handle a fighter, they had both agreed then, to keep their blokes apart, for as Barny had told him, that way, they could both make a good living.

Hence the reason Bob had never taken Matty south of Durham. For it was decided that he would have the northern towns, like Sunderland, Durham and Newcastle. Whilst Barny would take Darlington, Middlesbrough and the North Yorkshire towns.

Then, by the end of the night it was all settled. Bob would bring Matty down to The White Barn farm, just outside of Darlington, on Friday night. No money would change hands because it was felt that none would be needed. But Bob had told Barny, that if his bloke did a good job on Matty, he would see him alright.

So, as Bob drove back to Houghton in the early hours of Wednesday morning his mood was considerably brighter and, he kept getting excited at the thought of what damage Barny's bloke was going to do to Matty.

Come the Friday morning, Matty decided to go for a run, but as it had been snowing and was very slippy underfoot, plus the fact he hadn't had a run in ages, he only got a mile before deciding to turn back.

So instead of training, he bought a couple of pork pies and a half bottle of brandy, then went back to the caravan for a lie down.

He tried to sleep, but found he couldn't, for something was niggling him, yet he couldn't put his finger on what it was. Things seemed a little strange, like not seeing Bella around since that day Bob had almost caught them. Like the fight taking place at Darlington. Then there was Bob's calm attitude, as though he didn't have a care in the world. But surely, Matty felt, Bob would miss the fight game as much as he would.

Yet when he analysed these things, he found logical answers to them. Like Bella's mother really being ill and she had gone to Redcar and, may be the fight down in Darlington, was the only one Bob could get at such short notice, even though it did seem strange, never having gone down there before. Then finally, he concluded that the reason Bob seemed so at peace with himself, was the fact that he was getting rid of him.

Yet he still couldn't help feeling something was amiss and, by the time he put his coat on, just before seven that night, his mood was both one of depression and anger.

It showed too when he walked into the bar, for he totally ignored Bob and Cuddy and only nodded to the Hetton lads, then barked at Bob, "Come on, let's get the fucking thing over with."

When they reached the farm, Bob and the crew got out of the car without saying a word and went straight into the barn, leaving Matty on his own to get ready for the fight.

When he had stripped down to his pants and boots, Matty too got out of the car and looked around him. The feeling that something was wrong came back to him again as he noticed there were only three other cars parked outside of the barn.

He knew why no one followed him these days, for no one liked him anymore. 'But surely' he thought, 'If this fight is for as much money as Bob said it was, a fair few gamblers at least would have turned up. So why only three cars?'

Then he took a few steps towards the barn and suddenly stopped. "Unless" he told himself curiously, "Not many eyes are supposed to see what happens in here tonight." Then as his anger rose at the thought of what Bob might be trying to do to him, he went storming into the barn.

Bob was standing over to his right with the Hetton lads and Cuddy, talking to a couple of people Matty didn't know. One was Bob's age, but the other was an elderly bloke of about sixty, who was very smartly dressed and, by the manner in which Bob was talking to him, someone of importance too.

To Matty's left were four blokes sitting on bales of hay and, at the far end of the barn, he could just make out two more blokes, standing in front of someone else, sitting down on another bale of hay.

He knew instinctively that this was his opponent, but as there was only a small paraffin lamp swinging from one of the rafters, that only lit up an area of about twenty feet in the centre of the barn, he had no way of seeing what the bloke looked like.

Then he had a sudden feeling of isolation, as if at that moment the whole world hated him, but this only served to steel his resolve, as he uttered to himself, "Come on then you tossers, let's get at the bastard" and as his temper began to soar, he felt positively evil.

As the call went up for the fighting area to be cleared, another odd thing happened. The bloke in charge of the fight, simply told them to get stuck in, he never searched either of them for weapons, or checked their hands for knuckle-dusters or rings and, as he walked over to the well-dressed bloke Bob had been talking to, he gave him a thumbs-up signal, which struck Matty as very strange indeed.

Then the barn fell silent as Matty walked slowly towards the circle of light, as did his opponent. But when they came into full view of each other, they both stopped and, with a look of surprise on both their faces, they stood staring at each other in amazement.

"Well, I'll be buggered" Matty said to himself and smiled, as he noticed the horseshoe shaped scar on the bloke's left cheek, "So this is who they've set me up against, Bomber Foster, the Durham jail hardman."

Then he saw Bomber's distorted mouth twitch and wondered if he too was smiling. For if Matty was pleased to see him again, which he was, he knew that Bomber would be just as pleased to see him.

When the initial shock of seeing each other wore off, the smiles disappeared and they both took up a crouched position, with their arms spread wide, then slowly they began to circle one another to the left.

Neither blinked as they continued to circle, waiting for the slightest opening, but Matty dropped his eyes for a second and looked at Bomber's legs. Then inwardly he smiled as he noticed how thin they still were. But then he looked back up at Bomber's upper body, the smile disappeared as he told himself, "There's still a massive lump of meat stuck on top of the bastards though."

For he had to concede that that lump of meat was awesome. His torso and arms were huge and even his shaven head looked as though it had muscles bulging from it.

Yet for all the power the lad generated, Matty wasn't scared of him, he knew that if he kept away from Bomber's arms and didn't let him get any kind of grip on him, he had a good chance of doing the bastard and, if he could wear him down a bit and get him to stand heavy on his feet long enough, he just might be able to land "The Bomber Drop", the move he had practised for so long whilst in solitary.

But he knew the hard part would be keeping out of his reach, so he began bobbing and weaving like a boxer, pretending to throw punches, in the hope that Bomber would have to move just as fast as him, to keep out of the way of them.

Sadly Matty had forgotten one very important point, that was how much out of condition he was and, as he feigned to throw a left jab, Bomber clubbed him on his right ear with such a force, he instantly burst Matty's eardrum.

Matty reeled backwards but didn't fall. He shook his head to clear his vision, then felt the blood trickling down the side of his face. He shook his head again, this time, to try and clear the high-pitched whine coming from his ear, but he couldn't get rid of it and, as Bomber was bearing down on him, with a twisted leer on his face, Matty knew he had to do something quickly, so he crouched low and drove his right shoulder into Bomber's stomach, causing him to "Whoosh" and stagger backwards, giving Matty a few vital seconds to get his head together again.

With his eardrum gone, Matty had difficulty hearing above the high-pitched whine, but somewhere to his left he could just make out Bob's voice, encouraging Bomber, "To get stuck in again and kill the bastard."

This fired Matty up even more and as he and Bomber came together again, he thought 'Don't worry Bob, once I've got this gorilla out of the way, you're next.'

Then Bomber lunged at him, almost managing to get his huge bearlike arms around Matty's waist, but in sheer panic, at the memory of what happened the last time Bomber had done that, Matty wriggled free and fell to the ground, then quickly got back up on his feet, just in time to arch his body away from Bomber's swinging right boot.

Matty was beginning to tire now, but he could tell by the way Bomber was standing, he was also tiring, yet the bloke came forward once again, which told Matty that he wasn't quite ready for "The Bomber Drop", just yet.

Matty eluded him though by ducking to his left and running behind him, calling as he did so, "What's up you ugly bastard, I thought you were supposed to be good."

His goading worked, as Bomber turned and charged at him again, but only missing Matty's head with a swinging punch, by a fraction of a second. "Fucking hell" Matty exclaimed to himself. "That bugger was close" but then he noticed Bomber's chest, heaving up and down with exertion and he knew it was almost time.

He let Bomber come at him again, only to leave the bloke grasping at thin air once more, then, as Bomber stood rooted to the spot, covered in sweat, with his chest wheezing, Matty quickly measured out the five paces he would need. But as he leaned backwards, ready to take off, he suddenly felt disorientated, for with the high-pitched whine in one ear and the baying voices coming from the shadows in the other, he was finding it difficult to focus himself. Then he remembered what he had done whilst in the darkness of his cell in solitary, he had closed his eyes.

So he shut them tightly for a few seconds and hoped that Bomber wouldn't make a move and, yes it did seem to dim the noise, so he quickly opened them again and was relieved to see old scar face hadn't moved a muscle.

In fact, all the effort Bomber had put into trying to catch Matty, had also disorientated him and, as he stood watching Matty closing and opening his eyes, he also became confused.

This actually turned out to be a stroke of luck for Matty. For as he ran at Bomber, the big man instinctively leaned backwards and stretched out his arms, thinking Matty was going to leap at him, as he had done in Durham jail.

Matty didn't though, for on the fifth pace, he dived feet first under Bomber and landed both of them, smack on the bloke's left leg, just above the ankle.

There was an almighty crack as the leg snapped like a twig, then an horrific scream, as Bomber fell to the ground, clutching at his leg and writhing about like some mortally wounded beast.

"Got you, you bastard" Matty uttered, as he quickly rolled away from Bomber then jumped to his feet. Where he stood glaring down at him, his eyes filled with pure hatred and, with venom he roared, "Now you ugly lump of pigshit, now who's top-dog eh?" and as he spoke, he kept digging him in the ribs with his boot, causing Bomber to cower away from him.

After a few minutes though Matty stopped tormenting Bomber. He knew the bloke wasn't going anywhere, so he turned and peered into the shadows, scanning the faces for Bob. Then when he finally spotted him, he walked menacingly over to him, grabbed him by the jaw with his right hand and distorting the bloke's face grotesquely, he hissed "Don't go too far away Bob, cos when I've finished with ugly bollocks over yonder, I'll be back for you." Then he shoved him backwards so hard, Bob yelped as he went thudding into two blokes standing behind him.

Then Matty cockily strolled back towards Bomber and began circling him again, laughing sadistically and feigning to put the boot in as he did so, causing Bomber to wince and cower away from him once more.

Alas though, Matty had made one fatal error, he had badly underestimated Bomber's guts. The bloke may well have had weak legs, but he was every bit a hardman. For not only could he dish out pain, he could also take it and, whilst Matty had stupidly ignored him and gone over to threaten Bob, it had given Bomber a couple of minutes to pull himself together. So as Matty continued his taunting, Bomber was watching his every move from the corner of his eye, just waiting for Matty to get cocky enough to come into range and he could finally get his hands on him.

Then suddenly Matty stopped circling and stood leering down at Bomber. He had at last decided what he was going to do, he was going to drop down on top of him and punch the bastard into oblivion.

But Matty was too over-confident and, as he casually fell onto Bomber, the big man shot up both his arms and caught him in mid-air. With his left hand grabbing Matty's throat and his right, Matty's balls. Then he began squeezing and twisting with all the strength he could muster, grunting and groaning with effort and pleasure as he did so.

If Matty could have screamed he would have, as terrible pains from his groin went shooting up into his stomach, but Bomber had such a vice-like grip on his throat, all that came out of his mouth was a faint croak.

Then white flashes began darting back and forth across his eyes as he felt himself begin to pass out. He knew that unless he did something quickly he was finished, but panic had gripped his mind now and all he could think to do, was lash at Bomber with his hands, only occasionally catching his face with his fingers.

But from somewhere, whether it was his will to survive, or simply fear, inspiration came to him and instead of lashing wildly, he reached down with his left hand and began to feel his face.

Firstly he touched the scar, so he brought his hand right and put his index and middle fingers either side of Bomber's nose, then slowly began working them up towards his eyes.

Bomber sensed what Matty was up to and tried to turn his head away, but as he did, his arms weakened a fraction, allowing Matty's hand to follow the face and, as Bomber tried to twist his head the other way, Matty's fingers plunged deep into his sockets.

Bomber gave out another horrific scream as he felt his eyes being gouged out and instinctively he let go of Matty, causing him to drop with a thud to the ground, whereupon they both began lashing blindly at each other, like two rabid dogs, oblivious to the blood and gore that covered them. For by now, they were both out of their minds with pain and rage.

Bob looked at Barny and they both nodded in agreement, the fight was over. So they indicated to the blokes standing by them, to pull Matty and Bomber apart, then told the cuts men to chloroform them as quickly as possible.

Matty was still kicking and swinging his arms deliriously as the two Hetton lads dragged him to the side and propped him up against a bale of hay, where Cuddy was waiting with a wad of cotton-wool dowsed in chloroform, ready to cover his nose and mouth.

After feeling Matty's body go limp, Cuddy quickly set about tending his injuries. He could see that the throat was swollen and badly discoloured, but he knew there was nothing he could do about that, "And if there's any internal injuries" he told himself, "There's fuck all I can do about those either, for I'm only a cuts man, not a bloody surgeon."

But when he looked down between Matty's legs and saw the huge patch of blood on his trousers, he quickly took his scissors from his medical case and began cutting them apart.

Matty's balls were in a hell of a mess and, after he had cleaned them, Cuddy saw that they were almost torn off. So he threaded a needle with some catgut and hastily stitched as much of the wound as he could.

As he was doing so though, Bob came over and asked, "It is very bad Cuddy?"

In reply, Cuddy simply looked up at him and, with disgust covering his face he slowly shook his head.

Bob turned then and began walking back over to Barny, but as he did so, a sense of satisfaction came over him and he chuckled as he uttered, "That'll teach you to fuck about with my wife, you bastard."

For the following three days and nights, Cuddy had to keep Matty doped up with chloroform to stop him from screaming out with pain. For with street-fighting being illegal, they couldn't take him to hospital, so Bob had decided it was best to get him back to the caravan where Cuddy could look after him in private.

At first, it had crossed Bob's mind to throw him out of the car and leave him by the roadside, after all, no one down here knew who he was. But then his nerve had left him and he began thinking what would happen if Matty died and someone just happened to trace him back to Houghton. He knew fair well the cops would be knocking on his door before long. So all in all, the caravan seemed the best place to hide him.

On the fourth morning though, as Cuddy sat dozing on a chair by the side of the bed, he woke up with a start to find Matty tugging at the sleeve of his shirt.

"Wha-what's up young 'un?" he asked with a touch of alarm in his voice.

Then when Matty slowly pointed to his lips, Cuddy's face took on a puzzled look as he asked again, "What's up Matty, is your throat bothering you or something?"

With great effort and much pain Matty shook his head in frustration, which only served to puzzle Cuddy even more. But when Matty made a drinking motion with his hand, Cuddy finally twigged. "Awe, it's a drink you're wanting" he said nodding, then went through to the kitchenette to get some water.

He came back, then lifted Matty's head slightly, tilting it forward so he could put the glass to his lips without spilling any, but the moment the cold water touched his burning throat, he went into a coughing convulsion, which not only stung his throat even more, but also sent pains shooting from his groin, up through the whole of his body.

So severe was the damage to his throat, Matty was incapable of screaming, but Cuddy could tell just how much agony he was in by the terrified look on his face.

Cuddy's first reaction was to get the chloroform, but as the pain subsided Matty weakly stayed his hand and indicated with a faint nod of his head that he was now ok.

So Cuddy waited for a few minutes, then tried him with the water again and this time, even though it was still painful,

Matty took it. Then Cuddy eased his head back onto the pillow, where with sheer exhaustion, Matty lapsed back into sleep once more.

Cuddy sat quietly by him for half-hour or so, to see if he would wake again, but when he didn't and Cuddy was satisfied that Matty was sleeping peacefully, he decided to call it a day, after all, he too was exhausted and he hadn't been home since he left that night for the fight.

He cleaned up the caravan as much as he could, but he could do nothing about the stench of the place. He had no disinfectant, so he decided to leave that to Bob, Matty was his pigeon now, so he could look after him.

He put on his coat and had a final look round the place, then he lifted up the old, off white nightshirt, Bob had found for him to put Matty in, to stop anything irritating his wound and he almost wretched. For he could plainly see, the wound was beginning to fester. So he let the nightshirt drop and as his face involuntarily screwed up in disgust, he said to himself, "Aye Matty my lad, I don't think you'll be shagging anybody else's wife for a long long time, if ever." Then he quietly let himself out of the caravan and made his way up to the pub.

"Now you're sure he'll be alright?" Bob asked Cuddy suspiciously, as he shoved twenty quid into his hand.

"Aye Bob, I'm sure" Cuddy lied, "All he needs now, is a bit of peace and quiet, then in a couple of weeks he'll be as right as rain, and you can take my word on that."

But as Cuddy walked off down the street, Bob stood on the doorstep watching him go, not knowing whether to believe the bloke or not. Then he thought 'I hope he is ok Cuddy, because if he's not you little shit, I'll know where to find you.' For although Bob might have admired the bloke's skill with a needle, he also knew what a devious bastard he could be too and the last thing Bob wanted on his hands, was a dead body.

After closing the door, Bob's first thought was to pop down to the caravan to take a look at Matty himself and to see just what state he was really in, but as it was starting to snow, he simply thought, 'Bollocks to him' then went into the bar and poured himself a large brandy, then sat down by the fire to drink it.

It was only an hour after Cuddy had left though, that Matty awoke again and once more his throat raged with thirst.

Cuddy had refilled the glass with water, but the silly sod had put it on top of the drawers, opposite the bed and just out of Matty's reach.

Several times he tried to get to it, but each time, the severity of the pain held him back, until finally, overcome with exhaustion again, he fell back to sleep.

Yet barely twenty minutes later he awoke again, but this time he was determined to get to the water. So with his burning thirst driving him on, he slowly edged his body to the side of the bed, turned himself sideways, then let his feet fall to the floor.

He lay like that for a few moments to let the pain subside a little, then with one tremendous effort he heaved himself up into a sitting position, but again, having to stop to let the pain ease before reaching for the glass.

Remembering what had happened the first time he had tried to take the water, he began to sip it slowly and, even though he was tempted to take a big gulp, he didn't, he just sat quietly sipping, until eventually he drained the glass.

But so exhausting had been the effort, that when he had finished, he let the glass fall to the floor and slumped backwards onto the bed, where he lay for a few minutes with his eyes closed.

When he opened them again, he found that he was looking out of the window, upside down and, a faint smile crossed his lips when he saw that it was snowing.

He lay for a while watching the gentle flakes fall onto the pane, then melt and trickle down the window. 'So gentle' he thought, 'Yet so sad, just like tears of sorrow.' Then as his mind turned to thoughts of his own Snowflakes, he drifted back to sleep.

But this time, somewhere in the darkness, he could hear voices calling his name and he smiled, for there was no mistaking who those voices belonged to.

Then suddenly they appeared, just as they had before, with Frank and Dotty sitting cross-legged on the ground, beckoning him to them with one hand, whilst with the other, stroking Billy The Buck.

Yet when he walked towards them this time, they didn't move away as they had done previously and, when he did reach them, he was shocked to see that they were crying, even the rabbit had tears rolling down its cheeks which instantly alarmed him.

"Why on earth are you all crying?" he asked sharply, looking firstly at Dotty, then at Frank, "Has someone been hurting you?"

It was Frank who answered him, as he shook his head and said forlornly, "No Matty, no one has hurt us, only you."

"Me?" Matty asked, puzzled, "How could I possibly have hurt you, every time I've tried to get near you, you've just moved away again, come on Frank, how the hell could I have hurt you?"

Frank looked deeply into Matty's eyes and still saw much anger in them. He shook his head sadly then stood up, as did Dotty. Then Frank took her by the hand and with Billy The Buck hopping after them, they disappeared once again into the darkness.

A sudden dread came over Matty and he felt so alone. He didn't want to wake up from his dream, he wanted to stay there with his Snowflakes, but it seemed as though they didn't want him. So in panic, he began calling after them, "Frank, Dotty, where are you? Don't go and leave me, please, come back." But there was no reply and in his sadness, he burst into tears.

Then as he stood with the tears streaming down his face, he became full of self-pity as he told himself "Oh god, I wish they'd come back and get me I miss them so much and I realise now, just how lost I've been without them."

Then suddenly a voice from the darkness called "Don't worry Matty, we'll always be here if you want us, all you have to do is come, we'll be waiting for you."

It had been Frank's voice and, as Matty awoke from his dream still crying, he felt so at peace with himself. It was as though he had been on some terrible journey, but he had now somehow, reached the end and he smiled through his tears, as he realised it was Frank's final words, that had ended it. For now he knew the meaning of his dream.

He got up and painfully shuffled his way over to the door, where he turned the latch and let the door swing open. Then he pulled one of the chairs across to him and slumped heavily down on it.

The pain was excruciating, but he didn't mind. The stitches in his groin wound had also burst open, sending blood trickling down the insides of his legs, but he was oblivious to that also. All he was intent on doing, was watching the flakes of snow drift gently down and, as he reached out his hand to catch some, once again the words echoed in his mind, "So gentle, yet so sad."

Then he cast his mind back over all the bad things that had happened to him in the past two years, starting with Siddy, prison and Bomber, Bob, then Annie and finally, losing Dotty. Yet he felt no bitterness towards anyone, not even his father, who had turned him into a fighter in the first place.

For Matty now knew that this was their world not his. Like his Snowflakes he too was a misfit, he should never have been born into this environment either. But now, knowing the meaning of his dream, he knew exactly what he had to do.

He wasn't ready just yet though and, as tears of joy welled up inside of him, then cascaded down his cheeks, he said to himself, "Look world, it's me, hardman Matty Glave and I'm crying. Yes, just like the rest of you, I can also shed tears and I feel no shame at all." Then with his thoughts turning once more to his Snowflakes, he sighed contentedly, and whispered, "Ok Frank, I'm coming, tell our Dotty and Billy I won't be long, but first, there's something I've got to do before I come."

He got up out of the chair and again shuffled across to the drawers by the bed. He took out a pencil and writing pad, then made his way back to the table, where he began to do something he had not done in ages, he began to write a poem.

The following morning as Bob was taking some crates of empty beer bottles across the yard to the bottle shed, he happened to glance down the yard at the caravan. He stopped suddenly, when he noticed the door swinging lazily, back and forth in the breeze. "What the bloody hell is the simple sod up to now?" he uttered, as he spotted Matty's leg sticking out of the caravan door.

He stood for a few moments wondering what to do, then thought, 'Awe bugger him' then continued on to the bottle shed.

On his way back however, he stopped again for something was bothering him, things just didn't seem right. It was a bitterly cold morning, too cold to be sitting with the door open. 'So what in hell's name is he playing at?' he thought curiously.

Then a feeling that something might be wrong struck him. "Maybe he got up for some fresh air and can't get back to bed" he told himself, but as he said it, he had a feeling it was far worse than that.

So slowly he began to walk down to the caravan, for he was now filled with apprehension. Then as he neared it, his apprehension suddenly turned to dread, as he saw blood on Matty's legs and all over the doorway.

"Jesus Christ!" he exclaimed, then went rushing into the caravan, only to turn quickly away from the sight that greeted him. For not only was it Matty's legs and the doorway that were covered in blood, but also the rest of him and, so were the table and caravan floor.

Bob was scared witless, he didn't know what to do, but he managed to get hold of himself again and turned to look at Matty. His eyes were open and staring but they were lifeless, it was obvious he was dead. Then Bob spotted the bloodied razor blade on the table and panic took hold of him.

"Christ almighty, the stupid bugger's topped himself" he screamed. Then with his mind in utter turmoil, he ran back up to the pub to ring the police.

As he sat, nervously smoking a cigar whilst he waited for them to arrive, he began cursing Cuddy. "Aye" he told himself bitterly, "I bet that little bastard knew all along this was going to happen, in fact it wouldn't surprise me if the little shit had talked him into it." Then he put his head in his hands and shook it slowly, as he thought about Bella and how she would react, when she found out what had happened.

But his thoughts were interrupted by a loud banging on the front door and he quickly ran down stairs to open it.

As he did, his mouth fell open with shock, for the one person he had completely forgotten about, was now standing in front of him and, as Sergeant Shilton peered at him from under the rim of his trilby, Bob felt his legs begin to tremble.

So shocked was he, that all he could do was stand and gawk at the Sergeant and ignore the young, fresh faced constable who was with him.

But it was the constable who spoke, as he asked irritably, "Can we come in then, or are we going to stand here all bloody day?"

"Er, aye, aye. Come in" Bob stuttered as he stepped back, with his fear showing in the way he was repeating himself.

Then he walked quickly down the passage to the back door and opened it, saying, "He's down there look, in that caravan at the bottom of the yard."

The Sergeant, who hadn't spoken a word yet, followed Bob to the back door then looked down the yard. Then as he turned, his hate filled eyes towards Bob, said "Go on Evans, you go ahead, I'll be down in a minute."

When Evans had gone, the Sergeant indicated to Bob to let go of the door, which he did reluctantly, for he had a terrible feeling what was coming next and, as it swung slowly shut, he was to be proved right.

So rooted to the floor with fear was he, that even though he saw the Sergeant's huge, gloved fist come towards him, he just stood and took it, then went crashing against the wall, smacking his head against it then falling to the floor, spark out.

The Sergeant glared down at Bob's prone body, looking for the slightest sign of movement, but there was none. He wanted to finish the job and, if Bob hadn't been out cold, he would have done. But being the professional that he was, he didn't. He simply stepped over him and went out of the back door, uttering, "Bastard" as he did so.

It had started snowing again as the Sergeant made his way down the yard, so it wasn't until he actually reached the caravan, did he see the full horror of what had happened. But the instant he did though, he cringed.

Then with his detective's eye, he took in the whole scene. The blood-stained nightshirt, the cut wrists, the pools of congealed blood on the floor and the table and, the sadness in Matty's dead eyes. He also shook his head in disgust at the pathetic way in which his body was slumped in the chair, with his left arm on the table and his right dangling down by his side.

He lifted up the nightshirt and cringed at the dreadful sight he saw. Then he looked closer at his swollen and discoloured throat and concluded that he must have taken one hell of a beating. 'My god' he thought, 'It must have been some animal that did this and, I. know one thing for sure, I wouldn't like to bump into the bastard.'

Then Evans brought him back from his thoughts, telling him "It certainly looks like suicide Sarg, but I couldn't find a suicide note anywhere, just this blood-stained piece of paper, with a poem or something written on it."

The Sergeant snatched the piece of paper from Evans' hand and turned towards the light of the doorway to read what was on it. Then a sudden chill ran down his spine, as he saw it was a poem. He couldn't quite make out the words, so he stepped nearer the doorway, then he began to shake with emotion, as he read,

THE SNOWFLAKE

by Matthew Glave

The Snowflake fell without a sound,
As it came to rest, in it's given ground,
The Snowflake called, but no one heard,
Not a kindly gesture, nor loving word,

So the Snowflake melted, became a tear,
No one cared, no one came near,
Then the Snowflake thought, 'What was it all for',
Whereas once I was, now I am no more.

The Sergeant then turned his back to Evans and took out his handkerchief. He pretended to blow his nose, but was really masking the tears that ran freely down his cheeks. Yet the more he thought about the poem, the angrier he became and, as he folded it and put it into his pocket, he turned and glared up the yard at the pub.

'If it hadn't been for shits like him' he thought, as he pictured Bob lying in the passage, 'Maybe the kid would have stood a chance.'

Then he thought back to that night in the cell, when Matty had opened up to him and he remembered feeling then, that the lad was in some way doomed. Yet he had stood by and done nothing about it.

Even when he had bumped into him in the high street, he could have at least tried to warn him off fighting, but he hadn't. He could have even had a quiet word in Hunter's ear, but he didn't even think about that either.

He continued to chastise himself for a while longer, but eventually he thought 'What the hell. I don't suppose for one minute I could have changed the course of events. There was bound to come a time when the lad would realise, that the only way to get out of this shit-hole he was born into, was to do what he did. As he said himself, this environment is no place for Snowflakes.

If he had been born at another time, somewhere different, maybe he might have had a decent life. But as they say, "Once a slum child, always a slum child." You are born into it and you die in it, with nobody giving a toss either way.'

Then Evans brought him back from his thoughts again, as he asked, "Are you ok Sarg?"

Sergeant Shilton turned wearily to face him. He looked him up and down for a few seconds as he wondered what sort of bloke Matty would have turned out to be, if he had been given the same chance as him.

Then nodding his head slowly and smiling forlornly, he replied, "Yes I'm alright son" but then abruptly added, "Come on, let's go, there's nothing we can do here."

As they walked back up the yard though, the Sergeant stopped suddenly, then took off his right glove and held out his hand, letting some of the falling flakes drop gently onto it. Then, as they melted and the rivulets trickled down his wrist, he smiled as he softly uttered, "You were wrong you know Evans, the lad did leave a suicide note."

THE END

Printed in Great Britain
by Amazon